The Da Vinci Barcode
A Parody

Published and Forthcoming by New Academia Publishing

SCARITH Books (fiction)
ON THE WAY TO RED SQUARE, by Julieta Almeida Rodrigues.

THE DA VINCI BARCODE, by Judith P. Shoaf

VELLUM Books (non fiction)
A RED SOX FAN'S DIARY OF THE 2004 SEASON, by Derek Catsam

NEW ACADEMIA PUBLISHING (academic books)
ON THE ROAD TO BAGHDAD, OR TRAVELING BICULTURALISM: Theorizing a Bicultural Approach to Contemporary World Fiction, Edited by Gönül Pultar.

SHAKESPEARE'S THEATER OF LIKENESS, by R. Allen Shoaf.

GOD, GREED, AND GENOCIDE: The Holocaust through the Centuries,
by Arthur Grenke.

HERETICAL EMPIRICISM, by Pier Paolo Pasolini. Eds., trs., Ben Lawton and Louise K.Barnett.

SOCIAL PROPRIETIES: Social Relations in Early-Modern England (1500-1680),
by David Postles.

NATIONALISM, HISTORIOGRAPHY AND THE (RE)CONSTRUCTION OF THE PAST, edited by Claire Norton

ASPECTS OF BALKAN CULTURE: Social, Political, and Literary Perceptions,
by Jelena Milojković-Djurić.

AN **ARCHITECT OF** DEMOCRACY: Buildig a Mosaic of Peace, by James Robert Huntley.

LIVING NOVELS: A JOURNEY THROUGH TWENTIETH-CENTURY FICTION,
by Sascha Talmor

Russian History and Culture Series
RUSSIAN FUTURISM: A HISTORY, by Vladimir Markov. With an Introduction
by Ronald Vroon.

WORDS IN REVOLUTION: Russian Futurist Manifestoes 1912-1928.
Eds., trs., Anna Lawton and Herbert Eagle.

THE INNER ADVERSARY: Struggle Against Philistinism as the Moral Mission
of the Russian Intelligentsia, by Timo Vihavainen.

IMAGING RUSSIA 2000: Film and Facts, by Anna Lawton.

BEFORE THE FALL: Soviet Cinema in the Gorbachev Years, by Anna Lawton.

RED ATTACK, WHITE RESISTANCE: Civil War in South Russia 1918,
by Peter Kenez.

RED ADVANCE, WHITE DEFEAT: Civil War in South Russia 1919-1920,
by Peter Kenez.

The Da Vinci Barcode
A Parody

Judith P. Shoaf

 An imprint of New Academia Publishing, LLC
Washington, DC

Library of Congress Control Number: 2006923815
ISBN 0-9777908-6-X paperback (alk. paper)

An imprint of New Academia Publishing, LLC
P.O. Box 27420, Washington, DC 20038-7420
www.newacademia.com - info@newacademia.com

Everything's either
concave or -vex,
So whatever you dream
will be something with sex.

Piet Hein

Everything in this book was meticulously researched. However, any time I found that the actual facts didn't fit my story, I ignored them.

As those who have visited the Louvre, virtually or physically, will know, there is no such thing as the Centre Commercial du Louvre ("Louvre Shopping Mall"). For purposes of this novel, I have replaced the the underground complex that lies beneath the Louvre courtyard with my own vision of what ought to be there.

Most of the material about Mary Magdalen is accurate, which does not mean it is true. Through the ages she has meant different things to different civic-minded men, artists, and writers of saints' lives. I have tried to express some of these ideas as the opinions of educated young women who have a personal interest in her history.

Spoilers: I have no idea whether Vézelay has kept the body of Mary Magdalen, a very important relic, after it was discredited in favor of the relics discovered in Provence around 1300. St. Martha (sister of Lazarus and Mary of Bethany) does have a story and a set of bones in Tarascon (dating from the late 11th century), a fact of which my characters remain ignorant.

Thanks to Norris Lacy, who in some ways begot this project, to J-C Kirwan, to Allan West for reading the first draft and being enthusiastic about barcodes, and especially to my husband, who got it.

ONE

In another moment Alice was through the glass, and had jumped lightly down into the Looking-glass room.... the pictures on the wall next the fire seemed to be all alive.

Lewis Carroll

Robert Longone, Professor of Symbology at Harvard Business School, on his way to the cash registers at the *Centre Commercial du Louvre,* bumped his head on a strut of the *Pyramide Inversée.* This gigantic upside-down glass pyramid was an awkward way of getting light into the underground shopping mall. The Louvre Museum architect, Pei, had designed its faceted glass planes to descend from the ceiling, stopping in a point a few feet above the floor level. Beneath it a smaller solid right-side-up pyramid helped to prevent people from getting close enough to run into it. At 6'1", Robert Longone did not consider himself excessively tall, however, and he resented a little having to be more careful than definitively short people. *An efficient skylight, yes, and worth its weight as branding for the mall. But it dazzles the eye and makes it hard to concentrate on the merchandise. Or if you actually think about what you're buying, you run into the darned thing.* He'd nearly dropped the Georges de la Tour coffee mug.

The choice of Paris for the June ERP Accounting and Asset Tracking conference this year had been satisfactory, though Robert Longone (unlike many of his colleagues) had not had a chance to share the beauty of the City of Light with a significant other. He was thirty-six years old, unmarried and, for the moment, free of any romantic relationships. Somehow all the women he met were too young, too busy, or too ambitious for serious purposes. Still, he had enjoyed yesterday afternoon, after the conference's closing session, wandering the streets, peeking into the shops and tiny supermarkets to sample their labeling and shelf-space practices, getting a haircut. Today, Monday, he had set aside mostly for visiting the Louvre. He had seen all the masterpieces on his list and some he hadn't even heard of, like the Georges de la Tour painting of a woman holding a skull and staring at a candle.

The person behind him in line bumped his back gently and apologized in some strange language. Robert glanced over his shoulder and saw that there was already a longish line behind him. In front there were only two more, now. *I really should have taken a shopping basket. Too late now.*

He contemplated the Mona Lisa mousepad he was buying for his niece Jenny. The crowd management at the Mona Lisa approach had impressed him deeply.

Disneyworld, eat your heart out! If only you could line your attraction approaches with twelve-foot-high 17th-century paintings.... Interesting paintings, too, Bible stories and all that by painters I never heard of, like Caravaggio. The key is to have something people have never seen before, but it also has to be something really worth looking at. Hmm... now, Disney could try twelve-foot-high rear-projection screens showing old Duck and Mouse cartoons, silents maybe, for people to watch while they waited....

Forehead itches.

Robert juggled his double armful of purchases and found the medieval reproduction ivory mirror. It was too small to give him a view of his entire face, but he knew the whole well enough to understand how the segments fit together.

His forehead had not been skinned by the encounter with the *Pyramide Inversée*, but he could see a ruddy crease above his right eyebrow. It didn't look as if it would bruise. He wished he could touch it but he could only look, since he was holding a boxed paperweight and the Mona Lisa mousepad tucked between his body and the arm holding the mirror.

He checked his teeth for bits of lunch, which he had eaten in the Museum itself, in a café. He congratulated himself for having his goatee shaved off yesterday, when he got the haircut. He had a good chin, after all–he didn't need that thing. He had retained a neat dark brown moustache, which was good for keeping students' eyes focused on his mouth, and therefore on what was coming out of it. The salon girl had been very clever, telling him in Franglais that he didn't need to comb the front hair back over the potential bald spot, not yet, not for years yet. He kept visualizing his Dad's bald spot, and he was overcompensating, probably. He winked one grey eye at himself in the mirror and slid it back into its box.

He had reached the check-out. He dumped his treasure on the counter and surreptitiously stretched his arms. The cashier methodically arranged the items with the barcode labels facing up, ready for her handheld barcode reader. He glanced at her with approval, and noticed that she was a very attractive redhead.

She was more elegantly dressed than he would expect in a store clerk. She would not be out of place in a boardroom. Her deep red hair was beautifully rolled up in a smooth coiffure. He met her eyes, which were startlingly green. More makeup than he liked in a woman, but still that heart-shaped mouth in a heart-shaped face was very pleasant to look at. She did not smile but took his Visa and began checking his purchases, softly reciting the names and prices as her scanner read them.

Robert wondered if she knew that he understood French–at least, he knew the numbers and he recognized the names of the items when he was looking at them as she spoke. He thrilled to realize that she was muttering conversions–not only the euros price which showed on the cash register readout, but also the French Francs price. *Accurate, too. Do they train cashiers to do that or is she performing some private ritual?*

She scanned the tiny magnetic Venus de Milo for which he would find some use or other, a packet of *Raft of the Medusa* cocktail napkins, and the Mesopotamian Legal Contract paperweight, representing a lump of clay with cuneiform writing. He had not been able to resist it in the shop, though he had skipped the Mesopotamian galleries, thinking an American might not be welcome there this year. He had hesitated for a long time between the Mesopotamian Legal Contract and some other paperweights, two metal globes labeled Terrestrial Orb and Celestial Orb. But he had no use or room (or budget) for *two* paperweights, and they seemed to him to be a pair. So the Mesapotamian Legal Contract would be his desktop conversation piece.

Then there was the blue Egyptian Lotus cup or chalice thing for his sister–an expensive and fragile item. He was already planning how to pad it with his underwear in the carryon going home. She would eat it up. She was into Grails this year. The reproduction ivory mirror would be a Christmas gift for her. *Two gifts for Nell in one shopping trip, very efficient.*

The cashier paused over the coffee mug and looked up, approvingly. "*Ah, la Madeleine.*"

"*Pardon, excusez-moi, je ne comprends pas.*" O.K., he had been working on his French, but had no idea what she was talking about. There was a church called *La Madeleine* somewhere in Paris–he remembered seeing it on the Paris by Night bus tour, a vague impression of something like the Supreme Court building in D.C., enormous, all columns with triangles on top.

"You're American?" She sounded rather American herself, in English. Obviously he sounded American in French. "The painting of Mary Magdalen by Georges de la Tour. On your cup."

"Is that who she is? I didn't have time to check, but I liked the painting. That's why I bought this book, to back it up, learn a little more. She's in there, too. I checked." Robert patted the volume of *Masterpieces of Painting in the Louvre Museum,* a bit heavy but it probably wouldn't put him over his weight allowance on the flight home tomorrow.

"Yes, she is a repentant Magdalen. Unusual, since she has such dark hair. There are many paintings of Mary Magdalen, you know. She's in nearly every crucifixion scene ever painted, of course, and then in many other scenes in the life of Christ, besides being presented as an icon, a saint to be revered. In so many of those images she is blonde or red-haired." She angled her head, letting the light catch her own smooth, brilliant red hair.

Is she flirting? Robert shifted gears and got ready to say something along the lines of "I like red hair myself." However, she didn't pause and he realized she belonged to a type he knew well from Harvard–a type to which he himself perhaps belonged. The type of person who knows a lot about a topic and is just itching to download it for your entertainment.

"Georges de la Tour painted four—no, five!—different dark-haired Magdalens. He was not a court painter, and probably he used whatever model he could get. You can see that he worked from models. He may have been in the first generation of painters to use a *camera obscura* to train his hand in drawing."

"A *camera obscura*? That's Italian, or Latin–dark camera, dark room?"

"It's Latin, and it is a dark room."

"A darkroom for photography? But Georges de la Tour certainly was not taking photographs with cameras in the Middle Ages?"

"He lived in the 17th century. In France we generally count the end of the Middle Ages with Francis the First, who was born in 1494. In art history, Georges de la Tour would be classified as 'baroque' for his lighting and his preference for peasant-type models."

Robert nodded. He felt the person behind him in line grow-ing restless, muttering in the unknown language, but this was in-teresting, the kind of thing he had bought the book to learn. He stood with his shoulders at their broadest, protecting the talkative cashier, who clearly knew something about art, from the sight of the long line of waiting customers.

"This 'dark room' was not exactly for photography as we know it. His *camera obscura* would have been a kind of photographic stu-dio in which the only way to print the picture was to trace it. The principles of the technology were known to the ancient Greeks, and probably before then, but painters probably didn't figure out how to make use of it until the 17th century. You arrange and light what you want to draw in one room, and then you use a partition or curtain to create a second, completely dark room. In the partition or curtain there is one small pinhole. Through that pinhole the light comes, showing an inverted image of what is in the other room."

"An inverted image–you mean upside down?"

"Well, yes, of course. What else would I mean– a mirror image? Alice's looking-glass land? You know that our eyes see things up-side down, too, and camera lenses of any kind...."

Yes, young lady, I know it perfectly well. How charmingly you scold me. "So it is a camera in fact. A camera without lens or film, nothing but the aperture and the dark box."

"Yes." She had scanned the mug and the big book. Robert considered how to prolong the lecture.

"So he traced the picture? Like one of those children's toys that lets you trace a projected image?"

"Yes, though he would have had to use mirrors to get it right side up. There's your looking-glass. The mirrors did the work the brain does for our eyes. The use of the *camera obscura* would train the artist's hand to drawing human beings in perspective. But for a painting like this, it might have been used to prepare the sketch directly on the canvas."

"But wouldn't that be cheating?"

She laughed. "So why did you buy the mug and the book? Georges de la Tour's vision of the Magdalen is unique. Museum-goers here, and in New York, and Los Angeles and Washington, D.C., all stop before these paintings and feel something within them change. Do you think he cheated you?"

"No." Robert made a mental note to find out about the American paintings, and asked, "Have you seen the ones in the U.S.? Are they different from this one, or identical?" *Were you studying art history in the States, and that's why you sound American?* "It's odd to think that this is like a photograph, that there was once a real woman holding a real skull staring at an actual candle, back in the baroque 17th century." *At least I know how to listen to a woman.*

Her scanner moaned and bleeped. Robert Longone glanced down at the Mona Lisa mousepad, the last item, which was giving the scanner trouble.

"Let me see this." He took the mousepad, which was in a plastic bag, smoothed the barcode label with his strong fingers, and held the scanner to it carefully. The machine beeped gratefully. The girl smiled at him. Then he caught sight of the readout on the cash register. She followed his glance and gasped.

"I guess it must be an original Leonardo da Vinci, then," Robert said.

"Exactly. I mean, it's in the same ballpark, anyway."

"A nice *round* number!"

"Pi million," they both said almost at the same time, and laughed.

The readout showed 3.141.592,65. *The French are so stubborn they use commas and periods backwards. Really they should reprogram their cash registers here, for us Americans to understand. Well, when in Rome....*

TWO

I was not far from believing that each spectator in the theater looked, as if through a stereoscope, at a personal stage set, similar, however, to the thousand others at which the other spectators were looking, each at his own.

Marcel Proust

The distinguished longtime Director, retired, of the *Centre Commercial du Louvre* Monsieur Aspro was alerted by the sound of a tiny bell. It was a real bell, with a clapper, though activated by an electrical impulse, concealed in the cabinetry of his office. The office was underground, but still above the floor of the Louvre mall. His office and his secretary's shared a little mezzanine, reached by elevator or staircase from the main sales area. A platform outside their doors looked down on his domain of goods and shoppers.

The bell meant that it had happened. Already, here at the Louvre Boutique. *It is happening now.*

He got up from his desk and very carefully replaced on it the huge custom-made blotter.

He shut the communicating door with a nod to Madame Rosamonde at her computer. When he retired officially eight years ago, just as the new *Centre Commercial* under the *Pyramide Inversée* was beginning to fulfill its role in the *Grand Louvre* projects, it had been agreed that he could maintain an office in the new complex and continue to advise on the administration of the *Centre*. Madame Rosamonde had at that time already passed from being his secretary through a number of advancements and titles, and at his retirement she was asked to take on the post of Acting Interim Director, pending the appointment of a properly qualified *Directeur ad interim*, preliminary to the search for a new *Directeur*. Since *Monsieur l'ancien Directeur* Aspro himself seemed unlikely to budge from his office, and the *Centre* was prospering, no appointments or searches had been made. Madame Rosamonde continued to consider herself Monsieur Aspro's secretary.

Aspro turned to the shelf of books on his wall, the prestige Pléiade editions of the French classics. Gently he removed a volume–Marcel Proust's *Remembrance of Things Past*, the first of the old three-volume edition (he had refused to buy the revisionist four-volume one), and located in the space it had occupied a button, which he pressed.

The paneling on the wall beside it slid back to reveal a bank of video monitors. They blinked on, one by one.

Before returning the well-worn volume to the shelf, Aspro opened it for a moment and adjusted his bifocals to read a paragraph so familiar he could think his own thoughts as he read it.

The algorithms of perception. Tomorrow when I wake up I might be the little boy Aspro, afraid that the boys will make fun of me because my name is slang for "aspirin." If not, I might be the young man passionate about all things beautiful, including the beauties of computer programming languages. If not, the grown man scheming to create my own corner of a new Paris here under the Pyramide Inversée. If not, Ser Aspro, the old warrior who is feared and, I hope, loved. One man, slowly programmed with this unique information.

He put the book back on the shelf and began to examine the images which now appeared on the monitors. They were at a default setting, showing the various entrances to the underground mall and the shops themselves. He pressed a button on a little console, calling up images of all the points of sale inside the Louvre Museum itself–the displays of books and postcards relevant to a particular exhibit. Each of these had its own cash register. All looked calm, however. He didn't bother to call up the cameras in the independent boutiques which shared the *Centre* with the Louvre shops–they were not likely to be attacked.

His fingers on the buttons asked the console for views of the checkout cash registers for the main store.

A hundred years ago Proust invented television, he invented the computer monitor. He understood that we are each alone imagining what we see and hear, that the universe is a private performance for each of us. A terrifying thought, yet it made him happy.

The disturbance was at cash register number 3. The line was long at the checkout, but number 7 had just opened up, and someone was directing the people waiting at number 3 towards 7. Excellent. Even in the small black and white image, the commotion was obvious.

He toggled a switch and the camera zoomed in on number 3. He could see the customer and the cashier.

Ah! Marie. What could be more perfect? My own Marie is to be the first in the first battle, my warrior in the front lines.

He zoomed in further, on the object that had tripped the program. The *Joconde*–of course! Or as the Americans called it, the *Mona Lisa*. That Grail of reproducible, recognizable, beloved art.

The attack had of course come through a Leonardo da Vinci barcode.

He would be working late tonight. Now that he had some of the enemy's ammunition, he could build a better defense against it. They had been foiled and soon they would realize it.

There were many who would need to know that the war had begun. The enemy knew it already.

THREE

This invention relates to the art of article classification and has particular relation to classification through the medium of identifying patterns.

Patent application
Norman Woodward and Bernard Silver
October 20, 1949

Robert Longone, the Harvard Business School professor, expected the red-haired cashier to call the manager to void out the monstrous price, and a stock boy to go get another mousepad with a properly coded label. He picked up the Mona Lisa mousepad again to examine the code. It looked O.K. Odd that there should be a problem with a flat object. Suddenly he realized what had happened–the mousepad actually had two barcode labels, one on the pad inside the plastic bag and one on the outside. He opened the bag and pulled out the pad to show the cashier the second barcode.

"Here's your culprit," he said. "Your scanner saw the old code through the bag, and read both at the same time."

He was distracted for a moment by the suspicion that this mousepad was old stock, left long enough in the store to need a new code.

"What are you talking about?" She peered at the black bottom of the pad.

"Here." But when he took the pad from her, the label had disappeared. He moved the pad slowly until the label caught the light. *Not an old label at all. This is a very new label indeed.*

"It's printed on clear plastic, but the surface is reflective. If you tilt it so it catches the light, you can see it. I saw this type of label a few years ago at a conference, but I hadn't heard that anyone had actually used it."

The girl looked again and, now that she knew the trick, almost immediately found the code. She looked up at him curiously.

"That's not a barcode! I don't know what it is.... It looks like–like the *Arche de la Défense.*"

"Well, I guess most people wouldn't recognize it as a barcode. The Arch of Defense, you said? That's that gigantic building like three sides of a square that I saw on the bus tour? Hmm. Maybe they tried out a symbology based on that just for the French government or monuments, do you think? And it never really caught on?"

She shook her head, incredulous.

"To be frank, I have never seen a barcode like this, but it is certainly a barcode. Visually it reminds me of a very early type of barcode, the bull's-eye, which was used in California for a year or two, back in the 1950s. Before I was born, long before you were born. I've only seen it in archives. I can't understand why this Mona Lisa mousepad, which is not that old, would be labeled with such a maverick barcode."

"How do you know all this?"

"The fact is, this is my line of work." He pulled out a business card and handed it to her. "I've written a textbook on American barcodes. But I've never seen one quite like this. I'm actually here in Paris for a conference on symbology."

"Symbology?" She looked at the card in disbelief.

"Yes, the science of automatic identification technology, or you could call it the *art* of article classification through the medium of identifying patterns. Symbologists create and apply identifying codes, like this barcode–well, like the one on the mousepad packaging, anyway. That's EAN-13, European Article Numbering system. EAN-13 is getting to be the worldwide standard–a very adaptable symbology with thirteen digits, exactly the right choice for this place. Symbology is the general science of barcodes, which is why I'm a Professor of Symbology"–he tapped the card in her hand–"but the word also refers to any particular coding system."

She gazed up at him, following his explanation. *I'll give her a little return gift for the lecture on the camera obscura.*

"There are of course many symbologies with many purposes. You think of barcodes as a universal commercial system–to put it more exactly, you think of the Universal Product Code, whether twelve or thirteen digits, as the system that makes commerce possible! But barcodes have other uses–identifying medical products such as blood plasma, identifying ships and airplanes with giant barcodes that can be read from a distance, identifying packages for shipping companies. The next step will be Radio Frequency Identification, but it will be a while before the cost-benefits ratio works out and it can be widely implemented." The cashier still looked alert and interested, like a student in the front row on the first day of classes.

"Now this one, though"–he touched the strange square emblem on the back of the mousepad–"this one beats me. I don't know the symbology, and they weren't kind enough to print the actual numerical code under the barcode itself. It doesn't look two-dimensional–that would be a barcode that required a special reader that could scan it both vertically and horizontally. Anyway, I can't read it."

"You can sight-read other barcodes?"

"Some of them, if I've used them a lot–or if I designed the code. I can usually tell what symbology is being used, anyway, and I know some of the numerical codes of companies I've worked for. However, I would need a database to turn all the codes into useful information. For example, your cash register has a database of all the items in the store here, with their current prices, how many you have in stock and how many have been sold. The scanner sees the code but it needs the database to tell us what it means.... I'd love to know what joker programmed your cash register to pump out *Pi million* when the scanner was confused."

Her smile was delightful. That cold, elegant quality about her seemed to melt before his eyes. He decided she was worth a few more minutes of his time.

"There are scanners now that are so sophisticated they can read codes that are well beyond thirteen digits, mademoiselle. How about a scanner that would read your DNA?"

"To what purpose? Do you propose to 'create and apply' DNA codes?"

"Not yet, of course. But think of the possibilities. Forensic possibilities, to begin with. You could use any bit of a murdered body to identify the victim, no matter how unrecognizable the corpse. You could identify the perp by any bit of physical matter he, or she, left at the scene...."

She thought for a moment. "But that would only be possible if you had a file of all the DNA of everybody in the world, so you could match it up. Even now we only keep fingerprints of known criminals, not of possible victims or murderers!"

He couldn't resist her intelligent skepticism. "Ah, that's the beauty of this software. The analysis examines certain parts of the chromosome, and the program exploits that to produce an image, like an Identikit sketch.... but in three dimensions and color too. Actually it was developed for medical diagnoses, but there are plenty of possible applications–which is why I happen to have a prototype. Wait, let me show you." He drew the Personal Sampler from his pocket and took her hand.

"This won't hurt a bit," he said. He touched the Sampler to her wrist, saved the data, and then punched in the code for 20 years. The three-inch monitor slowly formed the picture of the woman standing before him. He hit the modesty button before showing it to her.

"But that's me! That's marvelous! No, it's a camera and you took a photograph of some kind, didn't you?.... but the hair is different, and the clothes.... well, if you can call that black bag clothes. And the glasses–I wear contacts."

"Yes, but the Personal Sampler doesn't know that. It just knows that at the age of twenty you are myopic and have red hair." He looked more closely at the tiny screen in her hand, leaning towards her to get a better view. "And blue eyes, not green. And you are right-handed." He showed her a little red x on the right palm of the image.

"I'm twenty-five, actually."

"I can't set it for twenty-five. It will do a readout of what you probably look like at the ages of ten, twenty, and forty. Beyond forty, there are too many environmental variables for a reliable image.

You have to project from one of the set ages, imagine what that person would look like at fifteen or thirty or eighty. Usually it works–if you know an eighty-year-old person well enough to identify him, you probably know what he looked like when he was forty, or even twenty."

"It's remarkable... this is my DNA barcode, you think?"

"In a sense, yes. In a sense, no. The barcode on each of these items for sale in your store depends on their being identical to others. The DNA is a code, but it's also a huge database with only one item, just lots and lots of data about that one. Your DNA is unique to you, and its value depends on the fact that no other object in the universe is carrying the same pattern."

She smiled an odd private smile, and he took this as encouragement.

"Moreover, these objects in the store must be classifiable to be barcoded. Someone chose the symbology, the EAN-13, that would express the most important categories about all the objects in this store. So if I had only the label I could find out the manufacturer from that, and that it came from a Mona Lisa mousepad. Thanks to your database, I could also find out that the item affixed to the label came from the stationery department of the Louvre Boutique and cost 11 euros. Without the label, with only the mousepad, the information I can get from it is different–I could do a chemical analysis of what it's made of, for example, but I couldn't be sure that it came from the Louvre, or guess what it costs. I could look up the painting and find out who painted the original, if I didn't recognize the Mona Lisa, but I wouldn't know who manufactured this copy."

He paused, and she looked up from the little screen in which she was admiring herself.

"The barcode is arbitrary and purposeful. Your DNA is not. You are a walking bag of information, with your entire body coded in every cell of your being. So am I. We are learning to read the code and understand what bits of it mean, but the expression of DNA is not the same as the purpose of a price code."

She inspected the small image one last time, and handed the Personal Sampler back to him. "It makes me look fat," she noted critically.

Robert felt awkward, all of a sudden. "Well, I think I'll skip the

Mona Lisa mousepad with the bad barcode, after all." *I can get Jenny a T-shirt or something at the airport.* "Can you void it out?"

"Mmm, I've voided it already. And the mousepad is free, whether you want it or not. Courtesy of the *Centre Commercial du Louvre*." She deftly bagged up his goodies, with extra tissue around the chalice box. "Your local address, Professor Longone?"

He was startled by her use of his name and title, then realized she had his business card as well as his credit card. "The *Hôtel Prieuré*," he said without thinking. Then, thinking, he added, "Mademoiselle...?"

I want her name. But she simply smiled and nodded, handing him back his Visa card with the receipt. Robert glanced at the total just to be sure—no, she hadn't charged him at all for the mousepad, much less the Pi million. As he walked past her toward the exit tunnel, he heard keys turning and drawers sliding. She was cashing out.

He looked back. The line of people behind him had disappeared, though the other checkout lines were still long. His beautiful cashier had already closed up and was disappearing into the dark offices in the shadows beyond the light of the Pyramid.

FOUR

Man is the animal that draws lines which he himself then stumbles over. In the whole pattern of civilization there have been two tendencies, one toward straight lines and rectangular patterns and one toward circular lines. There are reasons, mechanical and psychological, for both tendencies.

Piet Hein

Pi. A tool of the devil. A ruse to snare simpletons. We will square all the circles someday. Pi killed Di.

Fibonacci the one-eyed hunchback stood across from the entrance to the tunnel under the Seine River. It was growing dark. Street lights were coming on, and the headlights of the cars coming through the tunnel shone brightly. The place drew him. It was a Grail which he could never achieve, for he could not bear to enter the hole in the ground.

This was the Alma Tunnel, where in 1997 the British princess died with her Egyptian lover. Fibonacci was on his way to the Louvre Pyramids tonight, but he stopped to consider the tunnel. *He should have taken care of her, kept her above ground, among the obelisks of the Place de la Concorde. She would have been safe there.*

The tunnel entrance was not round, but square, or rather a double square if you counted the exit lane. But it was no squared circle. *All tunnels are the shape they are, and that shape is tubular. A tunnel is always a hole in the ground, a seductive arch of brick or concrete luring the unwary. Those who know too little are liable to enter, to be trapped, to be bitten off.*

Gazing within, Fibonacci could see the thirteenth pillar. The sweeping headlights would reveal for a moment its memorial graffiti, and then it would fall into darkness. Above it was the gilded flame, the Torch of Enlightenment. Though he could not walk up to it, because it was directly over the tunnel, Fibonacci thrilled to see that Masonic emblem memorializing his personal goddess.

All tunnels are round, even when they are square, just as all towers are beacons, even when they are round, and all bridges are potent even when they are supported by arches. A tower inspires, a bridge takes you across without wetting your feet. A pyramid is always triangular even when it is foursquare. But a tunnel is a damp hole where no hole should be, and it weakens the earth's fabric.

Paris, more than any other city on earth now, was tunneling into herself. One day soon the tunnels would bring down the towers, the foundations would be so riddled with holes they could no longer stand. Notre-Dame would be a pile of sculptured dust collapsed in on an underground parking garage. The Louvre would lie in pieces in its own courtyard. The Madeleine church, closest thing in the city to a Greek temple, would fall like Sodom and Gomorrah.

The mighty, foursquare *Arche de la Défense* was not quite foursquare because it stood over a subway node. There had been no place in Paris with enough solid ground to build the gigantic cube as it should have been, true and foursquare, in the perfection of the architect von Spreckelsen's design.

Fibonacci knew all this. He had known the uses and abuses of Pi since he was a child, a child of the square and the triangle. He knew where the subways of Paris ran under its streets, the excavations, the sewers, the catacombs, the underground parking garages, the deadly tunnels. He had studied maps. He could cross Paris without ever having to step on hollowness for more than an instant–one wide stride, foot on the empty air supporting him for a moment, then another wide stride would carry him to the other side. The empty air looked like street or sidewalk or café floor, but you could not trust it for longer than that instant.

It was just as well that one of the places for him to avoid was the well-excavated area around the Cathedral of Notre Dame. The tourists there would have laughed at his twisted, hideous body and one-eyed, distorted face if they saw him standing in front of the cathedral. Perhaps they would have thought he was an advertisement for a new play or movie of Victor Hugo's famous novel, *The Hunchback of Notre Dame*.

He turned away, zigzagging slowly towards the Louvre. This was another area he normally avoided, and crossing the fragile crust of garden, street, and courtyard would be a dangerous business. He had a task tonight, and the thirteenth pillar gave him the strength to begin it.

FIVE

Roland puts the Olifant to his lips, gets a good grip
and blows the horn with great power.
    The mountains are high and the road stretches far.
Thirty long leagues away they hear the echo.
    Charlemagne hears it and all his companions. The
king says, "Our men are fighting!"

Song of Roland

Alone in his office in the little mezzanine above the dark *Centre
Commercial du Louvre, Monsieur l'ancien Directeur* Aspro understood
that time was short. He had expected the assault on the cash registers, the deadly barcode. He had long prepared for battle on the
ground his opponent had chosen.

But it had not occurred to him that a physical assault might be
involved in the sabotage, that he might have to fight for his own
life.

He had been just a boy, coming into the wonderful wildness
of puberty, during the Occupation. Nothing in life since then had
compared to the thrill of espionage, of working for the Maquis, the
Resistance, against the Nazis. His thin muscular old body felt again
the surge of adrenalin.

For a long time after that he had not known the pleasure of being on the Right side against an enemy who was unquestionably
Evil. Fools and madmen he had met and vanquished, certainly. But
fools and madmen did not have the commitment to deeply wrong
principles that he saw in this enemy who had arisen, armed with

a barcode and a bad idea. For eight years Apsro had schemed and studied, waiting for the blow he knew must come.

The old man had seen, on one of the video monitors in his office, a stranger appear in the *Centre Commercial*. Oddly enough, the stranger did not enter the mall via the tunnel leading from the Metro, the Paris subway, though that was the easiest way whether by stealth or honestly. This odd invader had climbed down via the maintenance stairway up near the top of the *Pyramide Inversée*, near the base of the *Arche du Carroussel*. Few people knew this stairway existed, very few had keys to the little door to the gardens above.

The building alarm had not been triggered.

It was nearly midnight, and the mall guards must be dozing, for Monsieur Aspro had not heard from them. Perhaps the stranger was not a stranger, but a friend of one of the guards. Still, the stranger's avoidance of tunnels alerted Aspro to the possibility of attack. He knew that his enemies did not like underground places.

The old man had commandeered his secretary's equipment. His slim, liver-spotted fingers flew over the computer keyboard to finish his task, and then his white-haired head bent over the printer as the sheet of square labels slowly emerged.

On the desk lay seventeen envelopes, quite ordinary-looking white envelopes, with their individually printed blue addresses and complementary blue-and-white Marianne postage stamps, first-class for anywhere in the EU. The envelopes had no return address, but each bore a blue barcode printed below the address.

Also on the desk, upright on their grey felt skirts, stood the three pneumatic cylinders, each about two and a half inches in diameter. They were his own cylinders, custom made, dark blue vinyl with paler blue caps. So few people used the pneumatic service nowadays that one could afford to "sign" a message in this way, with a color scheme. It was like horseracing–everyone knew from the colors who owned the horse. The recipients would as a matter of course return the cylinder to the owner.

The metal bands on each had been carefully charged with their destination codes. In front of them lay three envelopes, but these were not ordinary-looking at all. They were long but unusually slim, to fit in the cylinders, and a lovely blue. Each bore a bar code in a darker blue, and two of them were hand-addressed already.

He must not get confused and put the envelopes in the wrong cylinders. Two of them would reach their addressees anyway. His blue cylinders shot under and over the Paris streets to these destinations often. When those cylinders reached their destinations, the intermediaries who received them would recognize them and know where to take them even without the addresses.

Of the third, he must be most careful. Only this afternoon he had discovered that this man existed, and could help him.

That envelope remained to be addressed. He picked up the business card Marie had given him and copied the name from it, and then turned it over to find the hotel address he had written there when she had told him her story. *Hôtel du Prieuré.*

He gazed at the three envelopes in front of him, fingering the business card itself, unsure what to do with it. It would not be a good thing if it fell into the enemy's hands.

He heard slow, unrhythmic steps on the stairs which led up to his office. His fingers tore the white labels from the sheet which the printer had finally expelled. He stuck one on the inside of each envelope, under the flap.

The business card went into one of the three blue envelopes.

He licked the flaps, one after another, with a dry tongue. He took a quick sip of Perrier water and licked again until all twenty envelopes were sealed.

All but those three blue ones went into the mail chute.

The three last letters into the three tubes, one after another. With the domed lids screwed on, the capsules looked like two-tone blue dildos of impressive size.

He slid aside one of the pictures on the wall, an exquisite reproduction of Fra Angelico's fresco of Christ and Mary Magdalen. He had chosen the subject carefully: *Noli me tangere*, "Touch me not." Christ, newly risen from the dead and still glowing with his otherworldly experience, tells the woman not to touch him yet. It was a warning and a reminder that the pneumatic console which lay under the painting was not to be used casually.

The picture moved to one side on a groove, revealing a beautiful wooden console with lights and switches and a row of holes for storing the cylinders upright. Then there was the hole in the wall for the actual sending of the cylinders, a little less than three inches in diameter. Above it were two lights, one red and one green, neither lit at the moment. Red was to alert for incoming cylinders, and green recorded the sending of one. Aspro fed the first capsule into the hole, gave it a good shove, waited for the green light to flash on, and then, an eternity it seemed, for it to turn off again. The first one had passed. The tube was ready for another. The second one went into the hole.

Waiting, he fiddled with the key card coder, setting it to maximum security. His coder was capable of producing that Grail among keys, a pass with full Louvre Museum security. He was merely the Director (retired) of the Museum's mall, so he rarely coded such a card. But sometimes he needed to, those times when he had to check on the sales points inside the Museum during off-hours. Well, tonight he might need a pass that would open all doors. After coding it, he scrambled the coder. There was no security at all in it any more.

The light over the pneumatic tube at last went off again, and he fed the third capsule into it. He did not wait for the light to change, but slid the panel closed again to hide the console.

Monsieur Aspro had done what he needed to do. He took the key card, which would allow him to escape in any direction, if only he could find a direction.

The man was standing at the door. It had a small window, and Ser Aspro could see him. The door was locked, but it would not be hard for a skilled felon to enter. Dimly outlined against the giant nightlight of the Inverted Pyramid, he saw the man's head and shoulders. *Something wrong with the shape.*

Since the light was on in his office, no doubt the man could see him quite well.

Was he waiting for Aspro to come out?

Of course, the office was underground, though high above the mall floor. There was no handy window to jump out of, no vent or chute large enough to let Aspro's slender body pass. He could try making a run for it through the inner office, his own office, but it would be obvious what he was doing, and the door to the inner office gave onto the same platform, suspended above the mall floor, where the man was waiting. Suddenly Aspro knew that he must confront this monster, that he must show he was not a rat in a hole.

This hole, his office, had been his tunnel to the light. It had always taken Aspro where he wanted to go. From here he had ruled and defended his small empire, made the decisions about management and marketing, brought in new lines without overinvestment, developed relationships with the British Museum, the Bibliothèque Nationale, the Vatican, and the Metropolitan Museum. *He had never compromised either the Louvre's prestige nor his bottom line.*

He glanced at the computer. It was all there–all of it. All the web of relationships, the records of transactions, the two-dimensional barcodes themselves.... and it had been backed up automatically on tape at midnight last night. It would survive. Also there was the record of what he had just been doing, a record not yet preserved, not yet backed up. It was only 11:30 now.

To his horror, the door opened. The creature outside must have had a key card after all, or have been quietly working with a decoder to pick the lock.

The light fell on him and Aspro saw that his spine was hideously curved in a hunchback. Moreover, the bones of his forehead were distorted, lumpy, and asymmetrical, and one eyelid seemed to be sealed shut by tumors on the eyelid. His other eye, wide and brown, returned Aspro's stare.

The one-eyed hunchback carried a gun, and it was pointed at Aspro.

"*Qui vous êtes?*" asked the creature, and then, as if to be doubly sure, in a strangely accented English, "Who are you?"

Aspro clutched his key card so tightly in his hand that the plastic edges cut into his palm. He answered in neither language, with the one word, "Aspro."

The man closed the office door and stepped towards him.

SIX

I hardly recognized the useless, lonely lines of my own writing in the address of the *pneumatique*, under all the round postmarks stamped on it by the post-office and the penciled inscriptions of the mailmen–these signs that it was being activated, becoming real, these seals of the outside world, these purple symbolic ribbons of life, which for the first time joined hands with my dream to make it come true.

Marcel Proust

Harvard Business School professor Robert Longone had been awakened from a somewhat restless sleep in his room at the *Hôtel du Prieuré*.

He was to leave Paris the next day, and was only half packed. He had become distracted in the process by, of all things, the Mona Lisa mousepad he had purchased for his niece Jenny. Perfectly packable. But he was stopped by the famous face as he was about to slide it into the suitcase. It had been strange, that day, to stare at the actual object, carefully encased and housed on a wall by itself.

Yes, it really was like a Disney attraction–waiting in line together, waiting for the big adventure. The origin of all the Mona Lisas you ever saw or didn't see, in books or posters or neckties or cereal boxes or playing cards or all the places in the world they put her picture. And there were people from all over the world in that line, too.

Not much of a ride, though–kind of a small picture, really, and sort of dark. But it was what we all came for.

The mousepad design had trimmed the rectangular painting to a circle, surrounded by white space. Of course you lost some of the landscape that way, but that vague dreamy part of the painting wouldn't reproduce very well on the textured plastified surface. The woman's face was what counted. That strange dignified face could survive any kind of pixel abuse or printing errors, even moustaches.

There was nothing about her that resembled the pretty red-haired cashier, but of course he found himself thinking of her. *A very small adventure, but a nice one, on my last day in Paris.* He turned the mousepad over and then removed it from its plastic bag to examine the extra barcode on the underside of the pad. In the bad light of the hotel room, he could hardly locate the label on the dark rubber mat, so he removed it and held it up to the lamp. The label itself appeared clear against the light, a rather heavy plastic, easy to handle, with the barcode printed on it in matte black ink.

It was an oddly beautiful thing. As he had thought at first glance, it was linear. That is, it was essentially of the same kind as the barcodes used for price tags and so on, a series of black vertical lines of varying width, the first few of which coded a "start here" command and the last few of which coded "stop." Yet it seemed also to be almost an architectural drawing of a box or hollow cube. *As if someone did origami with a linear barcode.*

There was a top, trapezoidal code set inside horizontal lines that made the inside top of the cube, then a middle range which varied greatly in the darkness and frequency of the lines, giving the impression of two monoliths flanking a blank space. That was the two sides and the back. At the bottom was another trapezoidal area filled with code. *I wonder where the start code is. I wonder why this square code produced that round number, Pi million. Somebody's joke, I guess.*

He stuck the label on a white card, so that it would be visible for further study, and slipped it into his wallet.

Suddenly, though he had still plenty to do, he decided to go to bed and finish packing in the morning. *So long as the hotel doesn't forget my wake-up call.*

In bed, he started reading a book he had picked up in his wanderings the day before, an English translation of a French classic. He got as far as some story about a cake dipped in a teacup before he fell asleep, into a strange dream about a hairy chalice. He was trying to understand why the cup had red hair instead of blonde when the telephone rang.

"Yes, *oui*, is this my wake-up call?" He stared at the bedside clock. It was only a little after midnight.

"Monsieur Longone?" They pronounced it "Lawn-GUN." He liked that.

"*Oui*. It's not my time. Not time to get up. I mean, what's going on?"

"*Monsieur le Professeur* Longone, you avanpneu."

"Avump, unwhat? Say again, *répétez s'il vous plaît*?"

"You–have–*a*–pneu."

Robert turned on the light and reached for the little French-English dictionary. There can't be too many words that begin with *pn*. Here it was. *Pneu*.

"I have a tire?" Maybe they were using an English-French dictionary, and had looked up the wrong word. "I *am* tired, yes. It's midnight and I need to go back to sleep. *Fatigué*."

"Non, Monsieur Longone. I am sorry. Not a tire, like Michelin. A telegraph. A letter. A pneumatic letter. For immediate delivery."

"A pneumatic letter?" He sat up and began to think. *Of course! Like the vacuum tubes the drive-in banks use for transactions at home.*

He had taught a course in postal history a couple of years ago and he knew that big cities used to have vast networks of vacuum tubes for quick delivery of messages. They were called Pneumatic Systems. A great advantage for Victorian insider trading on the stock market, but handy in other ways too, especially in congested cities. Instant communication, rather like email today. Packets of cards were always being unloaded from a capsule at one station and re-packaged according to the next stations on the route towards their final destinations.

The Paris system was particularly famous. A "blue," *bleu*, they called it, the pneumatic postcard you could send from one end of the city to the other. They had used some kind of electrical routing–electrically charged metal bands coded the destinations, and the codes were read at the station mechanically. In Prague, the system was still used, but Paris had closed down its network at least twenty years ago.

"Monsieur Longone, do you understand? May we deliver your *pneu* to your room?"

"Um... so this is an urgent letter?"

"Yes, it is urgent. It is a telegram."

He sighed. The dream was still lurking in the back of his head, inviting him back to his pillow. He felt as if he had fallen into a time warp, receiving an urgent telegram from twenty years ago. "Look, I'll get dressed and come down. Can you give me a cup of coffee?"

"Yes, monsieur, I will send for it from the bar next door."

"Perfect. See you in five."

He was downstairs in only three minutes, in the dim lobby. The night clerk apologized that the coffee was not there yet, and handed him an envelope. He had hoped to see something of the technology of the pneumatic system, but there was no sign of it. The clerk explained that it had been delivered by a messenger who had not waited.

Robert was still turning the envelope over in his hands when the waiter from the bar arrived with his coffee–in a tiny white porcelain cup topped with its saucer, on a tray with a little aluminum sugar bowl. To Robert, still befuddled by sleep, it was the Grail. He tipped generously, pleased to have such a comfortable way to get rid of a couple of his last euros. He drank the tiny cup of coffee black in two gulps, and the night clerk removed the tray to some shelf behind the desk. Presumably the waiter would be back for it later.

The envelope was long and narrow, slightly curved from its ride in the pneumatic tube. The stationery was blue, heavy and luxurious, a lined envelope which concealed its contents. Yet there was something odd about it, which Robert decided to postpone investigating for the moment. He slid his finger under the flap, which was a little loose. Stuck to the lining under the envelope flap was a blank white label, a large one, overlapping onto the inside of the envelope. To his astonishment, the envelope held nothing except a printed two-inch square of thin colored cardboard, some kind of commercial packaging torn off a lightweight box. It had a barcode on it, a standard EAN-13, and the numbers suggested to him a supermarket item.

Robert Longone felt foolish. Was this a joke? Some friend from the conference teasing him about his early-to-bed ways? Who else would send him a barcode? The espresso was coursing through his veins. He would never get to sleep now, and tomorrow there would be packing, taxi, airport, customs....

The street door opened again, but this time it was not a waiter who entered the lobby.

The girl, or young woman, seemed very out of place in the quiet and dignified hotel. Not the kind of girl Robert Longone was used to seeing at all, not the kind who would make it into the Harvard Business School classrooms. Her hair was a mess of pale colors, blonde to white and possibly pink, and it stuck up in tufts on her head. She wore very tight jeans rolled up above her knees, and a sort of short vest for a top, leaving her belly to swell out over the jeans waistband. To top it off she had a bright pink feathered jacket, hanging off her shoulders so as to expose tattooed upper arms.

As she approached the desk Robert saw that she was pierced– she wore small studs in her right eyebrow, nostril, and earlobe, but none on the left, so that her heart-shaped face had a lopsided look. She had no makeup on, and didn't need it–her skin was perfect, with a few pale freckles. She wore plastic sandals of the kind now called flip-flops, though in Robert's youth he had unblushingly referred to them as thongs. Her eyes were blue, disturbed and disturbing.

Stop staring. She's none of your business.

He was turning away when he saw what she had in her hand.

A long, narrow blue envelope, slightly curved as if it had spent some time in a tube.

SEVEN

"Durendal, you are beautiful, bright, white!... I am tortured and burdened by this sword. I would rather die than let it fall into the hands of Pagans!"... Roland strikes the sword on the dark stone, pounding it harder than I can say.

Song of Roland

Monsieur Aspro, former Director of the *Centre Commercial du Louvre*, had kept up the kick-boxing of his youth, as a kind of casual exercise, the way another old man might play golf or practice tai chi. But he could only chance one movement, and it would gain him time, not victory. A blow below the belt buckle, or in the face, would be most effective. But the bony growths on the face of the one-eyed hunchback facing him seemed to protect it. He could aim for the good eye. *The Greek hero Odysseus put out the single eye of the giant Cyclops using a heated stake, and so escaped him and saved his own men. Can I save myself and my people?*

The gun unnerved him, though, and he went for the gun hand. He shifted his weight to balance on his right foot, and then his left rose abruptly.

Fibonacci screamed as the gun flew across the room and his hand became a focus of agonizing pain.

Aspro had ducked into the dark inner office, lit only by the ghostly security monitors.

By the time Fibonacci had retrieved his gun from under the printer stand and followed the old man into the dark office, it was too late. The office was empty, and the door out onto the platform over the mall was open. Fibonacci dashed through it, looking around for the old man.

He can't have gotten far. It won't matter, though, unless he triggers some kind of alarm or calls the police. But of course that's exactly what he will do.

There wasn't supposed to be anyone here....

The pyramid's soft glow filled the mall below with shadows, confusing his single eye. But any footfall in the giant space should have been audible. All was silent.

He hated this place, underground, claustrophobic despite the huge pyramidal window. Better out here than in the little offices, but he would have to go back in to finish what he came for. To give himself courage, Fibonacci began to sing softly:

"Up the close and down the stair,
In the house with Burke and Hare.
Burke's the butcher, Hare's the thief
Knox, the man who buys the beef."

He moved slowly along the platform towards the staircase. He stepped into the rectangle of light streaming from the door window of the secretary's room. Light along the edge of the door caught his eye.

Just now I closed it tight behind me.

The old man, Aspro, was in the office, standing at the computer, swiftly tapping out commands. He had not escaped–he had returned to his hole from the platform!

Aspro turned to confront his enemy. He had finished. Now either the right people would find out his secret–or nobody would. *I think this man Longone will understand even if....*

Fibonacci looked past him at the computer for a moment. He was holding the gun in his left hand, and it seemed that he was ambidextrous.

"Step aside, there. And no more of that kicking."

Monsieur Aspro stepped out from behind the computer and stood right in the middle of the room. He stared at Fibonacci with a defiant smile. Fibonacci saw that he was shifting his weight to kick again.

The gun spoke twice quickly. Aspro felt the warm, vivid pain instantly in his chest and, shatteringly, in his left shin. As if the gun still resented being kicked.

"Take two, Aspro, and call me in the morning." The creature spoke in English.

That old joke. I'll never hear it again, at least. Aspro smiled, and repeated the words as if they had some private meaning. "Take two," he gurgled.

EIGHT

"Galahad," said she, "I want you to arm yourself and mount your horse and follow me. And I tell you that I will show you the highest adventure ever seen by a knight."

Queste del Saint Graal

The strange punk girl ignored Professor Robert Longone and spoke to the *Hôtel du Prieuré* desk clerk.

"*Il y a ici un certain Professeur Robert Longone?*" She pronounced it as if it were Italian, Lawn-GO-nay.

"*Ce serait Robert Lawn-GUN, je crois. Mais vous savez, il nous est interdit d'offrir des détails sur nos clients. Et ce serait bien indiscret, en desssus, n'est-ce pas?*" The night clerk caught Robert's eye and winked, not very discreetly.

Robert turned to her, holding his *pneu* so that she could see it. "Are you looking for me, Mademoiselle?" he said in English.

She faced him and took in the fact of his blue envelope, twin to the one she held in her hand. Looking at her, he was struck by something faintly familiar. She fumbled in the mass of pink feathers under her armpit and evidently found there a purse or bag, from which she took a pair of wire-rimmed glasses. When she had put them on, her facial jewelry looked even odder.

"I have this." Her English was strongly accented: "Uh av deess." From her slim blue envelope she withdrew a business card. Robert recognized it as his own, and took it from her. On the back was written in handsome penmanship the name of his hotel.

He had seen that script recently. *It's the same as the address written on the blue envelope.*

"Yes, this is my business card. Where did you get it? You received it in the, um, letter?" He couldn't quite manage to say a word that apparently, in this country, began with *pn*. When he had taught the class on postal history, he had just said "noomatic."

"Yes. You know who sent it to me?" She searched his face, peering through the glasses.

"No. I can't imagine." *Unless this really is a joke that Albert and Sadie are playing on me, sending me a tart with a barcode at midnight.* "I don't know who sent me mine, either." He displayed the back of the envelope. "No return address."

Barcode.... he realized now what had bothered him about the *pneu* envelope. There was a code printed in dark blue on the outside of the envelope–a complicated width-variable and height-variable pattern of the sort the Post Office uses. Dark blue on pale blue, very pretty.

He took her envelope from the young woman and studied it. It also had a blue barcode on the back and, he discovered when he turned it over and looked under the flap, a square blank label stuck on the inside, like his. The barcodes on the two envelopes were quite different, though, he saw at a glance–the same symbology but only one short sequence of patterns, a digit or two, the same.

She was watching him intently as he examined the two envelopes. "Do you know Aspro?" she asked, finally.

He shook his head. The night clerk helpfully dived under his desk and came up with a bottle of aspirin.

The girl smiled for the first time. "*Non, non, il s'agit d'un homme qui s'appelle Aspro.*"

"*Il s'agit toujours d'un homme chez toi, paraît-il,*" retorted the clerk.

She shrugged disdainfully.

"Uh, this is a man called Aspro?" Robert wasn't sure he followed even that much.

"If you don't know Ser Aspro, I think I should take this *pneu* from you. It cannot be meant for you. And yet there is the address, which he wrote himself. I know his writing. And there is this little visiting card of yours which he sent to me. He meant for me to find you." She tapped the business card against the edge of the desk, thinking, for a few moments. "I think we need to find Aspro, now. You, me. *Now.*"

She met Robert's eyes again, her own blue ones blazing behind the glasses, and grabbed his sleeve. She was pulling him towards the door. She was like a dog that needs to go for a walk.

Robert patted his breast to check his inside jacket pocket. He had his wallet, ready for tomorrow, with his passport and airplane ticket. Well, it was only midnight. Why not?

NINE

Now go, dear Wiglaf, and look there in the dark cave for the hoard. The dragon has lost its treasure, it lies dead from its wounds. Hurry, so that I may see these ancient treasures sheathed in gold, these wonderful jewels....

Beowulf

Fibonacci had some time yet. The security guards were drugged, and it wouldn't wear off for at least another hour. Yet he was sweating, in an agony of claustrophobia.

He had watched Aspro's death with some pleasure. He was startled at his own vindictiveness. He had not planned to kill the old man, far from it. But the pain in his hand had maddened him. Then the stupid games, escaping out onto the platform only to return again.

You could have gotten clean away. Why didn't you run for it? Didn't you know I wouldn't be able to follow you into the tunnels?

You came back here for something. Something on this computer.

Whatever Aspro had been doing on the computer was important enough to risk his life–no, to sacrifice it. But when Fibonacci went to examine the screen, it was dark, with a cursor pulsing at top left.

His right hand throbbed and seemed to be swelling from the blow of Aspro's shoe. He pecked out a few commands and moved the mouse, but the cursor didn't respond. He fumbled for the on/off button but the reboot ended quickly with the pulsing cursor again.

On the edge of the monitor was a post-it note with several sets of names and numbers written on it. Passwords. But they didn't do him much good, since the operating system wasn't responding to his restart attempts. He must go back to his original mission.

Fibonacci turned the computer off and went after the box with a screwdriver in his left hand. He located the hard drive and removed it. He bundled it up with a CD, apparently of Charles Aznavour songs, from the CD drive, and a floppy he found beside the computer, in case these might have evidence of recent activities.

He began to search the room.

There were plenty of papers to look at in the secretary's desk drawers. Letters, minutes of meetings, drafts of proposals. The file cabinets along the wall held more such, plus specifications for items to be sold in the Museum shops, invoices, receipts, orders, and so on.

The bottom file drawer held, mysteriously, nothing but folder after folder of sheets of printed barcode labels. The folders were unmarked–evidently the contents were in some well-known order. These he pulled out and spread on the rug. He took from his pocket a handheld computer and an object rather like the nozzle of a miniature hairdryer: a powerful barcode reader. He produced a power cord and plugged it into the wall, then a little cable which connected it to the handheld computer. He began to scan the barcodes. The pain in his hand discouraged him, but he persisted, the sweat dripping from his hideous brow. He passed the scanner over one label on each sheet in the first folder. It seemed that all the labels in the folder were identical. After that, he just checked one or two labels from each folder.

TEN

Among these women, Magdalen seemed to have forgotten her feminine sex, for fearlessly she pierced the darkness and found the one she sought.

Pseudo-Anselm of Lucca, ca. 1085

The young woman with the lopsided facial jewelry and pink feathers was named Mado. *Short for Madonna? Even in France American culture is dominant*, thought Robert Longone. She told him her name in the taxi she hailed outside the hotel.

I suppose I'll be paying—I may have to change more dollars for euros tomorrow. Today, I mean.

The reservoir under her fluffy pink wing produced a cell phone, and she punched in a couple of digits—speed dial, presumably. The first number didn't reply, so she tried another speed dial, then a third. She left no messages. She seemed to expect the person or persons she was trying to contact to pick up at midnight. After the second call, she changed the cab driver's instructions, and Robert caught the word "Louvre."

Robert felt the espresso leap in his veins. The business card with his hotel handwritten on the back, that she had found in her letter.... of course he had given out a dozen or so during the conference, but he had also given one to the cashier at the Louvre Museum shopping mall—the lovely redhead. Suddenly it seemed he had a lot to discuss with Mado, but the taxi had stopped and through the arches of the old palace he saw the glass Pyramid shining in the night. To his surprise, Mado paid the driver.

She led the way. They did not go towards the Louvre courtyard, but to the Metro entrance, down the stairs into the great subway system. Evidently the trains were still running, as the gates to the turnstiles were open. However, they took another direction, the tunnel marked for the Louvre Museum's subterranean entrance.

Her confidence impressed Robert. She walked briskly up to the heavy, closed security doors at the end of the tunnel. He was not, therefore, much surprised when she pulled out a key card which, when swiped in a well-hidden slot, produced a tiny green light. He was almost not surprised when a numerical keypad opened in the wall and she entered a valid code, so that the door opened without sounding any alarm.

ELEVEN

Wiglaf, still in armor, went in under the cave's roof. He saw jewels, gold lying bright on the ground, painted walls, and the den of the dragon, that old high-flyer. There were dirty damaged bowls that had once served proud men, old rusty helmets, finely woven rings for the arms of dead warriors.

Beowulf

The scanner beeped and beeped again as Fibonacci the one-eyed hunchback scanned the barcodes. There must have been several hundred file folders. Fibonacci stared at the tiny red-on-black read-out, concentrating, but whatever Grail he sought was not there. He clenched his left hand and pounded the floor in despair.

It was supposed to be here! Where did they keep it?

The telephone rang in the inner office, and he got up off the floor, too slowly for his own satisfaction. *Why did it ring in the boss's office and not out here? What is a secretary for, but to take calls? Maybe any person who might call at midnight knows a direct number?*

He turned on the light in Aspro's office and stared at the phone on the desk. After a few rings, there was silence. Any voice mail had been routed somewhere else.

Now that he was inside the former Director's office, he began to look around it. He glanced at the wall of monitors, and was pleased to see that the visuals of various parts of the complex showed no movement anywhere. The carpeted room was clean and tidy, the big desk bare except for a blotter and suite of desk accessories. No computer visible, no file cabinets. He lifted the blotter to see if it concealed anything. It did.

A sea, a spiky dome, a vortex of tiny women's faces stared up at him. Some were solemn and reserved, many twisted in grief or agony. Some gazed upwards with a look of glazed rapture, tears glistening. It was hard to see any one face, though, in the great round pattern made up of all of them. Although the images lay like a giant jigsaw puzzle flat on the desk, the overall impression was of a concavity, a great circular hole that might suck you down. A wave of nausea swept over Fibonacci, until he focused on one of the faces, larger than those surrounding it.

She was blonde, and she reminded him of Princess Diana. *The same halo, it wasn't just her hair, she looked like this, with the light around her. And she looked so sad. But she smiled at me. She was so sad because of the others, the poor sick children who might die. But she bent close over me and she smiled because she knew I was not like them.*

A telephone rang back in the secretary's office. It had an odd, muffled ring. It had stopped before Fibonacci reached it, but he realized that it was a cell phone in the dead man's pocket.

He knelt beside Aspro's body.

What were you doing, old man? What were you doing with them? Were you there, that night, in the tunnel? Did you kill her?

Energized, he bent over the body and rolled it roughly around, checking the pockets, patting the body all over to discover any papers. He turned off the cell phone and threw it across the room. He glanced at the identification in the wallet, The security key card had fallen from Aspro's hand and lay on the floor with drops of blood on it. Fibonacci ignored it.

Then he heard voices, far down in the mall. Voices speaking both French and English. He must leave. He shuddered at the thought of redescending into the underground mall. *But then I'll be out, outside!* With a final kick at *Monsieur l'ancien Directeur* Aspro's limp body, he staggered out the door and towards the stairs.

TWELVE

At first light of surging dawn on Sunday, Magdalen, burning with love, arrived, but when she realized the tomb held no Savior, weeping she moaned and lamented, torn by pain.

Pseudo-Anselm of Lucca, ca. 1085

Mado's flip-flops slapped the mall floor as she charged in, heading straight for an open door with lights on. A barrage of screeching French followed. Sleepy-sounding men's voices replied.

She came flying out. "*Drogués!* That's the guard room. All asleep like babies. But what I saw on the monitor for the office...!"

Robert Longone followed her in the dark, apparently straight towards a wall. But the shadowy wall concealed elevator doors, and they opened immediately when she passed her key-card through a reader on the wall. The ride was short and, from the way Mado looked anxiously upwards, they were ascending. They stepped out on a platform or catwalk, facing out towards the Inverted Pyramid, about halfway up. Into the shadows below ran a staircase back down to the dark mall. Two doors stood open on the platform, letting the light from the rooms inside stream out.

Below, footsteps could be heard, in a strange, irregular run away from them.

"Let the guards take care of him, or them, or her," Mado said.

For the first time Robert hesitated. Up until this moment, the whole thing had been an adventure. Not even his own adventure. The strange girl, the *pneus* with their bizarre barcodes, the tunnel with its magically unlocked gates, had entertained him like parts of a puzzle which he might or might not bother to fit together before his flight home took off from Paris's Orly airport. He had taken both *pneus* and had them in his pocket–those bits of the puzzle he planned to decipher back in Cambridge, Massachusetts, with plenty of time and equipment.

But the running steps in the huge dark space, the girl's increasingly frantic energy, the drugged guards who would "take care of" the fugitive, suddenly presented him with quite a different kind of picture.

Something bad had happened, and he was no longer sure he wanted to know what it was.

Mado had let go of him and run into one of the rooms. Alone on the shadowy platform, with just some distant scuffling scraping noises coming from the other side of the huge pyramidal skylight, Robert felt balanced over a chasm, a strange underground abyss. He was not at all sure he would be able to get off this platform by himself, without Mado's hand to guide him.

He braced himself. This was, after all, the Louvre Museum, or at least an annex of it. One of the most civilized places in the world. He felt his pockets, knowing that he had packed the only possible weapon he owned, a pocket knife, in the suitcase to be checked. To his surprise, he found he was carrying the Personal Sampler, the experimental pocket-sized DNA analyzer/imaging computer/diagnostic tool he had shown the cashier at the Louvre yesterday. It seemed a long time ago now. Maybe this would come in handy.

He went to the door where Mado had entered, cautiously since she had not called him–in fact, there had been no sound from the brightly lit room at all. The smell was there before he saw what there was to see.

Run!

It was not a thought, it was an impulse in every nerve of his body. He wanted to run, he wanted desperately to get away. The smell was like a great wave, just a rusty smell of blood, not an unfamiliar smell but very strong. He gripped the edge of the doorframe to keep himself there. He couldn't even close his eyes or look away, because some stronger part of him made him want to understand what he saw.

Two bodies lying on the floor.

THIRTEEN

"Wherefore I say unto thee, her sins, which are many, are forgiven; for she loved much: but to whom little is forgiven, the same loveth little."

Luke 7

Monsignor Poquette-Filiposi awoke in the almost-dark treasury. It was as if a cool breath had touched his face. The candle in its chimney burned steadily, but it was quite low–it must be after midnight. He felt at his waist for his keys. The rectory was not always locked at night, but sometimes the housekeeper or one of the priests remembered to turn the latch. They would assume he had gone to bed early–they wouldn't leave it open just for him.

Usually Monsignor Poquette-Filiposi did indeed go to bed early, but tonight he had a bad conscience. He had come to the church to pray for forgiveness, and had fallen asleep.

Since he awoke thinking of Ser Aspro, it seemed to him that his prayer had not been granted. If the Monsignor had been a superstitious man, he would have said he felt that Aspro's soul was there in the room with him for a moment, instead of where it belonged, in the old *ancien Directeur's* body, no doubt asleep in his bed in Paris or awake plotting some new twist in his fantastic barcode crusade.

The Monsignor did not regret what he had done for Aspro, so he could not confess it to another priest and ask God for forgiveness. Besides, it would be embarrassing to confess it. It was not even a sin, exactly. He knew that Father Pater had refused to do it, and that the Bishop of Sens-Auxerre and no doubt the Pope would disapprove. But he had not asked permission and he had no intention of discussing it with anyone except the parties involved.

The parties involved were Ser Aspro and the contents of a couple of boxes in the treasury of his church, the Basilica of Mary Magdalen in Vézelay.

Ser Aspro was a strange man, but the Monsignor was fond of him. Moreover, Aspro was a generous supporter of certain of the Basilica's projects, despite the fact that he rarely came to Vézelay. The Monsignor had not been able to interest Aspro in community projects, in funding for the youth group or even new chairs for the congregation, but Aspro had been most helpful in such matters as restoring the reliquaries and parts of the building.

He is not a good Christian, but he will be, I am sure, before he dies. Right now he cares too much for these absurdities. His fancies about Mary Magdalen are not pious. His fancies about barcodes are rather paranoid—history is not kind even to those whom the Pope blessed on the medieval Crusades, and Aspro's crusade has no virtuous purpose, I think. All these toys of his mind get in the way of prayer and peace. Even his request....Yes, it was motivated by love, but also by his own cleverness. Was it right for me to do what he asked?

Monsignor Poquette-Filiposi's neck and back were less stiff than he would have expected after a couple of hours asleep in a chair in the cool, closed room. He looked forward to breathing the fresh June night air and returning to his bed. First, however, he went over to the marble table where he had laid the golden box. He pressed his ten fingers on the edge of the table and knelt down.

"Holy Mary, forgive me. And you also, my dear holy one." He moved his left hand down to a great marble box resting on the floor under the table. "Forgive me but take my action and make of it a blessing on those who are touched by it. Bless Ser Aspro, and those young women, and guide them to Our Savior Lord Jesus Christ. Let that man's small and ill-motivated desire become a source of love and peace for many."

He gripped the table again to help himself to rise. He took the candle and left the treasury, locking the door.

FOURTEEN

But Mary stood without at the sepulchre weeping: and as she wept, she stooped down, and looked into the sepulchre, and seeth two angels in white sitting, the one at the head, and the other at the feet, where the body of Jesus had lain. And they say unto her, "Woman, why weepest thou?"

John 20

On the floor lay a man, clearly dead, a dark-rimmed gunshot wound in his chest. One leg was mangled from another shot. Her tousled blonde head on his abdomen, Mado lay, limp, her eyes closed. For a long moment Robert Longone thought she must be dead too, and her murderer in the room. Then he remembered the fleeing footsteps–surely that was the man with the gun, and he was gone now.

I would have heard the shot. Even with a silencer. She's not dead, she's fainted. I know because I feel faint, too.

Robert bent over her. Mado was certainly breathing. His hands shaking a little, Robert removed her glasses and called her name. Looking half-blindly around the room, he spotted a bottle of Perrier on the desk and, since the man obviously had not died by poison, used it to moisten Mado's temples. After a moment she moaned and opened her eyes.

"Who is he?" asked Robert.

She seemed unable to speak, and her eyes looked dazed, the way his own felt, as if having seen the dead man put everything else out of focus. *She needs a quiet moment.* Robert put her glasses into her hand, which curled around them like a baby's fist. He stood up straight and walked around the office. To keep from thinking about the dead body, he pretended to be a detective thinking about the dead body.

That man was murdered and we heard the murderer running away. Who is he, why was he killed?

Mado belongs here. She had a key.

She knew something like this had happened. And she brought me because.... someone who had my business card thought I could help? The redheaded cashier from the store? It must have been her.... she also belongs here, after all, she works here....

Can I help?

The first thing that attracted Robert the detective was, of course, the computer. But it had been gutted of its hard drive, rather crudely. The screws were scattered on the floor in front of its carcass. He turned away.

The walls were full of framed pictures, alternating lovely large art posters with smaller black-and-white photographs. The dead man appeared, recognizably, in all the photographs, posing or shaking hands with various other men. Robert recognized one of the French presidents, and a finance minister, and oddly enough Bill and Hillary Clinton. In another photo, the man stood alone in front of a display that was obviously in the Louvre Museum shop. He was holding up a Mona Lisa T-shirt, and among the many items behind him bearing the face of Leonardo da Vinci's model was a mousepad. It was a different design from the one Robert had tried to buy that day. The dead man looked rather younger, too, in this picture, than in the Clinton one.

On impulse, Robert returned to the body and touched his Personal Sampler to the wrist of the corpse. Mado stirred.

"What are you doing to him?" She sat up, but kept her hands on the dead man's body, almost caressingly.

"It's just a bit of identity information. Then, if we can find something the murderer left behind, we can tell them apart."

"The guards didn't stop him?"

"No, I don't think so. I didn't hear anything." He looked down into her despairing eyes, and noticed that she still had her glasses in her hand. She followed his gaze and fumblingly put the glasses on. When she looked up at him again, her eyes were just as despairing.

"You knew him. Who was he?"

"His name is Salvateur Aspro. He is *Monsieur l'ancien Directeur du Centre Commercial du Louvre*. He is the director since it opened."

Robert remembered something she had said earlier.

"Salvatore—Sal Aspro for short?"

"Ser Aspro. That was how he liked to be called. Ser is like Sir, Monsieur, Signore. I think it was the old way of calling a man in Italy, or maybe the Languedoc." Robert looked puzzled, and she added rather impatiently, "Languedoc, that's the old South of France."

She paused. "Always the joke about *aspro*, aspirin, like at the hotel. But he was a very great man, Ser Aspro." She caressed a neatly tailored shoulder, then turned over her hand and saw a smear of blood. With the back of her hand she caressed his face, as if she were checking to see whether he had shaved recently. "A very great man."

Suddenly she straightened up, as if an idea had pumped energy back into her. Her hand traveled down his damaged left leg, not stopping until it reached the wound. Then she raised it, as if to caress the air above the messy red site. "Something the murderer left behind, like blood?" She moved down to examine the old man's shoes, but shook her head. "He fought back. He kicked the assassin. You can see where there is a little mark on the edge of the sole of his shoe. Maybe from the gun." She stood up and mimed a kick, shifting her weight to one foot and stabbing out with the other several times at an invisible adversary, as if to discover an angle that would leave such a mark on the shoe. She shook her head and knelt down again to peer at the shoe. "But I can't see any blood or flesh. Maybe the police will be able to get something."

Robert bent down to look over her shoulder at the sole of the shoe, which she held up to the light, unconcerned for her own fingerprints or for the way the leg bent the wrong way and made a slight noise at the site of the wound.

"So he kicked the assassin?"

"Yes. I hope he went for the face. That's what I would have done." She laid the shoe back, gently, aligning the leg a bit more naturally than it had been before.

Robert realized he still didn't know why the girl belonged here, but evidently she knew the old man well. Now that Robert had seen the photographs, he could look at the body and perceive that it was quite an old man, with beautiful white hair, clean-shaven and handsome in a thin, French way. His eyes were closed but his mouth was a little open and looked rather pitiful, with the yellow teeth showing. Perhaps Mado had worked in the shops.... she might have stolen the keycard. Or she might have been the old man's mistress, and stolen the keycard.

He said, "Do you know who did this? Or why? Did he keep a lot of money here? The day's receipts? Was it theft?"

"No." She turned her attention to him. "No, not money. He still used the *pneu* system to deliver all the money to the bank." She got to her feet and walked over to the wall, a little unsteadily. She slid the Fra Angelico picture aside and displayed the pneumatic tube console. She opened a hidden drawer and pulled out one of the capsules.

Robert smirked uncontrollably, watching her handle the phallic object. He wanted to laugh as badly as he had wanted to run away a few minutes earlier.

"When this office was built, he insisted on having a terminal, even though the *Télécommunications* was planning already to discontinue the service. A few private persons and societies still use it, especially the banks. Ser Aspro loved to send us *pneus*." Robert was still smirking, so she added, "Not very sanitary for the use you contemplate, Professor Longone."

Robert looked at the floor, feeling himself blushing. Then he saw the spread of folders of barcode labels on the carpet. The barcode reader was still plugged into the wall and into the handheld computer. *The murderer was after–barcodes?*

He looked up and really took in the whole room for the first time. There were the security cameras, recording his and Mado's activities. It must be ten minutes at least–well, maybe only five–since Mado had alerted the guards. Where was everyone? *I guess we're in charge of the place for now.* He saw Mado slide the picture back into place, having apparently checked the mechanism for any unsent or returned messages.

He hesitated a moment, then took his clean handkerchief and, using it in the best Crime Scene Investigator manner to protect any fingerprints, he gently unplugged the two electronic devices and put them in his other jacket pocket, to balance the Personal Sampler. He would like to find out what kind of codes this fellow was looking for.

Mado was looking through the papers from the wastebasket.

Robert wandered into the other office, Ser Aspro's private den. He paused at the sight of the bank of video monitors. But after a moment he realized that they were recording no movement at all–he and Mado were evidently still the only ones alive in the complex.

He was attracted to the desk by the bright pattern exposed by the removal of the blotter. When he saw what it was, he began to work his way around the desk, trying not to touch anything but fascinated. Although the edges were jagged instead of forming a circle, the general effect was of a circle made up of many small faces, women's faces, some larger, some tiny.

A jigsaw puzzle–but not really. Damn, they're all postcards. Museum postcards, I guess. Hundreds of women's faces–five hundred, maybe? He cut them up, no, he just cut into them so that they would fit together and show the faces. What was he doing? Ser Aspro must have been a dirty old man... that redhead looks to be naked... and that one... but this one is certainly fully dressed, she looks like a nun... and these others with the fancy hats on... The horrible expression, agony, sorrow, on all these blondes with long hair–was he a sadist? Or a foot fetishist–all these feet in the pictures of women's faces, ugh. But this one is smiling, and then that one looks like she has a devil behind her but she's smiling too. And this is the woman on the painting that hides the pneumatic terminal in the other room. There's my girl, my Georges de la Tour, that painting I liked so much! No, wait....

He remembered what the red-haired cashier had told him. Georges de la Tour had painted four or five different Mary Magdalens. It must be five, because there were five dark-haired women looking at candles, along the outer curve where the corners of the postcards were visible. He wasn't sure which was the one he'd seen today, the one on his coffee mug. He realized then that the circular arrangement of women's faces really did have a pattern, a pattern of light and color that created an optical illusion of domelike concavity and depth.

Pale small ones near the center and the right edge. Engravings, some of them, like on paper currency. Larger faces on the outside, all pale blondes on the right, redheads and dark hair on the left. Very cleverly done. It's like looking up in the State Capitol rotunda.

He looked up and saw Mado standing at the door. He felt embarrassed without knowing, or wanting to know, why.

"Did you find anything in the wastebasket?" he managed to say.

"Not really." She handed him a sheet of blank, shiny paper. *Label stock, used,* he thought automatically.

Mado was staring at the display on top of the desk. With an abrupt gesture, she swept both hands over the huge circle, pulling and pushing, until she had collapsed it into an untidy pile of postcards. She pulled off her feather jacket and used it to wrap the cards into a package.

Now that she no longer had her feathers, her secret underarm compartment was revealed to be a good-sized pink purse, dangling from a shoulder strap.

An alarm sounded, then another, echoing all through the building. Lights went on outside.

Mado glanced up at the wall of video monitors, which were finally showing some activity. "Let's go," she said.

On the way out she stooped and picked up the blood-clotted security key card which lay near the old man's corpse. She handed it to Robert.

FIFTEEN

Through wisdom is an house builded; and by understanding it is established: and by knowledge shall
the chambers be filled with all precious and pleasant
riches.

Proverbs 24

Fibonacci had made it to safety. Hidden in the courtyard of a five-
story 19th-century apartment building on the Rue Jacob was a small,
oblong building, windowless. It was built of fine stone and deco-
rated with simple but exquisite pilasters and pedimented niches.
Every aspect of the elements and decoration was according to the
Divine Proportion. It gleamed clean and white in a neighborhood
where the buildings tended to be grimy. All the same, the residents
of the building that surrounded it assumed it was a kind of fancy
toolshed. But it was a piece of the Temple.

Most Freemasons thought of their organization as a social
or business asset. They knew of course that it had a long history
of power and influence, but felt that their own power and influence were more interesting than history. Paris in the 18th century had been one of the great centers. The Prince Regent, Philippe
D'Orléans, was Grand Master, but the Revolution had brought to
power an even greater supporter, Napoleon himself.

Then the Parisian Temple of the Grand Orient had been seduced
by the Satan-worshiping Illuminati, and the glories of French Ma-
sonry were tainted forever. The Louvre *Pyramides* and the great
square *Arche de la Défense* were empty gestures, pretenses of angles
in a city that was growing hollow underneath, literally.

Fibonacci, born in Edinburgh on the solid rock of the Royal Mile, was part of the true Temple, the servants of the square.

The bastion against Pi.

Now, at nearly one in the morning, Fibonacci was the only person there. He found the first aid kit and tended to his right hand. The pain was stronger and he thought a bone might have been broken. The Doctor would know, but the Doctor was not in Paris. Well, the Doctor would know everything soon enough.

Right now, Fibonacci was alone in this Temple. Some French Brothers had welcomed him there when he arrived a few days earlier—friends from previous visits. They were gone, but Fibonacci knew the resources of the tiny building well. There was an office with several computers.

Fibonacci selected the most powerful Windows box and began working on connecting the hard drive from Aspro's computer. He had assembled ahead of time the hardware he was likely to need, jumper pins and ribbon cables, and had practiced this task a little the day before with a spare hard drive.

The telephone rang.

"Fibonacci? Laddie, is that you?"

"Aye, sir." He felt his Scots intonations flooding back into his own voice, responding to the Doctor's.

"The day has eyes, the night has ears, lad."

"The line is secure, sir."

"And so, I am glad to see, are you. It's good to be out of harm's way. Tell me, now, did you find anything?"

"I got the hard drive, sir." There was a pause. "He that has a good crop doesn't mind a few thistles. I didn't find the barcode labels. Not the kind you told me about. All the labels they had were linear, but I checked them anyway to make certain."

"You'll gut no fish till you get them. Have you looked at the drive yet?"

"Not yet. I know that say-well is good but do-well is better, sir, and I was just going to set it in. But... there was a man there, at the museum. I caught him doing something with the computer. We'll soon know what he was about, I hope."

"Did you speak to this man? Where is he now?"

"I asked him who he was. He told me, Aspro. Was that a joke?"

"No, that is his name. Where is he?"

"He's dead. I shot him."

The voice on the phone paused a long moment before replying.

"That was not the plan, Fibonacci Fibonacci. Not to kill, especially this man. We were.... I would have liked to speak to the man. After we had the hard drive and knew what he was about."

"Aye, sir. But he... he attacked me, sir."

"He was the bee that made the honey, my boy. Well, what cannot be cured must be borne. It is long past joking when the head's off. You are a murderer, now. That's a terrible thing, but I will find out a way for you. And you found no barcodes there?"

"I found them, I scanned them, hundreds of them, sir. But nary a one like we were looking for."

"Well." The man on the telephone seemed to be thinking. Fibonacci waited, hoping for a kind word after his long ordeal. It came, sort of. "Well, when you've had a look at the drive, perhaps it will turn out that you did a good night's work after all. What we seek you may have found. I know Paris is a terrible place for you, lad. I know you suffer there. Do not leave the Temple until I call you again." He hung up.

Fibonacci returned to his task, a little more hopeful. He would redeem himself! He began to work to register the drive. At first the computer's BIOS was not detecting the drive at all. It was as if it were not there. He checked the connections again, tiredly. Was it somehow protected? He tried again. He wasn't sure he could troubleshoot if the automatic detection didn't work.

On the third try, the drive was detected and he was able to finish the configuration. He felt almost faint with joy. He restarted the computer and found it–drive L: for Louvre. He clicked on the drive, ready to unlock old Aspro's secrets.

To his horror the friendly blue-and-white interface disappeared. The screen before him began to scroll rows of numbers, green and white on black.

He reached impulsively for the Restart button and pressed it. The computer monitor went blank and did not light up again. Slowly he realized what he had done.

The computer was dead. The hard drives were lost. And all his night's work was for nothing at all.

He limped over to the cabinet where he had put his marbles.

SIXTEEN

The blessed Thecla observing, saw the rock opened to as large a degree as that a man might enter in; she ... bravely fled from the vile crew, and went into the rock, which instantly so closed, that there was not any crack visible where it had opened.

Acts of Paul and Thecla 11

This time Mado took them down farther in the elevator, skipping the mall level. They stepped out into a huge cool room, quite dark. There were a few lights burning overhead but he could not see them directly. Tall structures blocked them from his line of sight. "The stockroom," she whispered.

The outlines facing them and the obstacles Robert sensed at knee level resolved themselves into shelving and boxes. He felt alive and frightened. He had been wanting to run away for so long—it seemed like hours though it must be only minutes. Now at last they were doing it.

Mado started moving. She seemed so sure of herself that Robert reached out to touch her shoulder to follow her in the dim aisles. She turned corners several times and suddenly Robert felt they had left the stockroom. The walls were closer and it was even darker, and there were no more obstacles or turns. The girl's weird pale hair caught what faint light there was, so it seemed as if he were following a fairy fire.

After a few moments a faint light ahead began to glow. Robert thought it was still a long ways in front of them, but suddenly they were bathed in a very soft light coming from above, the light of the Paris stars shining down through a street-level skylight very far above. Robert forgot his fear and paused to look up. He realized that between them and the skylight there was a walkway suspended in the air, over which he had walked that afternoon going in the other direction, between the Louvre Museum and the mall, between the Louvre Pyramid and the Inverted Pyramid. He lowered his gaze and looked around himself, seeing the mouth of the tunnel from which they had emerged and another one, opposite it, leading apparently deep under the museum.

Mado had paused too, but now she moved on into the new corridor, pale shoulders and hair and a twinkle of bright pink that was her purse. Robert hurried to follow her. They came to a door and she slid her keycard. The door opened into a very large, softly lit room, the ceiling held up by thick columns. They stepped in and she closed the door behind her. They kept walking across the room—there was another set of double doors beyond them, on the other side. Robert gazed around at the strange ramps to nowhere, curved staircases, and sloping platforms parked around the room. Beside one column was a pile of women's shoes, stiletto-heeled sandals, all in turquoise and pink, all jumbled together, perhaps ten pairs. He stopped, distracted.

Mado stopped, too, and turned back, beckoning him. "This is under the place for the parades, the mode.... the couture houses...." She stopped, frustrated.

"Fashion shows?" Robert had heard that there was a special area for fashion shows somewhere in the Louvre underground. He looked up, as if he could pierce the ceiling and see this perfumed, no doubt very elegant room with its stage and catwalk. He looked at Mado with a bit of a smile to express his surprise. Even at a couple of yards' distance he could see how sad she looked. If she stopped now, he thought, looking at her downturned mouth, she'd dissolve with sorrow.

"Yes, yes! But look, let's just go...." Mado pointed up to an obvious security camera hanging beside the door towards which they were heading. Robert looked back and saw another that would have recorded their entrance.

"But then—should we just give ourselves up?"

"No, no, it doesn't matter, but come on, quick quick!" They hit the second set of doors running and Mado swiped her keycard fast to get them out.

On the other side, everything was pitch black. Robert hoped this was because his eyes were dazzled by the gentle security lights in the fashion basement. Mado herself moved forward more slowly, and he followed the sound of her, but stepping carefully. They seemed to be moving between walls again, and this corridor, if it was one, ended in what felt like a wider space, but with no lights at all. Mado stopped. Robert reached for her, and she took his hand and guided it to touch a surface. He felt along it. A wall, darker in the darkness. He leaned against it, so he wouldn't lose it.

"The Museum is on the other side, here. Have you seen the excavated medieval walls, the old castle?" she was whispering, very softly.

Robert shook his head, then realized it was too dark for her to see. "No, I don't think so. I've only visited the museum once, and I went inside upstairs, on the ground floor, past some paintings. I saw a sign for the other direction, like a tunnel entrance, to the Louvre Museum, when I was there yesterday, but.... "

"Well, there is an exhibition area, but we are lower than that. This is excavation level. We need to wait a moment here." She paused, then went on.

"You know, in fact the eighties and the Grand Louvre renovation were not really about the pretty glass *Pyramides*. When they redesigned the buildings and added those new entrances, it was not especially a matter for the museum, any more than for the museum boutique. It was the possibility of excavation under the Louvre itself, and the courtyards. The Louvre looks modern...."

"Modern? You mean *not* modern?" Robert felt there must be a language problem.

"Well, I mean, it looks 17th- and 18th-century. A lot of it is 19th-century additions, in fact–those wings reaching out towards the Place du Carrousel. Napoleon meant to recreate the ancient idea of a Temple of Knowledge–you know that he was a great franc-maçon–a Freemason? You know what that is?"

Robert knew what a Freemason was. *Odd girl, who looks like that and calls the 17th century modern.* They had drawn close in the dark, and he realized that now she could see when he nodded. Their eyes were getting accustomed to he darkness. He smelled her too, some perfume and some sweat and a little of Ser Aspro's blood. Or perhaps this was partly his own smell, unfamiliar in the slightly chilly darkness. He was still holding Aspro's security card, which Mado had given him, with blood on it.

"Anyway, underneath the *cour carrée*, the central square of the Renaissance palace, was the old, medieval fortress of Paris. It was not a castle for living in. It was a prison and treasury, and also for the people, though the king built it. This was a place where they could come when the river got too high or some enemy attacked. The first city of Paris was really our island, the *île de la cité*, you know, where the church of Notre Dame is now. But the city was getting bigger and the people needed another refuge. That was, oh, around 1200. Philippe Auguste. He had made France grow by taking territories from the English and others, kings and dukes you know, so it was important to remind them not to attack Paris."

"And the later palace was built around this old fortress?"

"On top of it. That is, the medieval castle was torn down to build the new one. *François Premier*, the first King François, did that, quite early in the fifteen-hundreds. But of course during three hundred years of city life the level of the courtyard and especially the ground outside would have risen–just from garbage, you understand. We were pretty sure, back in the sixties and seventies, that François's architects laid their foundations on many feet of buried medieval town."

"*We* were very sure? *We,* meaning who? Were you born then, Mademoiselle?"

"We, the archaeologists of Paris. I have studied that, a little. I count myself one of them. The question was, how much of medieval Paris remained under the Louvre? And how could we get at it?"

"So the big renovations were just marketing for the archaeology?"

"Exactly!"

"The *Centre Commercial* is marketing for the scholarship."

"The underground parking garages have been designed to accommodate the 14th-century defensive walls built by Charles V.

Back there, where we passed, after the fashion show–behind those walls is still unsifted midden, garbage. More Paris garbage we are examining all the time. The beautiful *Pyramides* of Monsieur Pei are built on this passionating garbage."

A noise came to them from far behind them. Perhaps it was in the fashion basement. Mado and Robert kept very still. The sound was not repeated.

He saw her pull her key card out and he realized that they had been standing in front of a door–a normal-sized door, set flat in the wall. Now that his eyes were growing accustomed to the dim light, he saw a card swipe beside it. She slipped her card into the reader. A tiny red light came on. They both nudged the door, then tried pulling on the handle.

It was locked and it stayed locked

"Let me try this one."

The sweat of his palm had dissolved the blood on Ser Aspro's keycard, and he wiped it carefully on his jacket before trying it.

Mado whispered, "It will not march. Not work. Ser Aspro's card was the same as mine. He did not have a card to enter the museum, except maybe..."

But the tiny light blinked green.

SEVENTEEN

I gazed admiringly at the agate marbles, captives full of light, in a wooden chalice set apart, precious to me because they were smiling and blonde like girls and they cost fifty cents apiece.... They were as transparent and melting as life itself.

Marcel Proust

Fibonacci gazed at the marbles. They were ordinary cat's-eye marbles, a child's toy, rolled out on the table, yellow and orange and green and blue. Sometimes he found red or black ones, and added them to the bag, but right now there were only the more ordinary colors. He would see other kinds of marbles, some of them smaller in diameter, or larger, in the shops, sometimes–made of white glass with colored swirls, or of shiny metal. He felt these were of no use to him, and did not add them to his collection.

The Doctor had given him a large decorative glass marble, made he said by an artist from Seattle, in the United States. Fibonacci carried that one in a pocket in his jacket, but did not of course use it. Once he used a marble, it was gone.

He had been born to a good family, he knew, though he was not sure of the name. He thought it must be MacGregor or even Stuart. Not every Stuart is high-born, but he knew his birth was good. Good birth, he was good enough but not pretty enough. His mother, a countess probably, had given birth to him in a big house on the Royal Mile in Edinburgh. But when she saw him she would not give him milk. When his father saw him he would not give him a name.

The Doctor had stood before his mother when she gave birth to him, and he wanted the ugly baby, so they gave it him.

This much he knew by heart. The Doctor had told him the whole story when he was so small. The Doctor loved him, for he had chosen him. He had given him a name, not his own name it's true. Not the best name, either, for a boy going to school. Fibonacci Fibonacci. But the boys at school had so much material in him for cruelty that they rarely got around to mastering his strange double name.

When he was in school they had taken him away from the Doctor for a long time, to a Children's Hospital. For years perhaps—he wasn't sure. There were lots of doctors looking at him, National Health doctors of course, when he was in that place. One said he would go deaf if they did not operate. One of them said he would make it so that Fibonacci had two eyes to see out of like anyone. Another talked about taking away the hump. Could they do it? No. If he could have been made like other boys, the Doctor would have done it. He had the instruments, the knowledge, the numbers. But nothing could be done.

That was when the Princess came to see him. She had looked sad, seeing the other children who were deformed or had burned skin or hideous stitches on their faces. But she had smiled at him. She knew he was not like them, that he had a destiny of his own. That was when he saw the light around her head.

After a while he came back to live with the Doctor, and learned many good things. But he had to go back to school, and there he continued to learn evil things. He had tried at first to fight back, but as he grew he became weaker instead of stronger. He could only wait until it was over.

He knew, by both instinct and reason, that the marbles were bad. They were spheres, products of Pi. And they had been a special joke of the boys.

Look! Here's an eyeball! Swallow it and then you'll have two!

Really, it will go right up there and pop out and then you'll be able to see really good!

Eat the eyeball, Fibbo! Eat the eyeball!

Fibonacci chose a green one and began the familiar process of swallowing it.

EIGHTEEN

Indeed, we believe that female whom Luke called a sinning woman and whom John names as Mary, is the same Mary about whom Mark testifies....

Pope Gregory, Homily 33

Mado and Robert Longone were sitting on some very old garbage under the Louvre. The medieval fortress wall towered above them in the darkness, stopping somewhere below the level of the floor of Francis I's palace. *The new Louvre, meaning 16th-century. Well, at least America had been discovered by then.* The excavation area was if anything too well lit, and full of scaffoldings, boxes, and mechanical and manually-operated equipment. They had gotten here through several doors and dark corridors known to Mado. She had made Robert stand in one place, just inside the room, while she ran around on the planks set over the rubble. She found a place for them to sit comfortably, where they could lean their backs against the rough wall and sit on a couple of dusty cushions. She set down her pink feather package of postcards there, came back to escort Robert to his seat, then ran back to turn off some of the lights so that the room was not quite so bright. Finally she came back to rest sitting beside him.

"Now we're safe," she said.

Robert hardly dared to ask, "Safe from what?"

"From being found. From having to talk to police and fill out forms, tell stories and identify the body."

"What?" Robert half stood up, but the rubble under his feet was not conducive to a pose expressing the sudden anger he felt. The equipment he had taken from the crime scene swung heavy in his jacket pocket. "What do you mean? We were running away from the police instead of helping them? Do you realize we might actually be able to help? Obviously you *can* identify the body."

"They don't need me for that." Robert thought of the photographs on the wall and realized that the dead man must have been well-known. "Bothering with us would just distract the dear policemen from finding the assassin. You saw, that place is so full of camerascopes, for security. They will have us on video, and also the assassin. Even if he wore a mask, even gloves, I think they can find him with ADN. I am sure that the kick drew blood. It will be on the carpet, the floor, somewhere. If they have his ADN they will know who he is."

"DNA, you mean?" *I should have looked harder for something I could pick up with the Personal Sampler. Instead here I am, down the rabbit-hole with Alice the archaeologist.*

"The thing is, I trusted you, Mado, I followed you here, and now it seems like we are just running away from responsibilities. I might have been able to help the police. We have evidence, after all."

"Did you figure out anything about the envelopes Ser Aspro sent us?" Mado asked.

Robert stretched out his legs, trying to relax them. He fished in his pocket for the envelopes and came across his wallet, passport, and plane tickets. He glanced at his watch. It was nearly two in the morning. The flight was at noon, and he still had packing to do. He pulled out the envelopes.

"I haven't had much time to think about them," he noted. "Did Ser Aspro usually use these special envelopes for his letters, I mean..." He still couldn't bring himself to say *"pneu."* She nodded. "Yes, I can see these narrow envelopes would fit in that, um, thing you showed me." *Pneumatic capsule? Dead technology dildo?* "Custom stationery would make sense. But what about this–did the envelopes always arrive with these markings?"

She looked at the blue barcodes.

"No, I don't think so. I think I would have noticed. They're like those labels on things you buy, aren't they?"

"Barcodes–see, they're made up of bars...."

She interrupted as he gathered his thoughts for a lecture on the nature and use and history of barcodes. "Yes, but what good is it? He didn't send me any message. I can't understand why there was no message at all."

Suddenly she yawned hugely, and immediately afterwards began to cry. She removed her glasses and put them in a case in her purse, sobbing gently the whole time. "I can't believe he's dead. No more blue *pneus*...." She switched to French and murmured to herself a little longer, then relaxed against his shoulder, asleep.

Robert, glad she was quiet now, continued to examine the envelopes, but beyond his earlier observation that the two barcodes were in the same symbological language, he made little headway. He remembered the little barcode scanner he had picked up in Aspro's office, left there probably by the murderer. *Tell me again why I am hiding this evidence from the police...?* Perhaps it was programmed to read these barcodes, or could at least give him a clue.

Thinking about the barcode reader, sitting in the pocket which Mado's warm body made unavailable, he remembered the Personal Sampler in the other, easier-to-reach pocket. He took it out.

He brought up the data for Ser Aspro and took a good look at the man, at forty, at twenty, and then at the age of ten. *Strange, this slim, big-eyed little boy lived another–how many years? Hard to tell, but he must have been seventy at least. And now he is dead. So he was the Director of the whole museum mall. I wonder if he knew about the Pi million total yesterday. And what kind of relationship did he have with this bossy whory punk little woman? She certainly cared about him.*

The girl stirred against him, pillowing her strange head in the curve of his elbow. She slept jewelry-side-up. He looked down in the soft light at the tattoos on her near shoulder. *Basically a circular design, round, with little spikes all over it–no, I think they are words. How could they tattoo in such a tiny script? I can't make it out, but the markings on those lines are certainly numbers. Three something, seven something or that might be a one. Wait, it's some kind of globe, a round map of the earth! That line is the equator, and that's Europe, but Africa is not very well drawn at all.... What is that little thing swimming along there, a ship or a....*

She sighed and moved forward almost into his lap.

Robert sat up straight. He should try to sleep, himself. He

closed his eyes for a moment, then opened them and, almost without thinking, turned the Personal Sampler back on.

Touch. Save. Now, which? *Age ten, very pretty little girl, with freckles! Age forty, not bad at all. Twenty.*

The image showed a lovely young woman with glasses and red hair, naked of course. He had seen her before. Exactly the same face, exactly the same body.

Had he opened the wrong set of data?

Or was this bossy whory etc. individual in fact the lovely red-haired cashier in a bizarre disguise?

Was she a split personality?

This woman had the red x in the left palm, indicating left-handedness, though, and Robert could have sworn the cashier was right-handed. Could that happen in a split personality? He had read somewhere that schizophrenics were more likely to be ambidextrous, as if both sides of their brains were talking at once. But that was not the same as being genetically right-handed in the afternoon and left-handed at night.

I would have noticed if that cashier had a hole in her nose. I think so, anyway.

He tried to call up the data for the red-haired cashier, but all he got was a low-battery message. The conclusion seemed clear, though:

There were two of them.

NINETEEN

They reasoned among each other thus: The virgin is a priestess of the great goddess Diana, and whatsoever she requests from Her, is granted, because she is a virgin, and so is beloved by all the gods.

Acts of Paul and Thecla 11

Marie Navet, the red-haired cashier from the *Centre Commercial du Louvre*, had googled Robert Longone before she went to bed, on her home computer. His faculty bio on the Harvard Business School site was worth the trip. There was a small photo of him, with a goatee. She was glad he had shaved it off. Ten years ago, when he was in his twenties, a goatee would have been suitable, to make him look older. Twenty years from now he might wear it again, to look a little younger. But right now, he was a very good age indeed.

Many degrees, a teaching award, a few consultancies listed. Of course, he would make his real money as a consultant. *He could do better than just those few, he is quite good. Probably he does do better than that but is discreet about listing such things on a public website.*

She could not discover from the website whether he was married. He had worn no ring, and did not act married, to her mind. During her internships in Los Angeles and Washington, D. C., she had met plenty of American married men who were interested in her, so she knew the type.

Of course, it was important for her to remain a virgin. In Ser Aspro's mind, Sacred Love was a virgin with red hair.

Yet Ser Aspro had seemed quite excited about the business card from Professor Longone that she had given him. Ser Aspro had tried to explain something to her about the strange behavior of her cash register, but her mind was too full of Professor Longone and his little gadget. He must have seen her naked on that display–it made sense that such a device would produce an image of the entire body without clothing.

She turned off the computer and went to bed. She did not awaken to the knock at the door of her apartment around midnight. Only the next morning did she see the *pneu* slipped under her door. She could find nothing in the envelope, just the white label under the flap.

What awakened her, however, was a call from the Paris police. She was needed to identify a body.

Monsieur Aspro, retired Director of the *Centre Commercial du Louvre*, had been murdered.

She took her *pneu* along in the taxi to the morgue.

TWENTY

A dream is like a holy book...
Umberto Eco

Robert was dreaming about a swan. He pursued it, and it flew away from him down a dark, rainy Paris street. He felt a great need to sneeze, and an equally great sense of foreboding that if he sneezed something bad would happen.

A telephone rang. It must be his wake-up call.

His pillow seemed to be moving and he heard a French voice speaking French.

It was not his wake-up call.

He opened his eyes, gazing up into Mado's face. His head was on her lap. She was talking on the telephone.

He needed to pee, urgently. He stood up abruptly, his joints stiff, his shoes slipping around a bit in the rubble. Mado smiled up at him and pointed him towards the door, signaling to go left. He climbed back up onto the plank walkway, hoping he hadn't stepped on any important medieval garbage, and hurried along out the door. He was prepared to use a wall, historic or not, but was pleased to find a discreet door marked "W. C.," Water Closet, a favored euphemism for toilet facilities in France. It must be the archaeologists' restroom

When he returned, Mado was standing on the plank platform, stretching. She bent over and touched her toes. He looked at his watch. It was seven in the morning. In the castle midden, the lighting was the same as it had been five hours ago.

"I think we had better go," she said.

"Yes. Where? How?"

"We will leave the way we came. The police know that we were in the office, of course, they saw us on the tapes from the camera-scopes. They want to talk to us, but I was right, it's not too urgent. That was Marie on the telephone."

"Marie. Who is Marie?"

"She knows who you are! She told me all about you. Even that you used to wear a little beard." Mado pouted a little and stroked her own chin to illustrate, rather flirtatiously. "Marie spoke to the police. They want to take back anything we lifted from the office. What do you think?" She hugged the feathery pink package of postcards, as if unwilling to hand it over.

"I have a barcode reader and computer that may have belonged to the murderer. It's important evidence. But I'd like to have a go at scanning the codes on those blue envelopes with it before we give it up."

Mado frowned. "The detective on the case, we know him. He's sort of a family friend, sort of. *Monsieur le Capitaine* Bulle. Not a good name for him, it means "bubble." We have nicknamed him Faché because he is always *faché*, angry. He is not like a bubble, not a bubblehead, not bubbly. He has not yet caught the assassin. So maybe we can help, you and I. I didn't know about this barcode reader. What is all this about barcodes?"

"That's what I'd like to know! It wouldn't take me long. I just need.... a current, good light, paper and pencil to take notes. I'll handle the scanner with a handkerchief."

I hope I can do this. I'll have to try to hold the thing in a different way, where he didn't hold it.

"The scanner has its own readout, so we can at least get a record of the numbers and letters if it is able to read these codes. Then there's the computer that the scanner was hooked up to, a hand-held. I don't dare try to operate that–I can't press keys or touch-screen without messing up any fingerprints it has on it. Probably he wore gloves, or if he didn't he must have left fingerprints in plenty of other places. Still, it's important not to tamper with evidence. But if the scanner can read the code, chances are the little computer has a database that would tell us what the code means."

Mado hesitated. "Would it help if you had one more *pneu* barcode to put with these?"

"Another in the same group? Yes, of course. With three read-outs we would probably be able to see a pattern even without the database."

"Marie has a *pneu*, too. I think we need to see Marie before we see our dear *Capitaine* Faché. Even if it makes him more *faché* than ever."

TWENTY-ONE

He would joke with hyenas, returning their stare
With an impudent wag of the head:
And he once went a walk, paw-in-paw, with a bear,
"Just to keep up its spirits," he said.

Lewis Carroll

Captain Ogier Bulle sighed. He was *faché* indeed.

He loved his job. He had a couple of offices, one out in the relatively modern building in the 17th *arrondissement* and one here in the *Brigade Criminelle*, in the heart of Paris, the Île de la Cité. His responsibilities in the First District gave him the chance to meet many distinguished Frenchmen, and foreigners as well. His wife, who was rich and socially ambitious, loved his job too. He himself felt that, particularly with her money behind him, he could be ambitious without becoming corrupt, and he expected to rise to *Commissaire de Police* easily and soon. The First District was prime territory for high-ticket shopping, fashion shows, and charity balls–mostly the province of the Urban Police, but with thefts, vandalism, and white-collar crime, even mob activity, to keep the Judicial Police busy. It was not, however, prime territory for murder.

Today he sat in the old chair at the old desk in the old room on the Quai des Orfèvres, the historic *Brigade Criminelle*.

Monsieur le Directeur Aspro, active and retired, had caused the police a little trouble from time to time. Now that he was dead he seemed likely to cause much more.

His techs had edited the relevant bits of the Louvre security camera videos for *Capitaine* Bulle.

Of course there was no video camera in the guard room itself, so they couldn't see how and when the guards had been drugged, but it was probably something in their late coffee, around 11 p.m.

There was a scene of the shadowy figure entering the mall on a metal walkway near the roof, leading to a ladder down the side. The man was barely discernible against the lit-up *Pyramide Inversée.*

The security cameras in the old man's office had been turned off before that, but had been activated a short time after the assassin entered the *Centre*. Aspro must have seen his enemy coming, on his own video monitor, and turned the office security cameras on then.

There was no way of knowing what Aspro had been doing in his office so late. Why hadn't he tried to awaken the guards? Why hadn't he called the police? Perhaps he did not expect to be personally attacked. But he was responsible for the merchandise below. If it was a thief, he should have given the alarm.

They had a video of the brilliant kick, the brief chase through the offices, and the murder. The shooting itself was like a duel from a Western (Captain Bulle's favorite film genre). Old Aspro had positioned himself so that his hideous assassin was facing directly into a camera, and the firing of the shots was clear enough to convict as soon as they found the man. Another camera showed it from the opposite angle. Perfect–you could cut a feature film from it.

Then there were the strange activities of the killer. Then the arrival of the girl and the man. Of course he recognized the girl. Mademoiselle Marie Navet, when she was shown that segment of the video, had been able to tell him that the man was an American professor, Robert Longone, staying at the *Hôtel du Prieuré*. She seemed to know this fact by heart.

He replayed the murderer's fruitless search through the barcode labels again. The American had taken the barcode reader, but it looked like any scanner at any cash register. Why had he taken the evidence? And what was he doing with that thing like a pocket computer, waving it over the dead man's body? He had some questions for *Monsieur le Professeur* Longone.

As for Mado Navet taking the postcards, he understood that well enough. Her sister Marie had been able to help explain it. Poor children, he thought. Perhaps Aspro's death would be a good thing for them, in the end.

His assistant brought him his late-morning tea. He had asked for a calming *tisane*, or herbal infusion, today. He was pleased to see that it was *tilleul*, the flowers and bracts of the lime tree, with a cookie to dunk in the rich green liquid. Its medicinal powers would help him through this moment of stress.

It was strange, he thought as he dunked and sipped, how Ser Aspro had managed to live in several centuries at the same time, with his *pneus* and his computer-controlled video monitors. At least the old man had outfoxed his murderer. Although the security camera was not so well positioned to overlook the computer monitor, Bulle could see from the camera that Aspro had activated a virus on his own hard drive before he was killed. Unfortunately that meant that when the drive was recovered it would not have any more to tell the police than to tell his enemies.

TWENTY-TWO

So we grew together,
Like to a double cherry, seeming parted,
But yet an union in partition;
Two lovely berries moulded on one stem;
So, with two seeming bodies, but one heart...
Shakespeare

Marie Navet, driving her own car, a sea-green vintage Citroën DS, met Robert and Mado just about where the taxi had dropped them off last night. They had been able to slip along in the early-morning shadows from the elevator to the tunnel without alerting the police, who were busy up in Ser Aspro's office and even higher up, near the edge where the *Pyramide Inversée* dropped down under the *Arche du Carroussel*.

Robert was somehow not surprised to find that the mysterious Marie, who knew all about him, was the red-haired Louvre cashier. She smiled at him in a friendly way as they climbed into the car but gave Mado a look that was almost tragic. None of them spoke in the car, however.

Marie dropped the other two off at a grand-looking doorway on an empty street and returned on foot from parking her car somewhere nearby. She unlocked the door, and Robert gathered they were going to her apartment.

The moment the apartment door closed on them, the two young women exploded in French cries and explanations, embracing each other and weeping.

Robert took a good look at the two of them.

Marie was in flats, and the two women were the same height. They were the same body, too, except that Marie had the red hair and Mado had the slight plumpness that the Personal Sampler had presented as their common DNA heritage. Looking at the two women, the question in Robert's mind was, why had Mado done this to herself? Why the hideous spiky white hair, the piercings and tattoos, the childish clothes?

Mado clutched at Marie's shoulder, and where Marie's sleeve was pulled up Robert glimpsed a circular tattoo on her upper arm.

He exploded.

"Stop it! Look at me!"

They stopped, and looked at him.

"Explain this to me! Sit down!"

They sat down together on the sofa and stared at him. Suddenly he realized that he had too little sleep, no shower, no breakfast. He should have asked them for coffee first. He sat on the floor in front of them. He noticed that his clothes were dusty from his night down the rabbit hole.

"You are identical twins." They nodded. "Twenty-five years old." Marie had told him that. "Marie and Mado. Mado is short for Madonna...?" They both laughed, though their faces were tear-stained. This was particularly noticeable on Mado, whose face was dirty.

"We are Marie and *Madeleine* Navet. Mado is short for Madeleine," explained Marie. "The nickname for Madonna would be Monna, like the Monna Lisa–the lady in Leonardo's painting on your mousepad–she was Madonna Lisa, wife of Ser Giocondo."

"Monna Lisa? What happened to Mona Lisa?"

"Oh, Mona Lisa, Monna Lisa, there are different ways of spelling it and saying it...."

"Marie is the Madonna, the Blessed Virgin Mother Marie. I'm Mado, Madeleine, the whore."

"Madeleine is Mary Magdalen. But of course I am not the Virgin Mary, I am the Mary half of Magdalen."

"You are the virgin Marie, though. She is *l'amour sacré*, holy love, divine love. Wisdom. I am profane love. We are a beanery."

"Well, but the Blessed Virgin Mary is only a type of the Virgin Mother. The point is that Mary Magdalen was both...."

"Yeah, virgin and whore. A beanery."

Robert interrupted, trying to get the picture. "A binary?" Marie rolled her eyes reprovingly at Mado for the mispronunciation. Robert went after what seemed to him a more important point. "But, Mado, *you're not a whore*?" Somehow that seemed even more unlikely than that the luscious Marie was a virgin.

"If you are very nice, someday I'll let you scan my tattoo barcode." She grinned strangely at Robert, a bit too wild to be flirtatious. "But, no, I am not much of a whore. Of course Marie Madeleine was not a whore either—"

"Or a virgin, for that matter, probably. Or poor. She was rich and independent, and virgins were neither in those Gospel times."

"Right, see, it's all Pope Gregory's fault. Too many women in the Gospels for him to sort out."

"Exactly! Poor old Pope Gregory in the sixth century, he had better things to do than keep track of Jesus's lady friends. And most of them were named Mary, or else had no names. Mary the mother of Jesus—"

"Marie the mother of James and John, who was the sister of Marie mother of Jesus. Marie Cleophas, Marie Salomé. Marie of Bethany, the sister of Lazarus and Martha, who liked to hear Jesus preach, so Jesus said she chose the better part. Marie Madeleine, who also liked to hear Jesus preach, so much that she funded his tours."

"And then there is the woman taken in adultery—"

"'Let the man who hath no sin cast the first stone.' *She* was a sinner, of course, an adulteress however is not the same as a whore, technically. And then the woman who was a sinner who washed Jesus's feet and dried them with her hair—"

"Who may or may not have been the same as the woman who poured perfume on his head. But if any of these sinning women had been Mary Magdalen, the gospel would have said so! All the evangelists, those men writing the gospels, knew her name and who she was. They all mention her by name."

"Exactly! They would have said, 'Marie Madeleine was taken in adultery,' or 'Marie Madeleine washed his feet with her penitentiary tears and dried them with her hair.' And if those sinning women had been important disciples they would have given their names too—"

"The way they carefully specify 'Mary the sister of Martha and Lazarus of Bethany,' or 'Mary the mother of James and John.' But this was just too much for poor Pope Gregory in the sixth century, to imagine Jesus being friends with so many different women. So Gregory preached a sermon saying that they were all the same Saint Mary, just to make things tidy."

"And of course that saint was Marie Madeleine, because she was already quite important in those days, in the sixth century."

"Yes, by that time there were already so many stories about what she did after Jesus died that you couldn't fit them all into one legend. Even in the early Church, there were several traditions. The writers of other gospels, besides the four that became standard, mention her. She was supposed to have married St. John, Jesus's beloved disciple. She is supposed to have converted the emperor Tiberias in Rome. I am sure the cult in Sainte-Baume, where she is said to have died at a ripe old age, is very ancient. So she was the obvious choice to represent all Jesus's female disciples."

"Yeah, it was just easier to think of all those women as one virgin whore, as a beanery."

"A binary. But of course they weren't. Mary Magdalen was probably a widow, a woman of independent means, the most important of several who supported Jesus's preaching."

"Do you think they cooked for them and made their beds and that kind of thing?" This seemed like an odd question coming from Mado, but she clearly wanted her sister's opinion.

"Well, probably. After all, they were Jewish women and he was the Rabbi. They probably washed the men's feet and made them chicken soup. Anyway, the other thing we do know about Mary Magdalen is that she was possessed by a devil and Jesus cast it out–"

"I don't believe that one. I think they just made it up, or got it wrong."

"If she was a widow, maybe she fell into a depression after her husband died. And Jesus got her out of it, gave her something to do. Right? That would be what they'd call casting out devils. And then she is mentioned as being at the Crucifixion, and the first person who saw Jesus alive after the Resurrection."

"*Noli me tangere.* Not to touch me. That's what Jesus told her.

But at first she thought he was the gardener. She didn't recognize him. Do you think that was because he was sort of materializing again after being dead? He wasn't really, uh, *coincident* with his body yet?" She said "kwan-see-dent" but Robert was getting the hang of listening to her.

"Well, look, Robert met us both and didn't recognize me when he met you."

"That's because my soul doesn't *kwan-seed* with your body, Marie."

"Actually, your soul coincides better with our body, according to that machine he has. He has a machine that can tell you who you are. And we are a myopic plump redhead."

"I am not plump! This is the way I am, and you would be too, if you didn't diet like that."

"Exactly. And you wear glasses, so your soul expresses our myopia, but mine doesn't because I wear contacts to hide it. If you hadn't done that to your hair–"

"How can I be a whore without bleached hair? Ser Aspro said…"

They both became quiet for a moment and the tears began rolling down both faces again.

Marie looked at Robert and explained, "Did Mado tell you that Salvateur Aspro is, I mean he was our grandfather?" She took a deep breath and smiled. "He is, I mean he was very interested in the beanery, I mean binary, of Mary Magdalen. That's why Mado and I like to think of her as a person, not a binary."

TWENTY-THREE

Perfection consists in round things.
Ronsard

Fibonacci swallowed another marble.

TWENTY-FOUR

Martha ... had a sister called Mary, which also sat at Jesus' feet, and heard his word. But Martha was cumbered about much serving, and came to him, and said, Lord, dost thou not care that my sister hath left me to serve alone? bid her therefore that she help me.

Luke 10

Robert sat on the floor, cross-legged, gazing up at the twins. He felt quite light-headed. Mado stared back at him for a moment, then stood and picked him up off the floor and set him on the couch, telling Marie "*Du café, quand même. On n'a pas déjeuné.*"

"Café, coffee," echoed Robert weakly. "Is there... do you have... please, some bread?"

Marie went into another room, the kitchen, he hoped. Mado patted his hand. "Martha makes coffee while Mary sits at the Lord's feet. *Vita activa* and *vita contemplativa*, the Active Life and the Contemplative Life. That's Martha and Mary, the sisters of Lazarus." She said the name "Mary" with a strange flat pronunciation, as if the word was new to her, and then went back to using the French name. "Marie of Bethany, not Marie Madeleine, unless you agree with Pope Gregory who thought all the Maries should be rolled into one."

Mado stood up and reached for her purse. "I doubt Marie has any bread, so Martha Mado will go to the bakery and get some. I'm hungry too. I wish sometimes Ser Aspro had been passionate about *that* binary, the active and the contemplative life, instead of the virgin and the whore. But then he would probably have shut one of us up in a convent. This theory, it's that a woman can't think unless she's in a convent."

Robert had closed his eyes but he heard her moving around the apartment, still speaking in English and therefore to him. "Poor old Martha, the active life, doesn't get enough credit. Jesus told her *not* to ask her sister to help her in the kitchen, because listening to him was more important. Martha is a saint, too, but who wants to pray to a lady who knew what Jesus liked for dinner when they can fantasize about repentant whores?" Robert heard water running–Mado must be washing her face. Then the apartment door opened and shut and there was silence.

After a few moments Marie drifted back in with a cup of espresso and some cookies. Robert opened his eyes at the smell, smiled, drank, and woke up. The cookies were stale but he could have eaten a bagful, and the bag too.

Looking at Marie's tearstained face, what he had heard about Ser Aspro came back to him. Ser Aspro had said Mado had to bleach her hair to be a whore. Ser Aspro would have shut one of them up in a convent, as some kind of experiment in making a woman able to think. There was something very wrong here, but he couldn't speak to her directly about it.

"Marie, there was a, a thing on your grandfather's desk. Pictures of women, in paintings. A lot of blondes, some with red hair or dark hair. And my Georges de la Tour Mary Magdalen that you told me about. From the mug, you remember? More than one, just as you told me at the checkout.... Was that.....? What was it?"

"Yes, that was part of Ser Aspro's environment for thinking about Mary Magdalen and the mystery of sacred and profane love. The binary, as Mado said. He's been working on it for years. Did you get a good look at it?"

"Sort of. It looked like a dome with a hole in the center." She nodded. "Mado has it. In her pink thing. Her feathers."

Marie went over to the door, where Mado had dropped the package, and retrieved the cards. She came back and knelt down by the coffee table, deftly unhooking them from each other so that they turned into a simple, but very thick, pile of cardboard rectangles, each of which featured or included a beautiful woman. The circular pattern he had seen on Ser Aspro's desk had been made by cutting into each card to reach the head, then cutting around the hair so as to make it into a tab which could be inserted in a slot cut in another card. Some cards had several slots, others, where the whole was mostly taken up with a portrait, only one or two. It seemed unlikely that, once the cards had been pulled apart, they could ever be reassembled.

"Yes, you see, he collected these postcards. And directors of the other museum shops knew about it and would send them on to him when a new one was made. A few of them are from altarpieces in little churches that weren't worth robbing for the great museums and private collections, in fact–a bit too early or too late to be worth the bother. But there she is, Mary Magdalen, Mary Magdalen, Mary Magdalen."

Marie was dealing the postcards into piles. For a moment Robert thought it had to do with hair color, but then he saw that each pile had a particular type of scene, a Crucifixion, a kneeling woman with a standing man, a woman kneeling in front of a table with a long tablecloth, a naked woman being carried through the sky by angels. A thick pile of portraits of women with disorderly hair and one or both breasts exposed, clutching crosses or skulls.

"This is crazy." Robert hadn't meant to say that out loud. Marie looked at him with a pained frown. "I mean, how can you even tell, how did he even know all these pictures were of Mary Magdalen? Like this one." He picked up a postcard she had just laid on one of the thicker piles, showing the dead Christ surrounded by other figures, women and old men. "He cut out the head of this woman by the feet, but why not this one?" He pointed to another figure with a sweeter face, long curling hair, and a weighty-looking halo, holding the head of the dead man. *I still say Ser Aspro had a foot fetish.*

Marie sighed and stopped shuffling the postcards. She set her hand on the postcard Robert had selected, touching the long white dead body with her fingertips and then, in a strangely sensual gesture, with the base of her palm.

I shouldn't have picked that one. She doesn't need to be thinking about dead bodies right now. Robert reached for one from a smaller pile, showing the Virgin Mary with the baby on her lap and several men

and women bending around. But Marie was already answering his question, smiling a little.

"Well, you have to know something about iconography."

"Is that the study of icons, then? How about this one?" He shoved the second postcard at her. "How can you tell...."

"One at a time, please. Iconography is the study of images, the study of the vocabulary of images, especially religious ones but others, too. Particularly in the period before printing made people more word-oriented, people expected to be able to recognize a scene or a saint–they expected to be able to *read* a painting without needing labels. Now, this picture you chose first is what is called a Deposition or Lamentation, or a Pietà. I notice you didn't pick out *this* woman as a possible Mary Magdalen, this one with the heavy dark cloak and wimple"–*Wimple? I wonder how that is spelled or if I heard wrong*–"and the tragic expression. You know she is not Mary Magdalen because she must be the mother of Jesus. The painter has given you clues, and you can still understand them across all the cultural changes of centuries and oceans. Unfortunately, you cannot understand the clues relating to St. John." She tapped Robert's choice for Mary Magdalen.

"That's a man?" *Am I blushing? Does she enjoy making me blush? Of course.*

"Yes, of course. It would be obvious to you if you had seen enough Crucifixions and Depositions. For a crucifixion scene you need Christ on the Cross, the Virgin Mary, and John the Apostle. The gospel says Jesus spoke to them as he was dying–he told John to take Mary as his mother and Mary to take John as her son. So these three are the minimum cast of characters. Mary usually wears very dark blue, John usually wears red or red over blue. I suppose he does look like a girl, because of his loose hair and smooth face, but that is how he is always shown. He was supposed to be the youngest apostle, the one Jesus loved, so his iconography is the adolescent, rather androgynous apostle in red and blue." Marie had sorted out a half-dozen postcards, all of which showed the cross with the two figures at each side, and a tormented woman kneeling at the foot of the Cross. "Mary Magdalene became a traditional fourth personality in the scene, as you see, often embracing the

Cross. It's true she wears red a lot, but it's usually visibly a dress, with a neckline and a high waist."

"Tell me about the feet." Robert felt blushed out, and he was curious.

"Feet. You mean, why she is shown so often kissing Jesus's feet?"

"Yeah, why?" Robert reached for the stack of postcards showing the woman kneeling in front of a draped table. "She's reaching under the table to get his feet, look at this, Marie."

"Exactly. This is the scene of the sinning woman who perfumes Christ's feet while he is dining at the house of a Pharisee. She washes them with her tears and wipes them with her hair. That's why Mary Magdalen is so often shown with lots of hair flowing down. Hair like a towel, you see. In another gospel, it is Mary of Bethany, the sister of Lazarus, who perfumes Christ's head. But the first story was depicted much more often, it is so much more dramatic, and Jesus said that she was forgiven much because she loved much." She paused, and he saw tears rise in her eyes.

"That's very beautiful," he said awkwardly.

"And it must be true," she said, very softly. "My grandfather.... oh, he had much to be forgiven, but...."

She shook her head briskly, and tears actually flew off her cheeks. She took the card Robert had picked up earlier, of baby Jesus being admired by a group of men and women.

"Here is the Madonna with some saints, Jerome, Catherine, and the Magdalen. For this picture you really have to know the iconography, the emblems of the saints. Jerome is often an old man with the red hat of a cardinal, as you see here. Catherine is often paired with the Magdalen because both were preaching women, Catherine in Alexandria and Mary Magdalen in Marseilles, in the South of France. Catherine has a crown and a broken wheel in her hand, reminders of her martyrdom. You know, crown in heaven, and they tried to break her using a wheel as a torture device, though as I recall it didn't work and they had to behead her. The Magdalen is holding her ointment box, you see? Like a toy for baby Jesus, but also a reminder that she will anoint his feet and also that she will come to embalm his dead body after the Crucifixion."

"Um, but, Marie, she's a grown-up lady here. Wouldn't she

have been quite young when Jesus was a baby? I thought she was about his age, or younger–that's what it looks like in the other pictures....?"

Marie smiled and chose another postcard, a large one of a complicated painting. The head of a woman on the far right, with a prom-quality hairdo, was cut out for inclusion in Ser Aspro's mosaic.

"Here's another one where the Magdalen is actually watching the Nativity, the birth of Jesus. This is the Portinari Altarpiece, very important, painted by a Flemish painter for a family in Florence. The Magdalen was a patron saint of one of the Portinari women, these ladies kneeling in front of the infant Jesus. Probably Mary Magdalen got into so many paintings of the Madonna because they were for someone who had a special devotion to her. But look here. She did not come from over the hill, like the shepherds or the three kings. She comes from the future, from heaven. The Christ child seemed to medieval painters, and I suppose the philosophers also, like a.... like.... how can I express this? A gap in the time-space continuum. Inside this dark hole–the Nativity scenes always show a cave, or a dark stable open on one side, like a cave–is the shining baby, just arrived, older than the universe and yet brand-new. So modern people, like the Portinari family of 15th-century Florence or you and me, we can be there too–why not? Saint Margaret is in there, too, with a dragon, which was her special emblem. *She* probably never existed, but if she did it was in second-century Antioch."

"So that Grail thing Mary Magdalen is holding is the ointment box or jar or whatever?"

"Exactly. When Mary Magdalen sort of sucked up the identity of the anointing woman, the ointment container became her emblem or attribute. Like St. Margaret's dragon, or Catherine's wheel. Whenever you see a woman in a medieval painting with a covered cup thing like that, you know it's Mary Magdalen. And the closed cup also implies virginity, sexual purity, while the extravagant use of the ointment implies, well, something else."

"Is there more coffee?" She poured the second tiny cup from her tiny pot and went to the kitchen to start more coffee for Mado. Robert tried to sort the rest of cards out into the piles Marie had started, with special attention to the naked women being carried by angels and the half-naked women with skulls–evidently another iconographic trigger. He realized that he was looking at many centuries' worth of ideal sexy women, a kind of medieval Swimsuit Issue.

Marie returned and sat beside him. She reached for a postcard he had not been able to classify. "Now this is the oldest picture here, but it is only a guess that it is of Mary Magdalen. It is a painting from the catacomb of Priscilla in Rome, so it is from a time when Christianity was not legal there. It is a woman praying, and Ser Aspro liked to imagine that it was the Magdalen."

She chose another card from the same pile. "But here is an ivory carving from around the year 400, of the three Marys coming to the tomb to anoint, to embalm the dead body of Christ. You can't tell which is which, of course, but aren't they lovely. You can see from the way he clipped it that Ser Aspro picked out the woman in the middle as the Magdalen. Of course all these early women wear veils to cover their hair, as was proper for Jewish women. Only after Pope Gregory made Mary Magdalen the woman who dries Christ's feet with her hair do you get the images of her with flowing hair."

"So we don't have anything from her lifetime?"

Marie stared, and laughed. Mado, who had just returned with a bag of croissants and heard the question, laughed too. She answered.

"Robert, don't be silly! We have little enough art from that time anyway, our images of Jesus Christ from the earliest Christian period are mostly fishes. The only thing from the lifetime of Marie Madeleine would be her bones."

"And there are two complete sets of them!" added Marie. "Not counting the one that was stolen from Constantinople in the 15th century."

TWENTY-FIVE

They sought it with thimbles, they sought it with care;
They pursued it with forks and hope;
They threatened its life with a railway-share;
They charmed it with smiles and soap.

Lewis Carroll

Captain Bulle told himself that he had done everything necessary to locate Mado Navet and Robert Longone.

Thinking about this problem allowed him to let the larger problem of the murderer simmer on a back burner of his excellent mind. The murderer, so identifiable from the security cameras, so unknown to the Paris police and evidently to Interpol, though he still had hopes of news from elsewhere in Europe. It seemed that no-one but old Aspro had ever seen this hideous assassin.

Longone and Mado, at least, he knew to exist, though how they came to be together in Ser Aspro's office was more problematic, as was their current whereabouts. They were not at Mado's apartment, and he had men posted there on stakeout. The directress of the escort service who sometimes let Mado use a room denied having seen the girl for a week. Her young business associates, as she called them, and their clients agreed that Mado had not been around the place recently.

Robert Longone had been staying at the *Hôtel du Prieuré*. His room had been searched, of course. Most of his possessions were in a suitcase or lying on the floor beside it. He had left in the room a laptop computer and a cell phone. He had taken his passport and airline tickets, though. There were a lot of papers and two heavy ring binders relating to the conference he had been attending. He had obviously been shopping at the Louvre Boutique, just the previous afternoon according to the receipt. A connection with *Monsieur l'ancien Directeur* Aspro?

The night clerk, visited at home by a police sergeant, was clear that Professor Longone had received a *pneu* and had met a girl who was certainly Mado in the hotel lobby. And they had left together.

From the description of the *pneu,* Bulle knew that it must have come from Aspro, and this was confirmed by the café down the street, the local *pneu* terminal. Yes, these special blue envelopes were used only by Ser Aspro. Everyone knew that. No, none of them had come through this station for years. They had very little *pneu* traffic, but they were paid to keep the service up by the little consortium of *pneumatique* users in Paris.

Bulle thoughtfully checked Longone out of the hotel, so that he would not have to pay for another night. The police impounded his possessions. This afternoon, if they could not find him, they would start ransacking his computer.

Longone had been scheduled to depart Paris, in fact to leave France and go home, on a flight from Orly at noon. Captain Bulle had canceled the reservation, since Longone would need more time to answer questions about his relationship with Salvateur Aspro, but policemen were posted around the international terminal and the gate, and a photo of Robert, taken from one of the conference programs, was in the possession of the security guards.

It was nearly noon already. Still, very likely the flight would be late. No need to move the men off the gate yet. Longone might still show up. The airlines were to contact him if there was any further attempt to change his reservation, whether by telephone, computer, or in person.

He had spread his web. It was a pity, given how co-operative Marie had been, that these two others, Mado and Robert, were not willing to come have a little talk with him.

TWENTY-SIX

And certain women, which had been healed of evil spirits and infirmities, Mary called Magdalen, out of whom went seven devils, and Joanna the wife of Chuza Herod's steward, and Susanna, and many others, which ministered unto him of their substance.

Luke 8

Mado had been generous with her croissant purchase, and Robert devoured several of them before he began to feel fully conscious.

"Now, what's next?"

"Poor Robert! Do you want to go back to your hotel, to get a change of clothes?"

"No, I…" He looked at his watch. It was noon. "What time is it?"

"Mid-day, noon. Did you have some kind of appointment?"

"I have a plane ticket. I was supposed to be on a plane at Orly. Now. Leaving now. Right now."

"Poor, *poor* Robert! You were going home?"

"Orly to Logan airport, Paris to Boston direct. Not an easy flight to book, actually."

They stopped saying "poor, poor Robert."

I guess I'm saying it loud enough all by myself. Poor, poor me. But am I such a poor me? I have plenty to do back in Cambridge, but no classes for two months. I don't have much to look forward to except a visit to my sister. And working on that new system for Tech Corp.

It's O.K. for me to be here. It's a good thing I am here. These women are very confused. Their grandfather was murdered, and I may be able to help them find out who did it and bring this person to justice. For once

knowing something about barcodes may turn out to be really important.
Forensic symbology.

"I think what I need to do is see that third, um, message from Ser Aspro that Mado mentioned. I want to check the barcodes using the murderer's barcode reader. There may be a clue, or a message of some kind. Marie, your grandfather sent you one of those blue envelopes last night?"

"You want to see my *pneu*?" Marie took his hand to help him rise from the floor. "Also, I have my computer set up with lots of softwares for scanning barcodes." Seeing his look of amazement, she went on, "Ser Aspro wanted me to take over the Directorship of the *Centre Commercial* from him. Of course, that is not a hereditary job! Even though he has held it since before I was born, and didn't let go of it even after he retired. But he thought that, with my background in art history, if I could learn all about the commercial side..... That's why I was at the cash register yesterday. And that's why my computer can be set up like a cash register right now."

Mado frowned. "It won't happen the way he'd planned it, will it, now? They'll never appoint a young woman to that post. Maybe they would let you do the job while they wait to find some old man to do it...."

"An interim appointment?" Robert suggested.

But Marie took a deep breath and smiled an enormous smile. "Maybe I don't care who does it! Maybe running the *Centre Commercial du Louvre* is not my number-one choice of jobs!" Tears suddenly burst out of her eyes, while she was still smiling. *There should be rainbows on her face,* Robert thought.

Mado sat very quietly, expressionless. She was stunned.

Marie stood up, controlling her emotions. "Our lives have changed. I can start out as a sub-curator of medieval painting at the Louvre. I think they will offer me that job, you know, in his memory. And Mado, you can.... You won't have to...."

"Marie, I had already told the Egyptians that I would work on that dig next year. I couldn't miss such an occasion. You don't get two chances in a lifetime to excavate a site of such importance. I hadn't told Ser Aspro, of course. I was trying to figure out how I would explain it, how he would take it." She also began to weep, tears rolling down her cheeks as she smiled up at her sister.

The twins hugged each other, murmuring French in each other's ears.

This is where I came in. Robert rose from the couch and wandered over to the computer. *Ser Aspro wanted one of them to take over his own job, and the other to be... a whore? What kind of plan is that? And Marie wants to be an art museum curator, which explains how come she's so full of explanations about art. And Mado seems to want to be an archaeologist. That's right, telling me all about the Louvre excavations. I'll bet she sneaked in there to do a bit of digging alongside the professionals, a time or two. "We, the archaeologists of Paris."*

I wonder if I can check my email from here?

Robert sat down at the computer, finding that the familiar Windows desktop was a pleasant distraction from thinking about Ser Aspro and his unpleasant binary.

He opened Explorer and tried to go to his webmail site, but the keyboard didn't work properly. He opened a blank Wordpad document and began to hit the keys, one after another, starting with the top left. He did the top row with the shift on, then with the shift off. The same with the other rows. There were a few surprises, especially that the letter A was not where it should be. Using this page as a typing guide, he was able to keyboard the Harvard Business School webmail address. Marie evidently had some kind of DSL–he was in very quickly.

A couple of old students wanting to get together. A couple of incoming students, wanting to get to know him. His sister Nell, wondering what kind of present he was bringing her back from Paris. A notice from the Dean about rule changes. A note from his publisher about revising the textbook and adding an online interactive module using some kind of proprietary templates. Notes from Tech Corp. reacting to his recent proposal for an internal barcoding system. An email from a colleague, Lindy Teabag, a distinguished British medical symbologist whom Robert had run into from time to time. Teabag had not attended the Paris conference, but he was in Paris now and wondered if Robert would like to get together for coffee. Robert did not reply to any of these.

My plane left Orly an hour ago, if it was on time. I am sitting in an empty seat above, oh, maybe Ireland right now. Or maybe I am still in Paris, maybe it is still yesterday when I was supposed to be enjoying my last day in Paris. No, I don't think I'll plan to meet Lucky Lindy for coffee. I might wake up.

Spam, lots of it, too. For some reason there were a lot of porny ones lately. Holding down the CONTROL key, he selected the whole batch and deleted them. Then he logged out of webmail.

He spent a few minutes on the ESPN site checking the baseball scores–he hadn't had a chance to see them since Sunday morning. Boston (which he was sentimental about for social reasons) and San Francisco (which he was sentimental about for personal reasons) had both won their games. Satisfied, he closed the browser.

He opened "All Programs." Yes, Marie had installed several cash-register programs. There was the standard one they were using at the Louvre, and a very recent release that involved RFID, the newest trend, identification by radio frequency chips tagged onto items. More suitable, really, for Louvre Museum collection inventories than for the items in the shops. He wondered what kind of databases she had imported to practice with–probably standard Louvre shop stock.

Ser Aspro wanted her to inherit his position as mall director. She, the privileged one, Holy Love, or Wisdom, had they said? The Blessed Virgin? Marie was a virgin, attractive though she was. Had that been a choice, or a price paid for her grandfather's attention? And had Mado had to sacrifice her own virginity for the same reason?

Robert closed his eyes and listened to the two women weeping softly in the adjacent room.

TWENTY-SEVEN

[Merrick] often said to me that he wished he could lie down to sleep "like other people." I think on this last night he must, with some determination, have made the experiment. The pillow was soft, and the head, when placed on it, must have fallen backwards and caused a dislocation of the neck.

Frederick Treves

Fibonacci had a nightmare. It sometimes happened that he forgot to set the pillows properly on his bed, and his twisted body and heavy skull would produce deadly confusion in his organs and in his mind.

The first time he fell asleep it was some time before dawn, and he slept lightly, waiting for the Doctor's telephone call. He would call to check on Fibonacci's progress in searching Aspro's hard drive for evidence of the codes.

The call did not come, though, until it was light outside. Though the little Temple had no windows visible from the outside, light was cleverly let into the rooms by a series of translucent panels and hidden openings, and Fibonacci thought it must be around seven or eight o'clock. Evidently the Doctor had not been waking all night to hear the news.

There was no possible kind word for the Doctor to say to Fibonacci. There were words to the effect that sometimes if you want a thing done right, you had better do it yourself and not trust to servants or friends.

Fibonacci had killed the old man, an important old man, it seemed. He had not found the barcode labels he was assigned to find. He had ruined the *Centre Commercial* computer drive, along with a good Temple computer. They had lost their chance at finding the Pi code.

Fibonacci did not confess that he had left the scanner and his handheld, with its questionable database of possible Pi codes, in the Louvre office. In fact, the night's adventures were so blurred he was not sure he had done so. *Perhaps I unplugged it and took it with me, and then it fell out somewhere in the streets, coming here. Perhaps it fell out in this very room, and I will find it tomorrow.*

The Doctor said that Fibonacci must leave Paris. Fibonacci was happy to do so. However, he could not come home to Edinburgh. He was too horribly easy to identify at any airport or train station, or even in the streets. Undoubtedly the *Centre Commercial* was full of security cameras, and he had worn no mask. The French police would be looking for him, and he must not cross a border. There were many Brothers among the police, but this was not a case in which they could be asked to turn their heads and let him pass.

A friend would give him a ride to a safe place in the country-side, to a good part of the country, far to the south, where there were mountains and houses built of stone, on stone. The friend could be expected at the Temple in Rue Jacob that afternoon. This friend would keep Fibonacci safe.

Or is he my assassin? I know the Temple must not be connected with a murder. This murder. I would never mention the Temple if they did arrest me for murder, surely the Doctor knows that.

There would be a scandal among the Brothers, it's true, since they would know that one of us had killed a man. But they might see that it was an accident, when I was on a mission. And even the police—after all, they are representatives of order, many of them are Brothers. If they knew, they would understand why I had to kill that terrible old Aspro.

But, with all this, when he went back to bed again, the pillows were not set right. The throbbing hand kept him restless, turning and twisting his bedding around his ill-proportioned body.

In the nightmare, he was staring up at a dome made of women. The whole thing was naked women, standing on each others' shoulders, and more women behind them. The huge concavity of femininity arched over him, and he couldn't look down, or away–there was no away, they were all around him. He couldn't close his eyes (two eyes, in the dream). Far, far above him was the hole for light to come in. A beautiful, golden light was shining down on him from that round hole, but it was also revealing those masses of women standing together, row on row. He felt that something important was going to happen, someone was going to appear.

Bells rang.

He woke up, and heard the subtle sound of the coded ring on the hidden bell of his little Temple. Wearily he pulled his body together and rose to answer the door.

TWENTY-EIGHT

Though he looked an incredible dunce,
He had just one idea—but, that one being "Snark,"
The good Bellman engaged him at once.

Lewis Carroll

"So, you are telling me that there is a teeny tiny miniature centrifuge in there, to separate out the DNA and analyze it? That is physically impossible." Mado was extremely skeptical, but Robert assured her that it was true.

Marie and Mado insisted that Robert plug in the Personal Sampler. He wasn't sure he really wanted them playing with it, but the only data on it at the moment was for the three of them, their two sets and their grandfather's. Marie had quite a collection of charger cords and adapters, and he found one that worked. He showed them how to access the various data screens, and also, since Marie seemed to have figured out that it existed, the modesty button–though Mado said she'd like to see Ser Aspro stark naked, just once. Finally he let the two women sit down together and examine themselves, or themself.

He turned his attention to the three mysterious blue pneu envelopes.

He realized that he had four barcoded objects to worry about: the bit of cardboard packaging with a barcode on it, which had been enclosed in the *pneu* addressed to him at the hotel, as well as the three envelopes. He laid them all out and considered them carefully.

The code on the cardboard would be some kind of standard packaging code, like the American UPC code though with an extra digit for the European EAN-13 standards. It had been printed with the numbers underneath, as was normal for commercial barcodes. He might be able to find the numbers on the internet or call a friend to find out the identity of the product. Perhaps it was aspirin, Ser Aspro's humorous way of identifying himself? The bit of cardboard itself was pale green except for the white barcode element, with a fine design of leaves and small flowers. It was smooth on the two edges which had not been torn–probably the top of a small box.

The pneus, with their beautifully handwritten addresses, and their dark-blue on light-blue barcodes, were in a different class. He was strongly tempted to throw forensics to the wind and use not only the murderer's barcode reader but the pocket computer that had come with it. He was sure it contained the database with the key to the message formed by these barcodes.

He remembered then that Marie had scanner hardware and software on her computer. He went over and cruised her list of programs again. He was startled to notice a program called Apple Pi. It reminded him of the Pi million cash register charge. He opened it and found it was a program for creating and reading barcodes–but unusual ones.

The telephone rang, and from the corner of his eye he saw Marie rise to answer it. At about the same moment, there was a buzz indicating a visitor outside. They were on the second floor of an apartment building–probably you had to identify yourself below to have the door opened. Mado got up, too, to go answer the door intercom.

He heard both women's voices raised in vigorous protest, and a man's voice suddenly quite loud at the door.

Robert stood up, alert and angry at the thought of some attack on the twins. He looked around the little room for a weapon of some kind to defend them. There was a really hefty-looking old barcode scanner among the collection on Marie's worktable. *Must be an antique, from the sixties or seventies. Just the right weapon for a Professor of Symbology.*

But when he rounded the corner into the living-room, carrying his weapon of choice, the two women were looking rather ashamed of themselves, one on either side of a large, well-built man who spoke to him in a wonderful British accent:

"Professor Longone, I presume? I have wanted to make your acquaintance for a long time. In fact, for a little more than twelve hours. It had not occurred to me that Marie Navet would do anything so absurd and irresponsible as to invite you to her home when she knew that you and I had an appointment."

"Hi."

"Let me introduce myself. I am Captain Bulle of the Paris Judicial Police. Will you please show my assistant...." He stepped a little aside and a uniformed woman with rubber surgical gloves on appeared in his shadow. "Please give her the items you took from *Monsieur l'ancien Directeur* Aspro's office when you were present there shortly after his death. She will also take custody of any other items of interest, such as those remarkable blue envelopes of the type *Monsieur l'ancien Directeur* Aspro had made exclusively for his own use. Also, I think, the device plugged into the wall over there, which you seem to have had with you in the *Monsieur l'ancien Directeur* Aspro's office."

Robert held his jacket pockets open so that the policewoman could remove the barcode scanner and pocket PC, along with the power cord and cable. She put each of these into a plastic bag. She took out a forceps to handle the four paper items on the table–she took the bit of cardboard too. Then she went over and rather roughly jerked the plug from the electrical outlet and carried the Personal Sampler to her boss.

Marie began to speak rather quickly in French to Captain Bulle. Mado nodded from time to time. Evidently they were explaining the function and nature of the Personal Sampler.

Oh, yeah. They probably would prefer not to be the DNA pinups down at the police station.

Finally Bulle asked Robert formally, "Do you swear that the only data on this machine pertains to these two women and to their grandfather Salvateur Aspro?"

Robert swore it, in English and in French for good measure.

Bulle handed him back the Personal Sampler. "After all, we have an abundance, even a superabundance, of *Monsieur l'ancien*

Directeur Aspro's DNA right now. And we know quite well what he looks like."

Little boy, take back your toy and don't bother the grown-ups with it.

TWENTY-NINE

In the midst of the word he was trying to say,
In the midst of his laughter and glee,
He had softly and suddenly vanished away —
For the Snark was a Boojum, you see.

Lewis Carroll

Inspector Bulle did not need to touch Robert to have the effect of taking him by the arm and marching him down the stairs. But Robert felt a surge of distress that the twins were not coming with him. It was as though he were abandoning them, or maybe losing them. In fact, though, they were safe enough. Marie and Mado Navet were left at the apartment with a woman officer. They were going to be allowed to take a shower and change their clothes before being deposed by the police. Although Marie had already given a statement, evidently she was wanted too, again, at this point in the investigation.

Robert, however, as a stranger and a foreigner, was shoved into the police car and driven to a police station in an unwashed state. The driver seemed to prefer alleys to streets. Robert was not sure whether he was primarily murderous or suicidal in his intention.

Captain Bulle took him to an interrogation room of some kind, empty except for a few chairs and a long bare table. They sat silently staring at each other across the table for a minute or so.

A uniformed woman came in and hooked up an audio recorder, then left. Bulle asked Robert to describe the events of the night before, and Robert gave as clear and complete a narration as he could into the microphone. Evidently Captain Bulle knew nearly the whole story already, and the only thing that seemed to surprise him was the news that Mado Navet could get into the *Centre Commercial* at night and that they had found, near Ser Aspro's body, a key card that opened a door into the excavation level of the Museum itself.

A man in uniform came in with a big black trash bag. He set it down on the floor and removed from it what Robert recognized as his own laptop and cell phone. He left.

"Please– *s'il vous plaît–" Please may I check my voice mail, my laptop, whatever else in in that bag–and if you broke that Grail I bought for my sister, I will make you buy me a new one.* Bulle nodded and Robert went over to examine the contents of the bag. His electronics were on top.

He picked up his cellphone first. When he reached his voicemail, the Captain came and stood beside him. Robert held the phone so that both of them could hear his messages: Two long buzzy ones, which were the result of someone having hung up after reaching the voicemail. An automated telephone message from his telephone service, suggesting that he upgrade for a better international roaming rate. And one actual piece of communication, a call from his colleague Lindy, who still wanted to get together for coffee or drinks in Paris. Bulle took notes, but there wasn't much to note.

Robert opened the laptop and found it as he had left it, except that it no longer had a password dialogue. Captain Bulle commented that the police had managed to bypass the authentication process and examined his programs and files, finding nothing of interest. Robert had to sign a release, written in French, authorizing this invasion of his privacy by the forces of justice.

It occurred to him belatedly that he should probably call the American Embassy. If there had been a Miranda warning, he had missed it.

The big black trash bag contained everything else from his hotel room. They had had the grace to put his shaving gear, shampoo, and toothpaste into his travel bag before dropping them in on top of his carryon and suitcase, at least. Everything else loose had been stuffed into his suitcase and then it had just been folded over, not closed, so that a mess of dirty clothes, underwear, and papers overflowed from it. He reached inside the carryon and found a fold of the plastic shopping bag from the Louvre Boutique. Gently he worked it out until he could set it on the table and unpack the items.

The blue Egyptian cup for his sister had not been broken.

He was re-packing it carefully when the policewoman with the surgical gloves came into the room. She laid out on the table the barcode scanner and handheld computer Robert had been carrying around all night, and the three envelopes and the boxtop or whatever it was. In addition, there were two tiny clear envelopes with what looked like dirt in them.

She spoke to Bulle for a few moments, and he replied. She took a seat and another policeman came in, with a laptop which he cabled to the handheld computer–which presumably had belonged to Aspro's murderer.

"Professor Longone, now I want you to do your stuff. I mean, if you please, I want you to proceed to use the barcode reader the way you had planned to, in the apartment of Mademoiselle Marie Navet. All these items have been carefully examined by our forensics department and, while some of them are still in evidence, we can allow you to handle them freely. We have already copied the contents of the handheld computer to this laptop, as a backup, and my colleague, *Monsieur l'Ingénieur* André, will be able to monitor your investigation."

This is embarrassing. I don't even know what I'm looking for. Start with the boxtop, that's the safest...

"Professor Longone," said Bulle with a grim smile, "this is from an ordinary box of tea, what you would call herbal tea. It is a *tisane*, that's what we call it in French, vegetable matter to be infused in hot water and drunk to calm or revive the spirits. I am fond of drinking *tisanes*." He picked up the box and looked at it more closely. "Yes, you see, I recognize the box. You can see the leaves and flowers in the design. This is from a box of infusion of the *tilleul*, a tree whose leaves and flowers have a healing and calming effect. It is called in English the lime tree." He smiled broadly.

"Then I don't need to scan it. I can see that the barcode is normal for an item of that type."

"It is mysterious that *Monsieur l'ancien Directeur* Aspro sent you a barcode from a box of teabags, is it not? But *Monsieur le Directeur*

Aspro seems to have liked mysteries." Bulle sighed. "You have read Proust?"

"Proust?"

"*A La Recherche du Temps Perdu, Du Côté de Chez Swann...?*" Bulle went over to the trash bag and fished out the book Robert had bought on Sunday. "*Swann's Way,* they translate it."

"Oh, *Swann's Way.* Oddly enough, I read a little bit last night." *Last night, a long time ago.*

"Ah, he speaks of the magic of the *tisane,* even of the *tisane* of the *tilleul,* like this box. At least I believe so. I have not read the book myself."

"So you think the message in this bit of cardboard is a reading recommendation?"

"Why not?" Bulle stuck the boxtop at random into the book, as a bookmark, and handed it back to Robert, who repacked it in his suitcase/trashbag without saying anything.

Why not indeed.

THIRTY

The beauty that is borne here in the face
The bearer knows not, but commends itself
To others' eyes. Nor doth the eye itself–
That most pure spirit of sense–behold itself,
Till it hath travell'd, and is mirror'd there
Where it may see itself.

Shakespeare

Marie and Mado Navet had not had an easy time. The policewoman tactfully sat on the couch, reading a magazine, while they moved between the bathroom, the W. C., the kitchen, and the bedroom.

Left alone together, without Robert to distract them, they kept bumping into each other, not only physically but emotionally.

Of course Marie had to lend Mado clothes.

"But I don't have any clothes that fit your type. You'll just have to make do. There are shirts and shorts in that drawer. But all my shorts and slacks are very tailored, so the waistband might be too snug on you."

"You think so? I don't care, anyway. I wouldn't put myself through it, what you do to stay so scrawny."

"Well, then, you'd better find something with an elastic waistband, if you can."

"Besides, Marie, what is *my type* of clothes? I think we should dress as twins. I want a button-down shirt and a navy blue skirt. And a jacket to match, a suit."

"Is that what I'm planning to wear? So we can be twins? How many outfits like that do you think I own? I'm going to wear a dress."

"Which dress? This satin one with the wonderful plunging neckline.... oh, my, it still has the tags on. You must have bought it for a party, and then.... alas, Marie!"

"I bought it on sale. It was an impulse. I might return it, but anyway it was not a big investment."

"Not financially, but.... alas, Marie!"

"Shut up. Don't tease. How about this dress?"

"Beautiful! Beautiful red poppies to drug his eyes and make him fall in love with you. But the colors would look better on me. I think I should wear it."

"It would look ridiculous on you, with your hair! And I *can* wear red."

"And I can *change* my hair, dear."

And so on.

THIRTY-ONE

Taking Three as the subject to reason about–
A convenient number to state–
We add Seven, and Ten, and then multiply out
By One Thousand diminished by Eight.
The result we proceed to divide, as you see,
By Nine Hundred and Ninety Two:
Then subtract Seventeen, and the answer must be
Exactly and perfectly true.

Lewis Carroll

Robert scanned the barcodes on the three blue envelopes. However, although the scanner could read the barcodes, showing the series of numbers and letters, the murderer's handheld computer did not seem to have a database to which they meant something. Robert fiddled with it for a while, and the police tech fiddled with the copy on his laptop, but neither of them could find any meaning in the three codes.

"Since these codes were on Ser Aspro's envelopes, the database must have been on his computer," said Robert, hopefully. "Have you had a chance to access it?" Then he remembered that, in the office the night before, he had seen the computer gutted by the murderer.

The three barcodes produced these readouts, after the initial and checksum digits were removed:

Mado's: VZBPF50018
Marie's: STBSM50018
Robert's: BWRLT01010

"This is really peculiar," said Robert half to himself. "This is a very common kind of code. I create them all the time, myself, for various purposes. It normally uses a constant set of identifying letters for the first half, the alphabetical part. That's much easier to read than a numerical code and immediately identifies the manufacturer or company or whatever super-category is most important." Captain Bulle nodded. He had made a handwritten copy of the three codes, and Robert spoke up, sensing an audience.

"Then the numbers would be some kind of series. It might be 00001, 00002, 00003. Or it might be broken up into meaningful segments. The numerical section would identify the particular item or subset and item. Thus the first half tells you who made it, or to whom it belongs, and the second half tells you which thing made by that company, or belonging to that group, this is."

Bulle nodded again.

"Instead of which, Marie and Mado have identical numerical codes but very different alpha codes. The numbers could point to a product code of some kind, but they might be a postal code.... And the barcode from my envelope has yet another alpha code, and a numerical code that is just alternating zero and one, the basic binary unit on which all computer calculation is based. Or I suppose that if you ignore the first zero and read the last four digits you could read it 'ten, ten.'"

"Or X, X, in Roman numerals," commented Bulle. "Perhaps 'X marks the spot' as in a story of pirate treasure?"

"That would be nice! Or two kisses." Robert felt himself blushing. "X means a kiss when you are signing a letter...." *Better let that one drop.* Suddenly, he had an idea.

"You know, for me this whole thing started when I bought a Mona Lisa mousepad at the Louvre shop. It had a very strange barcode on it. Let's see if this scanner can do anything with that." The shopping bag from the Louvre Boutique was still on the table. Robert brought the mousepad out, then realized that he had removed the barcode. He found the card on which he had stuck the label, in his wallet.

Bulle looked over his shoulder. "This is a very fancy barcode. It looks like the *Arche de la Défense.*"

"That's what Marie Navet said. But it's a barcode, sure enough.

It did something strange to her scanner, to her cash register. The cash register read Pi million dollars, I mean euros. I mean, the number Pi, you know, multiplied by a million and carried out to two decimals."

Captain Bulle shook his head. Apparently he and Pi were not friendly.

Robert turned the murderer's barcode scanner back on and both he and the police tech got ready to see if the murderer's computer software would have anything to say about it. On the white card, there was no need to hold it so that the plastic reflected white light.

The barcode scanner bleeped and beeped, and went dead.

Robert watched the handheld computer's screen die. The computer tech's face reflected, literally and figuratively, the bright flash of the operating system closing and then the progress of the police laptop computer's crash.

THIRTY-TWO

Speed, bonny boat, like a bird on the wing!
Onward! the sailors cry.
Carry the boy that is born to be king
Over the sea to Skye.

Jacobite song

The Doctor's friend, assigned to drive the fugitive to a safer part of France, was not a man, as Fibonacci had expected, but a woman. She was tall, almost taller than he was. She had short dark hair and did not seem to be very old.

She was obviously taken aback when she saw Fibonacci. She had not been told about his deformities, and at this moment he looked his worst, after a nightmare-ridden sleep.

After a long moment, the kind of moment Fibonacci was used to when meeting strangers, she held out her hand.

"Hello, I'm Valerie Percy. Please just call me Val."

She was clearly British, and well educated. Fibonacci was relieved he would not have to try to speak French. All the same, he struggled to get the Scots burr out of his voice as he answered her.

"I'm Fibonacci."

"Yes. Good. Of course. I—my husband was supposed to drive you south, but he is detained in London. He asked me to do it instead."

Just in case I get any ideas about her, she wants me to know that she's married.

"This building is lovely. I had never been here before."

"It has been here so long, they say, that most people don't even notice it. They forget it's here. It was designed in the 17th century. The Divine Proportion is in every element."

"I can see that. I'm an architect, and I, like my husband, am a friend of Doctor–"

She broke off, seeing his hand. Fibonacci was not used to having people offer to shake hands with him, and he had gestured vaguely towards her outstretched hand with his intact left. She kept hers extended, however, and finally he had put his right hand in hers, bandages and all.

"What happened? This looks very bad, Fibonacci. Let me see."

He pulled his hand back. "I'm all right. We can just go, wherever we're going. It's not too bad." But he was almost crying, just from the pressure she had put on the bandage trying to keep hold of the hand.

"Oh, you are stoic, aren't you?" That pleased him, and he smiled through the tears.

"We must get you to the hospital, to the emergency room. If it's infected...."

I could lose my hand. A terrible thing for one already so crippled, wouldn't that be?

I thought the Doctor was sending an assassin. She is no assassin. She is kind, she is really worried about me.

She also has not seen the morning news. The murder must be everywhere, the television, the newspapers. They probably know what I look like, that place is full of videocameras, the way the Doctor said. My picture may be on the front pages–anyway, a description.

"Miss, Madame..."

"Please do call me Val. We must get your things and go to a hospital."

She is kind but she thinks I am as stupid as I am ugly.

"My dear Madame Val, I cannot go to a hospital. Surely the Doctor told you that I must not be seen by anyone at all in Paris."

"Oh. You mustn't be seen–of course not, I understand. But we must do something about that hand."

She thinks it is because I am so ugly, that I am afraid of what people will say when they see me.

In the end, they stopped in the suburbs at a pharmacy and Val purchased dressings, ointments, and a stiff narcotic painkiller. Sitting in the car, she unwrapped the hand from the improvised bandage of last night. It was ugly, but the signs of infection were still local. She cleaned the hand, anointed it, and wrapped it in a clean dressing. He had asked her also to purchase for him a computer user's wrist support, which would help immobilize the hand.

By the time the support was strapped on he had drunk the bottle of painkiller and was ready to be driven anywhere at all.

THIRTY-THREE

She was of all the feminine sex (except for the unique Virgin Mother of God) the most intimate with God, the most devoted and full of grace. No man of the Church could take away from her the performance of the task with which she had been honored.

Raban Maur, How Christ sent Mary Magdalen
as an Apostle to the Apostles.

Marie and Mado had quite a bit to do at the police station. A police lieutenant had a number of questions for them. First Mado was interviewed separately. She had to recite her night's adventures to a voice recorder. Then Marie rejoined her and a police lieutenant read off a list of names. She didn't tell them where the names came from, but obviously they reflected Ser Aspro's appointment book. After each one the lieutenant asked if they had ever heard of this person.

The Marquise de Saunière. *Designer of a line of "Goddess" costume jewelry based on the museum's antiquities, which sell well in the store.*

Richard Nouveau. *A museum donor who is interested in developing some prestige reproductions with grotesquely (says Mado) high price tags.*

Signe Soigné. *A graduate of the prestigious École Normale Supérieure, currently an associate head of the museum's cultural services, the obvious candidate for Aspro's job now (says Marie, with Mado shaking her head).*

Dr. Malcuore. *Not a medical doctor, an American Ph.D. He wanted the Louvre to stop selling certain Round Table merchandise, including pop-up books, jigsaw puzzles, and miniature armor reproductions labeled as King Arthur's knights. His theory was that Arthur was some kind of Russian who lived in the Dark Ages (says Mado) or a Roman general from the year 200 A.D. (says Marie).*

Snorri Clay. *A Swiss publisher who was a good friend of Ser Aspro's. They always had dinner together when visiting each other's cities.*

Adèle. Both girls shrug, the lieutenant moves on, nodding. *We all know who she is.*

Bébécé Canalet. *A TV broadcasting researcher who was badgering Ser Aspro for information and interviews for some educational program about the Louvre.*

Linden Teabag. *Never heard of him. Would remember a name like that.*

Monseigneur Poquette-Filiposi. *Mado: never heard of him. Marie: sounds familiar, but not sure who he is.*

And so on.

This took quite some time, and by the end of it both sisters were drained. It was as if they had been asked to write their grandfather's biography or obituary. They had not realized how much of their grandfather's life they knew. He had shared it with them, selfishly in a way, but apparently quite completely. Tears kept trickling down one cheek or the other, but they kept going.

Finally they were shown a video capture of Fibonacci. The camera had caught him as he stared at the array of Mary Magdalens on Aspro's desk. His expression was visible.

A monster killed my grandfather. A Quasimodo, but a cruel one, a wicked hunchback. Ugly form, ugly soul.

Disgusting man! Look at his hand! Good for you, Aspro! You did something to him, you marked him!

He hates grandfather's postcards of the Magdalens. You can see it. He hates them.

Grandfather's picture puzzle made him sick to his stomach. Maybe all beautiful women made him sick to his stomach. What woman would ever smile at him, except his mother? If only he had fallen down sick at that moment and retched his guts out.

"No."

"No, I've never seen him. Ser Aspro never mentioned anyone like that."

"Did you ask Madame Rosamonde, Ser Aspro's secretary–the Acting Interim Director of the *Centre Commercial*?"

The police had spoken to Madame Rosamonde, at length. She had never seen or heard of such a man. However, the evidence against him was complete–the murder was on camera, as if Ser Aspro had made his final stand with that intention. And it would not be hard to find a murderer who looked like *that*.

THIRTY-FOUR

A certain man put a pair of rabbits in a place surrounded on all sides by a wall. How many pairs of rabbits can be produced from that pair in a year if it is supposed that every month each pair begets a new pair which from the second month on becomes productive?

Leonardo Fibonacci of Pisa

Robert and the police tech, *Ingénieur* André, had spent the better part of an hour trying to reconstruct what had happened. The mini-computer had died almost instantly when Robert scanned the square barcode, but the laptop had taken more than a minute to close down completely. At first André, the tech, had hoped that it was a worm of some kind whose action could be reversed, and he had concentrated on what was happening on his monitor in order to understand it. However, whatever had hit the computers had been absolutely effective. Both computers were beyond resuscitation, and attempts to patch the laptop's hard drive into another police computer to recover the data were unsuccessful. The black barcode had completely fried both machines.

Captain Bulle was, of course, furious. *Capitaine Fâché.* He paced the room as the two other men sat with their heads together, but he kept having to pause to translate.

When the attempt to retrieve data had clearly failed, *Ingénieur* André began simply to write down, on a sheet of paper, sequences of numbers that he remembered from the crash. It had not appeared to him to be a conventional memory dump. There had been a quiet progression of numbers, which would appear and disappear in a regular rhythm. The numbers became larger and larger, starting he thought in the single digits but growing in some kind of geometrical progression.

It seemed that only three numbers at a time were on the screen. When the fourth one appeared, the first one would fade. Eventually, however, the numbers were wrapping the lines and then they grew so long that three of them filled the display. Then the machine shut down.

Robert examined the numbers. The tech had mostly been able to remember numbers of three, four, and five places.

21 34 55 89
144 233 377 610 987
1597 4181 6765
17711 or 11711 46368 75025
a 10-digit number beginning 77787
a 19- or 20-digit number beginning 28800 and another beginning 46600466
a number so long he was not sure where it ended, beginning with 2222322446

Robert felt André had done pretty well to catch this much. The man admitted he had been quite optimistic for the first few seconds. Bulle explained for him to Robert that André had been looking for patterns, and so he noticed 144 because he hoped for multiples of twelve, and then 233, maybe it would all be prime numbers, but of course it couldn't have been both.

"Well, it helped him remember them. Is he sure the sequence was 144, then 233?"

Yes, but he might have skipped the next number. He wasn't sure.

At least it seemed clear that the worm had done something to the computer's memory. That was the simplest explanation for the time it took to shut down the smaller and the larger computers. At the same time, it was inconceivable that a mathematical process could use more than a fraction of the computer's memory. Something else must have been going on.

André was positive that the barcode scan itself had initiated the process. The scanning software had been open and it had seemed to have found the database or program called for. Since a lot of the laptop's files had been copied to the laptop from the handheld computer, one of them might have activated the invasive program.

"What we need to do," sighed Robert to Captain Bulle, "is to try scanning it on another computer, to see whether the reaction depended on files which were on the murderer's computer. We need to know if it could have this effect on any computer at all. Ideally, we would want to see if it could shut down a server or local area network...."

Captain Bulle turned red. The police tech began speaking, in a kind of humble, no-eye-contact, you-are-the-alpha-wolf-but-I have-a-suggestion way, and Bulle turned purple. Robert gathered André was making the same proposal.

"It's like that *X-Files* episode," said Robert, hoping to distract Bulle before he exploded. Robert had not been a fan of the show, but this particular episode had been screened at the Conference on the Public Image of Symbology at UCLA a few years ago. Agent Scully confuses the cash registers in a supermarket by scanning a diabolical (literally) barcode.

"Lay zicks feels?" André asked brightly. *"Les Dossiers X? Bien sûr, là où la belle Skoolee passe le code à barres sur le lecteur de l'épicerie...."*

Bulle, who was regaining his normal color, claimed he could not translate this–he had no idea what the man was talking about. However, since Robert did, he and André grinned at each other. Robert went back to the list.

"Well, they're nice numbers," sighed Robert. Captain Bulle looked at him furiously. Robert began to make a copy for himself, to look for a pattern later. As he wrote the digits, the pattern hit him with full force.

"Fibonacci!" he said.

THIRTY-FIVE

And for to stire them to devocioun,
Thanne shewe I forth my longe cristal stones,
Ycrammed ful of clouthes and of bones:
Relikes been they.

Chaucer, Pardoner's Tale

The door to the interview room opened and Marie and Mado entered, accompanied by another policeman.

Robert gaped. Mathematics drained from his mind for a moment. His mind in fact drained from his consciousness, leaving him to the mercy of hormones. A real adolescent moment.

Marie, who was fixed in his mind as elegant in a businesslike suit or shirtsleeves and skirt, was wearing a gorgeous flowered dress with a bouffant skirt. Her deluxe hair waved gently to her shoulders. Her eyes were green as grass. She looked like a fifties Technicolor dream.

Mado–the only way he knew it was Mado was that she was clearly the twin of Marie. She had slicked her pale hair down on her head, so that the curves and angles of her face stood out. A face without studs, though later he found himself noticing the holes where they had been. She wore very high heels, dark slacks and jacket, and a white drapey blouse peeking out. She still wore the same glasses, though.

The twins seemed to be ignoring his response to their changed appearance. They were all business, talking seriously in French to Captain Bulle, who looked much less *faché* all of a sudden. *He must be enjoying a few resurrected hormones, too.* He was showing them the scanner's interpretations of the barcodes on the three *pneus*. They were shaking their heads–evidently they did not see any significance in the "messages."

The police tech had paused to admire the twins, too, but he had gone back to scribbling notes. He must be more used to seeing beautiful young women up close. Or gay, maybe.... He gestured to catch Robert's attention again.

"Vous avez raison, absolument, c'était la suite Fibonacci."[1] Even without a translator, Robert found he could get the idea of what André was telling him. He had filled in some more numbers, reconstructing the pattern.

The problem was, though the Fibonacci sequence can generate some complicated mathematical calculations, it would certainly not do that fast enough, by itself, to stress the computer's memory and cause a wipe of the hard drive—or even just crash the computer. Robert and André managed to convey this to each other with a few gestures and shrugs.

Robert shook his head in a melancholy way, assuming that André understood him. "Perhaps it was just a cover for whatever was really happening. It masked the actual processes." He spread his hand across the laptop's display, indicating masking, while wiggling his fingers in the general region of the machine's hard drive to indicate that something else was going on. "Or a signature of some kind. I would like to know how that much activity was packed into that barcode, though. It's a remarkable piece of programming." He tapped his finger on the card with the black barcode, and André nodded admiringly.

Robert turned to the girls and Captain Bulle. Marie was discussing the square barcode from the Mona Lisa mousepad with the Captain. Seeing Robert listening, she switched to English.

"Of course, the *Centre Commercial du Louvre* is closed today because of this tragedy, and also because it is Tuesday, the day when the Museum and its shops are always closed. But I think that we need to collect the staff immediately and search for barcodes of this

---

[1] For details on the Fibonacci sequence, see Dan Brown, *Da Vinci Code* (Doubleday, 2003), p. 61.

kind. It would be a further disaster if our cash registers were attacked by this virus, or whatever it is."

She turned to Robert. "Yet when you brought the same mousepad through the checkout yesterday, it did not put a virus on the scanner."

"We don't know what it did to the cash register, actually, Marie. Remember, it produced the Pi million readout...."

"Yes, but I could void it out immediately."

"You left the cash register after that...."

Oh, you were watching me? "Yes, I wanted to discuss it with Ser Aspro. But another cashier took my place very quickly. The lines were long. The cash register functioned normally the rest of the afternoon." She paused. "But perhaps there are different kinds of these dangerous barcodes, which have different effects on different computers. We don't know until we look."

The Captain offered to assign some policemen to help with examining the Louvre Boutique inventory for the square barcodes. He also had a stock of good flashlights which would help detect the labels, which were almost invisible when applied on black surfaces. The police tech, André, immediately volunteered, asking if he could examine the cash register which had read the code without crashing. Robert let Captain Bulle know he would like to do the same.

Mado was looking at the blue *pneus* and the debris in the little glassine evidence envelopes. These were still being guarded by the policewoman in surgical gloves. Mado turned to Robert and Marie, excited.

"Marie! There was something inside our envelopes, too!"

They gathered around the array of items on the table. The policewoman explained, and Marie translated quietly for Robert. The two little evidence bags which she had brought in with the *pneus* held the contents of Marie's and Mado's envelopes. As with the cardboard boxtop enclosed in Robert's *pneu*, these items seemed more or less like garbage, or in this case dirt of some kind. Under the microscope, the item in Marie's envelope was seen to be a small, matted clipping of hair, and the one in Mado's was a bit of leather.

Neither item seemed likely to have anything to do with the murder. The *pneus* and their contents would be returned to the three recipients, Captain Bulle added.

Though of course the scanner and handheld computer will stay in custody, not that they will do the police any good now that I've fried them, thought Robert.

Mado picked up her little cellophane bag carefully and put it back in the blue *pneu* envelope, then handed it to Robert. "You keep them for us. Keep them safe." Marie seemed to agree.

As he placed the three *pneus* in his inside breast pocket, Robert noticed one other item that had been there in his pocket for a while. He couldn't remember what it was so he pulled it from the pocket. The policewoman stepped forward with a frown and took it from him with her surgical gloves.

Bulle commented, "Yes, we should have asked you about that earlier. We saw on the security video that you removed it from *Monsieur l'ancien Directeur* Aspro's office."

It was just a blank, shiny sheet of paper, folded in half lengthwise to fit in the pocket. Label stock, with all the labels used up, leaving a rim of sticky paper around the edges. Robert pulled out one of the *pneu* envelopes again and opened the flap. Laid beside the sheet of label stock, it seemed very possible that the large blank white label inside the flap had indeed come from this sheet. If so, the sheet had held twenty such labels. Ser Aspro seemed like the sort of man who would take a new sheet of label stock every time he needed to use labels. So there may have been twenty *pneus* sent out last night, or up to seventeen regular postal letters with these blank labels. *Blank labels? Why was he sticking blank labels on letters when he was murdered?*

Both girls seemed to have finished with their time at the police station. Mado would be making the arrangements for the funeral, while Marie had to organize the hunt for the square black barcodes at the *Centre Commercial du Louvre*. Without speaking she pressed into Robert's hand a key–her apartment key?

THIRTY-SIX

The technique of reproduction ... substitutes a plural-
ity of copies for a unique existence. And in permitting
the reproduction to meet the beholder or listener in his
own particular situation, it reactivates the object reproduced.

Walter Benjamin

Robert had not been dismissed. Captain Bulle touched his arm and
asked him to step into another office.

"You can collect your possessions in a few moments," Captain
Bulle told Robert Longone. "I have a small proposition for you,
however."

"If you want me to do anything else, could you feed me first?"
Robert's croissant breakfast had been a long time ago.

"Certainly, *bien súr*. Do you eat ham?" Robert did, and a sandwich and coffee were ordered. He was given a bottle of fizzy water
on the spot. Bulle explained that Robert's interest in the technical
aspect of the case had been noted, and the Paris Police would re-
serve the right to call on him in the next few days for assistance in
the matter of barcodes, should that seem relevant to the case, and
should he wish to remain in France rather than going home immediately. He was free to go home, Bulle emphasized. When Robert
had finished eating, he gave Captain Bulle a business card, suggesting that email would be the best way to contact him.

Hesitantly he asked, "Captain Bulle, of course I had never
met Ser Aspro, and you had." The Captain nodded, looking both

amiable and mournful. Robert remembered that, after all, the Captain wanted a favor from him.

"Well, Captain, do you think he was responsible for these peculiar barcodes? Could he have been planning to use them on the competition, for example–other museum shops, or something like that?"

"It's possible." The Captain's tone was so neutral it seemed skeptical.

"This would explain why the barcode did not shut down the Louvre cash register, wouldn't it?" Captain Bulle nodded thoughtfully. "Did Aspro have the knowhow to design this code? Was he the kind of man who would try to destroy commerce this way?"

"Monsieur Aspro was much respected among museum shop directors, and even among museum directors, Professor Longone."

"That's not an answer." Robert surprised himself by going on, "Do you know anything about how he treated his granddaughters? I mean–it seems very wrong to me, from what I understand...." Robert stopped. The Captain was looking down at his desk, and he projected a stonewall quality that damped down Robert's questions.

After a long moment, the Captain said, "I don't think that really bears on the case. And as for whether it was wrong or right... I suppose the twins' opinions are what count. I would not question them about it right now, though, if I were you." He looked up and smiled a little.

"Now then, Professor Longone. Did you bring your marvelous toy with you, the scanner that reads people?" He nodded towards Robert's jacket side pocket, which swung heavy with the weight of the Personal Sampler. "I understand you can create a robot portrait from a very small sample of DNA."

"Yes, I did bring it. Just in case you changed your mind about wanting to see it." *I hope he doesn't want to see the girls naked. And I already traded his wish for a ham sandwich.*

"I would like to see what the materials *Monsieur l'ancien Directeur* Salvateur Aspro sent his granddaughters might be. I want you to show me the animal from which came the hair and bit of leather."

Robert started to reply, but the Captain held up his hand to stop him.

"I could have ordered tests. But these relics are so small, they would have been destroyed by our tests. It appears that your apparatus requires a far smaller sample of organic material. You understand, we have excellent evidence as to the murderer of *Monsieur l'ancien Directeur* Aspro, and we will catch and convict him. I cannot justify the complex of tests we would have to run, and depriving the young Navet women of their grandfather's last gift, however strange that gift may be. But–I am curious."

Robert found that he was curious, too. "The Personal Sampler is charged and I can use it. I want you to understand something, however. If the organic material comes from an animal, we may get a very strange picture on the screen. The program will interpret the data as if it were from human DNA. It could be something quite grotesque. Just a warning."

His sandwich and coffee arrived, and he ate and drank quickly. They waited until an officer had removed the plate and cup, and the two of them were alone. Robert drew the *pneus* once more from his inner breast pocket. He found the glassine evidence bag from Mado's *pneu.*

"O.K., Captain Bulle, here goes." The policewoman had said Mado's "gift" was leather, but it might be human skin. Ser Aspro seemed to have been capable of anything.... He tipped the bag so that the ragged bit of material lay along a side of the bag perpendicular to the opening, and slipped the Personal Sampler into the bag. He was relieved that the Personal Sampler's touch did not disintegrate this fragile-looking dark patch of organic matter. He saved the data and selected twenty years old.

The image developed quickly. The sample was indeed human

A woman, not very tall, with dark hair and eyes but fair skin. Good eyesight–no glasses added. A slender body type, rather large feet and hands. Left-handed.

The screen showed her frowning, with her eyebrows drawn up in the middle. This mournful expression denoted an inherited tendency to depression.

Robert flipped to the age of ten, then to forty. At those ages, she looked more cheerful. Presumably the depression had something to do with hormones.

Captain Bulle had come to stand looking over Robert's shoulder.

Robert handed him the Sampler after setting the age each time. The Captain seemed to be memorizing the woman, but he said nothing at all.

Robert was even more curious, now, about the bit of hair sent to Marie. He repeated the procedure to sample this second organic mystery.

He saved the data and called up the twenty-year-old image. This time it appeared very slowly, and with many gaps blurred where there wasn't enough information in the sample. Still, there were enough details to recognize her.

It was the same woman.

"Well," said Captain Bulle at last. "Now we know. Both of these came from the same woman. Perhaps she was their great-grandmother...?"

But this woman had a cross in her right palm.

"I think, whoever it is," said Robert, "there were two of them."

THIRTY-SEVEN

'Tis true my form is something odd,
But blaming me is blaming God;
Could I create myself anew
I would not fail in pleasing you.
Joseph Carey Merrick (possibly)

Fibonacci was awakened by a stab of pain in his hand. He came to consciousness as his adrenalin was stirred by unfamiliar physical sensations.

A woman's voice was speaking softly.

He smelled medicine, perfume, and a little mildew.

A hand reached under his neck to pull a pillow up under him.

There was air on his poor hand, and then the pain suddenly eased.

The light was bad but a bright light was shining at him when he opened his eye.

He sat up as abruptly as he could, making a fierce noise and trying to remember where his gun was.

He was ravenously hungry and he needed to pee explosively. He still didn't know where he was but when his eye fell on the startled face of the woman, he began to calm down.

After a moment he was able to speak normally.

"Sorry, Madame. I—where are we? Where is the toilet, please?"

She laughed abruptly, like one who has been badly frightened by something which turns out not to be terrible at all. "Right there. Let me help you get up."

She did help him, and he needed it. Standing turned out to be difficult, but once he got upright he was able to walk.

When he returned, he sat on the bed and apologized again. She reminded him to call her "Val" and he remembered her name, Valerie Percy.

It seemed that they had stopped at a motor inn of some kind, a modern place with a W.C. for each room. It was small and known to her to be friendly to their organization. He had been feverish and somewhat drugged from the painkillers, but she had been able to walk him from the car to the room.

It was not yet dinner time but she had seen a *charcuterie*, a shop selling cooked food, down the street, if he was hungry. He was.

She finished re-bandaging his hand and went out.

The room was small and not very nice, in spite of the plumbing, not really worthy of a member of the Brotherhood. Val was clearly not planning to share it. His own small suitcase had been brought in, though. The bed was not bad, though not as good as what he had in Edinburgh or in the little Paris Temple. She had arranged the pillows quite cleverly, to his surprise. He wondered if she had known other hunchbacks, but that seemed absurd.

She returned with a substantial ham sandwich, half a chicken with some fried potatoes, an apple, a chunk of some kind of sweet pudding, and two bottles of *limonade*. He felt like a child being given a treat. She left him while he ate, to go arrange her own room, she said. But she was back in a bare twenty minutes, just as he was dropping the well-gnawed apple core into the wastebasket. She sat in the one chair, and he sat on the bed.

"Fibonacci–where did you get that name?"

"The Doctor gave it to me. He adopted me."

"The Doctor *adopted* you? How very.... odd. I mean, I had never heard that he had a son. Are you a blood relation of his? A nephew?"

"No, no. But my family, my mother and father, were quite.... they were fine people. Well-born people. I was born like this, though, so...." He couldn't bring himself to tell her that his parents were of royal blood. It was not something he had ever discussed with anyone at all, except the Doctor.

"And the Doctor took you in when you were a child?"

"A baby. Before I can remember. He took me in and raised me. He saw my potential...."

"And nothing could be done?"

"Nothing.... done about....?" *That's right, about me, my body, my face...* "He looked into it, of course, but there wasn't any way to fix me up. When I was older they took me to a National Health hospital, but all I wanted to do was go home. Finally they let me out. They said in the hospital that I would have gone deaf if they hadn't fixed something. I think they did operate. I ought to know that, oughtn't I?" He laughed nervously, a little excited. *I'm not used to discussing this. I should be able to remember an operation. I can ask the Doctor some time to be sure.*

"Is it progressive? Is it getting worse all the time? I'm sorry, I'm being very personal, but I have to ask you–how old are you?"

"I'm twenty-seven. No, I'm twenty-eight, I think. What day is it?"

"It's June sixteenth."

"My birthday is June fourteenth. So I am twenty-eight. And it was progressive, but it hasn't gotten much worse in the past five years, I think. I remember when I was twenty-three I thought, it hasn't really gotten worse this past year."

"And the scoliosis, the way your spine is curved? Did you have therapy?"

"Therapy? You mean, like, braces or machines or things? In the hospital I did, but I hated it. It was like torture, and it didn't make things any better."

Val stood up and came over to him. Very gently she touched his deformed head, probing a little to feel the texture of the bone and flesh under the skin. He closed his eye so that she could see him more clearly. Then she picked up his two hands and looked at them.

"Your right hand, is it any bigger than the left? I mean, was it, before you hurt it? I can't tell because of the damage..."

"No, why should it be?"

She stood over him. "The soles of your feet, anything odd about them?"

He bent down and untied his sneaker, removed it and the sock, and presented the sole of his quite smelly foot for her inspection.

She felt along the length of the sole, tickling him a little.

"Sorry. No, your feet seem perfectly normal."

Except that I need a bath. "What were you looking for?"

"There's a disease that causes growths of the skull that look a bit like yours. But it usually affects the hands and feet. Proteus syndrome, what the Elephant Man suffered from."

"The elephant man! Yes, that's what I have! They said elephant man syndrome, neuro-fiber-something." *Why can't I remember that name? It's my own disease, after all.*

She smiled. "Your informants were out of date. Neurofibromatosis is what you mean, and it used to be called elephant man syndrome because Joseph Merrick was thought to have suffered from it. He was the actual Elephant Man, do you know about him? He died I guess more than a hundred years ago, quite young. He was horribly deformed. Compared to him, you're...." She hesitated.

You can't tell me that compared to Merrick I'm Mel Gibson, or Adonis. That would be stupid.

"You would be a very mild case indeed."

Good save, Madame Val. "Yes, I've heard of Merrick. I had a book, and I started to watch the movie once, but it was horrible and I stopped."

"Well, I don't think you have his disease, Proteus Syndrome, though it's so rare that not much is known about it. I think that your symptoms do fit with neurofibromatosis, the diagnosis you say they told you. Both Proteus Syndrome and neurofibromatosis are the result of genetic mutations. Neurofibromatosis causes growths and they are sometimes on the face and skull, as yours are. And these cafe-au-lait spots on your arms...."

"My freckles? I've always had those. Well, they got bigger as I grew, but isn't that natural?"

"They're a symptom of the same mutation that causes the skull deformations and tumors. Neurofibromatosis also is likely to involve spinal problems. You said the doctors were concerned about your hearing—that fits, too, because the tumors can cut off the nerves to the ears. Every case is different, of course. But...." She trailed off, looking distressed.

"Well, I've lived with it all my life. Nothing can be done about it. I just have to be tough. Nothing is going to make me straight or...

or nice to look at. But I was allowed to join the Brotherhood. The Doctor arranged that."

The woman looked at him very strangely. She looked very sad for a moment, and then she smiled at him, broadly, almost a grin. "Yes, that's right! Being in the Brotherhood is a fine thing. They won't initiate *me!*"

"Of course not." For a moment he felt quite sublimely sorry for her. She was, after all, just a woman.

THIRTY-EIGHT

No sooner had I glanced at this letter, than I concluded it
to be that of which I was in search. To be sure, it was, to
all appearance, radically different from the one of which
the Prefect had read us so minute a description.

Poe

Robert Longone's plane ticket from Paris to Boston could be re-
scheduled with only a small penalty, thanks to the assumption
that the police had made him miss his flight. He was not ready
yet, however, to make the reservation. He stood in a little reception
area downstairs at the police station, looking wistfully out through
a barred window. There was a basketball hoop and a few officers
were enjoying an informal practice in a tiny courtyard. Robert
would have liked to join them, but he felt exhausted and filthy. And
unfairly tall for them, and unfairly old.

He would need a hotel for the night, and the police had checked
him out of the *Hôtel du Prieuré*. Half-heartedly he called the *Prieuré*
to see if they had a room for tonight, but they were booked. They
kindly checked another hotel nearby for him, too, but it was also
full. It was, after all, high tourist season in Paris.

He decided to take himself and his things back to Marie's apartment. She had given him her key, which implied that she wanted
him to do so. He could scout hotels in her neighborhood when he
got there. If he was staying in Paris, after all, it was because his
expertise might help with the peculiar situation of the young wom-
en's grandfather's death. On the one hand, he was curious about the

problem. On the other, he felt that he wanted to protect the twins from whatever sorrows or dangers they might have inherited.

If old Aspro did come up with that square barcode as a device to decimate the computers of someone he considered an enemy, it will be very hard on Marie. Maybe even on Mado. But it's Marie who really believes in her grandfather's work.

When the taxi dropped him off, though, he was too tired to do anything but climb the stairs, drop his various cases, and lie down on the couch.

When he opened his eyes, it was dark. The apartment was completely still. The vague light of the city came in through the curtains, so he could see quite well the little apartment in which he had spent several pleasant hours that day.

I'm in Marie's apartment. She gave me her key. Where is she? Why hasn't she come home, or Mado either?

Marie went to the Louvre Boutique. Every object there has to be checked for renegade barcodes. Mado went — somewhere else. She doesn't live here. I may be here alone all night.

Might as well see about something to eat.

Marie's kitchen was not very helpful. Mado had made some snide remarks about her dieting, and it must be true. There weren't even any more of those cookies she had given him that morning– the empty package sat in the trash can. He would have to go out to find food.

The toilet and the bathtub were in separate rooms. The bathtub room had clearly been used by both young women, and the bedroom was worse, with clothing strewn all over the bed and floor. He found a towel that was not too damp, though, and managed a quick shower and change of clothing.

As he transferred his wallet to a different jacket pocket, he realized that he did not have many euros left to spend on dinner. He had a few dollars, though–perhaps a restaurant would take those. Or he could simply use a credit card, though he tried to avoid that during the summers when his teaching income dipped abruptly. He often ended up paying off the summer's extravagances right up until it was time for Christmas extravagance.

He returned half an hour later. Although it was ten at night, he had found a little corner grocery store open, and they had taken his dollars (at a terrible exchange rate) as well as euros. He made a meal of French junk food, enjoying the strange packages and tastes. He ate this improvised dinner in the chair by the worktable, in front of Marie's computer, though he scrupulously waited until he had finished eating and washed his hands before getting down to business on her computer.

He checked his email. Marie seemed to have gotten hold of his email address–there was a short message from her. She confirmed that she did not expect to be back that night, and he should make himself at home.

Amazingly, there was a message from Captain Bulle, too. The police had located a couple of elderly computers and another, quite ordinary barcode reader, and the tech, André, had networked them and set them up to imitate a cash register and a server. The Mona Lisa mousepad barcode, scanned onto the cash register, had brought down both computers, streaming the Fibonacci sequence until the hard drive was wiped clean. The police tech was now, indefatigably, at the Louvre helping Marie. Any insights from Professor Longone would be appreciated.

Professor Longone had no insights at the moment.

He wrote a brief reply to the email from his sister, stumbling a bit with the unfamiliar keyboard, telling her his return had been delayed.

He considered the saved email from Lindy Teabag, the colleague who wanted to get together. For the first time he realized that this could be just what the doctor ordered. Teabag was one of the most inventive symbologists around, and he might have some ideas about barcodes that carry viruses. Perhaps he could help Robert think himself *into* the box of the nefarious black barcode. But Robert would have to see Marie, and if possible Mado, before deciding his schedule for tomorrow, so he didn't reply yet.

Relaxed, he picked up the three blue *pneus* and examined them one more time. *Strange to send messages in a code they don't understand to your granddaughters. Or to a complete stranger, meaning me. Stranger and stranger.*

He opened his own envelope. He looked more closely at the blank white label stuck on the inside of the envelope–visible as soon as the envelope was opened. There was a similar empty label on each of the other two *pneus. Old Aspro printed twenty of these big white labels. I saw the empty sheet of label stock. He was not a man who would save partly used label sheets. He would use a fresh sheet of labels for a new project. Except he didn't print them, did he? He sent twenty blank labels to his friends and acquaintances, and to his granddaughters, and to me....*

Unless he printed them white on white, the sly old fox, the way he did blue on blue.

THIRTY-NINE

Here, lit up by the sky itself, the museum planned to offer from now on.... services designed to make the museum visit comfortable and complete: an art bookstore and shops with related products (CD-ROMs, cassettes, postcards, posters, jewelry, gifts, sculpture reproductions)....

Louvre website, "Les dix ans de la pyramide"

The *Centre Commercial du Louvre* was brightly lit under the glassful of night that was the *Pyramide Inversée* at midnight, and busy. The little mezzanine with Ser Aspro's and Madame Rosamonde's offices was still a cordoned-off crime scene, dark against one wall. Everyone was aware of it, and worked hard, as though to please the old man.

So far all the dangerous barcodes had indeed been found on black surfaces. Black on black, they were, in a sense, invisible.

The labels all appeared to be identical, black printed on a transparent plastic which reflected as white in certain lights, and located near the more conventional price codes on certain items, so that scanning one would scan both. They were not too hard to find with a flashlight, which blanched the label and made the distinctive pattern appear black on white.

Ingénieur André, the police tech, had arrived with the news of the deadly effect of the black barcode on an ordinary computer network. Now the mission seemed much more urgent.

"When we do inventory in January, we take three nights," sighed Marie Navet, who had gathered all available employees for the emergency night duty. The police officer assigned to co-ordinate the work with her, Brigadier Laurent, nodded sympathetically.

"I suppose that if we don't finish tonight, we can just put drop-cloths over the merchandise that hasn't been checked, so that we don't sell any of those items. But people usually want to look underneath a covered display. Some people find that kind of hidden merchandise more attractive. If one of these treasure-hunters brought one of the objects that hasn't been cleared to the cash register...."

"But, Mademoiselle Navet, you are clearing each product in the database as it is checked, aren't you? So if a product that has not been cleared is brought to the register, it will not scan."

"Not exactly. The barcode is the only way the computers can identify any piece of merchandise. Therefore, until the actual label is scanned the computer won't be able to identify it as belonging to a product category which has been cleared or not cleared. And when our product barcode label is scanned, the other barcode, the black on black one, would also scan. And break the computer. From what *Ingénieur* André says, it might be able to break the whole checkout system, and even wipe out all the records of the *Centre Commercial du Louvre.*"

She paused as the bookstore manager came up to hand her a scanner-full of barcodes that had been cleared. All the CDs had been checked quickly and easily, since most of them had so much printing on the package inserts that the dangerous barcode was easy to spot. In fact, not many had been found, but the staff were confident that the rest were clean. Marie began to download the numbers into the central database, marking them as cleared.

"No, my dear Brigadier Laurent, the only thing we can do, I think, is make up a paper checklist of cleared categories. Or uncleared categories–I hope that will be shorter! It will slow things down for the cashiers to be checking it, but what else can we do? A few of the older cashiers understand how to use a keypad to enter the numbers, but most of them never learned–I never learned it, myself, and I make mistakes if I try to do it quickly. No, it will be faster to check a list. They will get used to which categories have been cleared, the CDs, the mousepads, quickly, I think."

A couple of dozen mousepads, about half of them Mona Lisas, had the codes applied on the dark undersurface, inside the packaging which was in the form of an easily opened clear plastic bag. The clear bags had some printing from the manufacturer, mostly around the edges so as not to obscure the masterpiece portrayed, and on the back.

Almost immediately the stationery department manager had pointed out that normally the regular barcodes, the black-on-white EAN-13 labels which the Louvre Boutique used, were applied on the picture side of the mousepad, the "top" side.

The dangerous mousepads had been removed from the bag, labeled with the black code on the black bottom surface, then re-inserted into their bags upside-down. That way, the EAN-13 code was right over the other one and would be scanned with it.

So all they had to do was look for mousepads which had the white barcode labels on the back of the mousepad packaging. That speeded things along, but Marie was worried that it might give a sense of false security.

Objects sold in black or partly black boxes were also turning up with the square black barcode, placed next to the EAN-13. So far the objects so labeled were all relatively cheap, and they were items of which there were many in the store. A good way to ensure that the codes would get to the registers.

Marie wondered restlessly if the labeling had been done in the store, perhaps by agents posing as shoppers handling the merchandise, or by the *Centre*'s employees arranging the displays.

At least we don't have to go through every box in the stockroom. The mousepads arrive from the manufacturer in their packaging. Then we apply the barcode labels ourselves, before setting them out for sale. Whoever applied the black codes was working with mousepads that we had already labeled, on the front of the bag. The white label had to be there already, so that this saboteur could position the hidden black code in such a way that it would be scanned along with the white one. To do that, the bag had to be turned around so the white label was on the bottom.

She walked over to the cash registers. Of course, when she was serving as Robert Longone's cashier yesterday—by now it was day before yesterday—her register had not been shut down by the Mona Lisa barcode. *Ingénieur* André had finished examining Number 3, the one which had rung up Pi million yesterday. He hadn't said much, but from his glum manner when he left to go home, Marie guessed that he hadn't found out anything.

She wondered if it were an accident that the Mona Lisa mouse-pad hadn't crashed the whole system, after all. Had the plastic bag or a corner of the black-on-white EAN-13 label obscured enough of the black one to abort its effect? Or it might not have reflected the light clearly enough to read properly. She had been upset enough by its strange behavior to cash out and go speak to her grandfather immediately afterwards.

Ser Aspro was excited by this news of the Pi million. But he did not seem very surprised. It was as if he expected it, and he was congratulating me on a job well done. Yet I did nothing. The cash register did it all.

I can't bear not to understand. But that, Ser Aspro would have said, is the lot of all men and women, not to understand. We play games to pass the time. We pretend that the puzzles we make and solve mean something. That is not the same as understanding.

Marie was staring at her cash register, Number 3. André had shut it down before he left. She started the computer up again and turned on the big LED price readout and the scanner. Then she went to the next register and turned it on as well.

The system was designed so that the cash registers had to "see" the local network in order to function properly. If the central database, on a server somewhere downstairs, was not available via the network, error messages would pop up when one tried to scan something. Therefore, she had to risk the entire system in order to test it.

Yes, this is what Ser Aspro would have done. It's what he would have wanted me to do.

Marie called Brigadier Laurent over. She showed him the network plug that linked the cash register to the rest of the system. She explained what she was going to do. She would initiate a transaction and scan one of the black barcodes using the register where she had worked that day. One of three things might happen:

1) The scanner would not register the barcode because the item was not in the database.

2) The scanner would register it because for some reason it *had* been added to the database, perhaps as Pi million.

3) The computer would crash, possibly spreading a virus through the entire computer and cash register system of the *Centre Commercial du Louvre*.

Marie would be watching her cash register, and the instant it looked as if it would shut down–that is, possibility #3–she would tell Brigadier Laurent. He would disconnect the network plug from its jack, and they could hope that the shutdown could be confined to just this one register.

Marie began with one of the Mona Lisa mousepads. She removed it from its packaging so that she could be sure she was scanning the black barcode with no interference.

Nothing happened.

She called for someone to bring her a pile of different objects with the black barcode. One after another, she scanned them. Brigadier Laurent stayed alert. Nothing happened.

Perhaps the effect required an interaction between the the renegade label and the official one. She scanned again, giving the products a broader swipe of the barcode reader in order to pick up the normal product barcodes. They rang up as usual.

"O.K., that was the cash register I used yesterday. It's ignoring the black codes completely! Let's try another register."

Brigadier Laurent took up his station at cash register Number 4. Marie picked up the first mousepad she had scanned before, and directed the beam carefully at the black label.

The monitor at first seemed not to react. Then the LED readout flashed.

3.141.592,65.

Pi million.

Just in case, Marie nodded to Brigadier Laurent and he pulled the plug.

FORTY

After writing a message on a piece of paper with lemon or onion juice, make it invisible by drying it with the hair dryer on Low. Make the writing visible again with a dryer set on High.

Tip of the Day

Robert Longone sorted through the collection of scanners Marie had laid out on her worktable, near the computer. There were a couple of small flat ones, that looked like pocket calculators, and three wands, and one which had a computer incorporated into it with a little display screen and keypad. These didn't interest him. He handled each of the five "guns," though. They were sort of like little hairdryers or vacuum cleaner attachments, with a comfortable handle and a wide nozzle to point at the barcode label.

He picked up the largest of these. It really was the size of a small hairdryer, and it was clearly rather old technology. It didn't even have its own rechargeable power supply, like the others, but had to be plugged in to an electrical outlet to work at all. It was a heavy tool, like an electric drill. He remembered that he had considered using it to brain Captain Bulle some hours earlier.

It was an ultraviolet label reader, at least thirty years old. It was not designed to be cabled to a computer, or even to show a readout of the code. It would record the number onto a magnetic tape, of a kind so obsolete you probably couldn't find equipment to play it back except in a museum. But it would also make any UV light-sensitive printing visible.

There was no possible reason for Marie Navet to need such an instrument. Why did she have it?

He plugged it in and pointed it at the blank white label on the inside of his *pneu.*

The label glowed. Robert turned off the lamp over the table so that the UV light was stronger, to be sure of what he was seeing. The label turned pale purple, and on it stood out in white a series of concentric circles.

"Bull's eye!" he said aloud. *In more senses than one.*

Ultraviolet barcodes had been tried out early in the history of automatic product identification. But it was not a practical idea.

He remembered a student in class asking, "Why not? I think invisible codes would be really useful." He replayed that class in his mind.

"You think so, Dawson, and so did some other people back in the 1950s and 1960s. And these were not people smoking pot under a black light poster of Jimi Hendrix. They were important scientists and their clients. But for whom would invisible codes be practical? That's a military mentality, that we have to keep information secret and guard it from unauthorized eyes.

"What are the labels for? Identification by a machine, yes. Identification by human beings is based on other aspects of the object, not on a barcode."

He dove into his briefcase and found his lunch bag. He had packed an apple that day.

"What is this?"

The students were enjoying the demonstration. "An apple!" came several voices. "A Red Delicious!" said the young man who was going to inherit a grocery chain.

"O.K., you all know it's an apple. Some of you have more information—you have a mental database in which you can categorize it more fully than others. Now, could you tell what it was if it were invisible?"

Silence, then that woman who had been an English major, got married, and was coming back to school said slowly, "Well, if I was blind, or blindfolded, it would be invisible. But I could tell it was an apple from the smell. And.... and the shape and the taste would tell me it was a Red Delicious." A couple of other students turned around to look at her. Apparently they looked doubtful, because she added. "A Red Delicious has that shape like a big strawberry, with little points at the bottom. And almost always they are waxed, so I could tell it by the touch. And they have a particular taste, a little bland but really juicy."

The grocery chain heir nodded. "They're the best keepers, that's why they wax them. They keep all winter and so we have a supply year-round. The other varieties tend to be seasonal, we can only stock them in the autumn."

Robert picked up a barcode label at random from the sheet on the overhead projector and slapped it on the apple.

"Now, how much more do you know about the apple?"

"Nothing!"

"Not one thing!"

"Well, it changed because you put a label on it." That came from a former philosopher major.

"In a way, it did, yes. But the barcode has no secret information about the apple. All it does is take a couple of the facts that your eyes, nose, and common sense can tell you about it, and make those facts available to the computer, which has none of those senses."

Dawson put up his hand. Obviously, since he was being proven wrong, he wanted to do the same to the professor.

"Yeah, except that it doesn't tell you those things, because that barcode you put on it has Post Office codes, right?" Everyone laughed.

"Dawson, you are so right! It *is* the wrong barcode. The supermarket barcode reader would either not be able to read the label at all, or would produce the wrong information."

He paused.

The grocery heir raised his hand. "The produce manager who labels the fruit–well, of course, we only put barcodes on the bagged stuff, but you see what I mean. Well, whoever handles the barcoded fruit knows at least some of the code, like the last two digits, by heart usually. Plus, also, the codes are on the boxes the produce arrives in. And there are codes on the bins where the produce is on display for purchase. So you would know if the codes didn't match up, if it was the wrong code."

Dawson saw the point. "You would know it didn't match

because you can see the codes on all the labels. Because none of the codes are invisible."

"Well said, Dawson. Did everyone get that? And we have just covered the next point I was going to discuss, the decision to have the codes printed out in numbers and letters on the labels, as well as in bar form. The barcode readers, of course, ignore the numbers and any letters–they get their information directly from the bars and spaces. A few people are adept at reading that system of bars and spaces. Just by looking at the barcode itself, knowing the symbology or system being used, a trained technician can sometimes translate the code into numbers and letters. But most of the people who actually need to match up or read barcode labels are not trained technicians. So they learn the code for apples as a few numbers, not as a pattern of bars and spaces."

That class was a long time ago. Now we get those Royal Gala apples and Fujis from New Zealand and Chile even in the summer. I haven't had a Red Delicious in a couple of years.

And invisible barcodes are fashionable again. The mail services want to be able to cover a package with barcode labels for tracking. They also want the package to look the way customers expect, with just a "to" and "from" address on it. The solution? Invisible barcodes.

Robert remembered that there had been a session on invisible inks at the conference he had just attended. He had attended a different session in that time slot, however. He found the program in his suitcase and read over the abstract, a short paragraph summarizing the paper to be presented by the expert for discussion. Yes, they had made a lot of progress just recently. The goal was to have inks that could be printed or stamped on any mailable package surface, not just labels. He noted that the expert presenting this particular paper was in fact a French chemist. *A friend of Ser Aspro?*

The next thing to do, of course, was to scan the invisible barcode into a computer and see what happened.

FORTY-ONE

Apparatus for classifying articles having thereon concentric circular light-reflective outer classification lines and inner auxiliary lines....
Patent application
Norman Woodward and Bernard Silver
October 20, 1949

As soon as he saw the target-shaped barcode, Robert knew how to scan it. Well, he knew what would probably work.

He had noticed earlier on Marie's computer a program called "Apple Pi Codes"–presumably a Macintosh program for Apple computers, but not a standard one. It was an odd thing to find here, since her computer used a Microsoft operating system.

Apple Pi. He remembered the cash register readout, "Pi million." Almost too good to be true.

He opened the "readme" file and found it was to do with so-called two-dimensional labels, another recent trend, very popular with the post office. Basically, you took a regular bar code but you used the bars themselves to hold a second code, which was read perpendicularly to the main one. You could get in an immense amount of information that way.

Apple Pi, however, was 2D barcodes with a twist. Apparently it produced or read circular labels, shaped not like the usual rectangular barcode but like the old bulls-eye barcodes that had been used in California in the earliest days of supermarket barcodes. You could do spirals and superellipses, too.

One of the "gun" scanners was branded Apple Pi. The software and scanner combination were obviously designed to read the white-on-white barcodes from the *pneus*. Perhaps the software had been used to create the label.

The scanner required a connection to a computer, almost certainly to a computer with the Apple Pi software installed on it. Robert found the appropriate port on Marie's computer, then hesitated. After all, the last time he had scanned a strange-looking barcode, it had destroyed not only two computers but possible police evidence as well.

Without snooping, he saw that Marie's computer contained not only her personal and business files and documents—*maybe she's writing a book, a doctoral thesis, love letters*—but also materials brought in from the *Centre Commercial du Louvre* computers for, as she had told him, training purposes. Possibly she had copies of some of the lost files from Ser Aspro's secretary's hard drive, which had been destroyed to prevent the murderer from accessing it.

It would not be a good idea to fry that computer.

He got his laptop out of its case and set it up. He cabled it to Marie's computer and dumped a few of his most important files on her hard drive—notes from the conference he had just attended, a chapter of a book he had been working on during the flight to France. Most of his other files were backed up at home.

Then he reversed the direction and copied the Apple Pi program onto his laptop. In addition, he did a search for every database file type he could think of, and copied those onto the laptop, too.

Who knows? Maybe I can find out more about what this barcode means from one of these databases.

He discovered that all the database files were in a subfolder named SerA. That was unmistakable—files given her by Ser Aspro. This folder was in turn inside a folder named CCL–*Centre Commercial du Louvre*, obviously—which also held the various barcode scanning and cash register emulation programs. All quite tidy.

He disengaged the two computers. Now only his own laptop would be at risk. *Good excuse to upgrade.*

He had three of the invisible barcode labels, one on each *pneu*. He began with his own. Using the Apple Pi scanner, he moved the laser beam carefully down the label. On his laptop monitor, the Apple Pi program popped up a box which instructed him to scan it again–presumably this would pick up the information coded in the other direction. He finished.

Nothing was happening. The program just sat there, working. Then it presented him with a pop-up window full of letters and numbers. It looked like some kind of program. Before he had time to read it, the computer began to shut down.

Oh, no. Should I turn it off to stop whatever is causing the shutdown? Same difference, I guess. Robert was so upset he got up and went into the kitchen for a beer, although a beer at this hour was likely to put him to sleep quickly. *Good. I've done my day's work. I've killed three computers in twelve hours. Five, if you count the two that André and Bulle slaughtered at the police headquarters.*

When he returned to the worktable where the computers were set up, he saw to his surprise that his laptop had in fact restarted itself. It was ready to go again. When he looked at the laptop's files and structure he could find no changes. He went as far as checking the registry and some of the underlying programming.

It seems as if the label actually wrote something onto the computer, but where? And why?

He found his beer where he had set it down and took a swig. *Oh well, might as well see if the other invisible labels are the same.*

He scanned the invisible label on Marie's *pneu,* with two passes, as before. This time the window popped up but in it was a message reading, "ALREADY SCANNED."

He shut the Apple Pi program, re-opened it, and tried again, with the same results. *I want to see the readout of what is coded on my label, please.* He searched all the options of the program and read more of the "help" files than he had read for any program in years. None of it referred to a one-time-only kind of barcode.

He scanned the label from Mado's *pneu.* ALREADY SCANNED.

Finally he scanned the label from his own *pneu* again–the one which he had tried first. He would at least be able to read a bit of the program that it had initiated before the computer shut down. But no.

ALREADY SCANNED.

He heard a soft noise in the living room. He turned and saw that the apartment door was being opened, very gently and quietly.

FORTY-TWO

The method employed I would gladly explain,
While I have it so clear in my head,
If I had but the time and you had but the brain—
But much yet remains to be said.
In one moment I've seen what has hitherto been
Enveloped in absolute mystery,
And without extra charge I will give you at large
A Lesson in Natural History.

Lewis Carroll

Marie Navet came into the apartment.

"Robert, why aren't you asleep?" She yawned uncontrollably. "I would be, if I were you. It's...." She blinked at her watch. "It's probably after two. I took my contacts out in the taxi. Is that beer? Can I have some? Guess what happened!"

She was clearly both exhausted and triumphant.

"I bought beer. There's another bottle in your refrigerator. And I'll guess what happened to you if you'll guess what happened to me."

"O.K." She went into the kitchen and poured beer into a glass for herself. She came back and sat down on the couch. "One, two, three!"

"I solved the invisible code!"

"I solved the invisible code!"

They had both spoken at once, and they stared at each other for a long moment, both almost laughing. Then they untangled the explanations.

Marie had found that all the cash registers at the *Centre Commercial du Louvre*–even the ones in the little shops of the mall–either produced the Pi million readout when the strange black-on-black barcode was scanned, or simply ignored it. Only two of them ignored it on the first try, and one of those was the cash register she had used to scan his Mona Lisa mousepad. But after she had already scanned an item with the code on a particular cash register, and it had produced its Pi million total, it would afterwards ignore the code, behaving as if there were no code at all.

"I wish that *Ingénieur* from the police had stayed around. He told me that the black code does crash computers. He couldn't figure out why your Mona Lisa mousepad didn't crash my cash register yesterday. But it looks like it doesn't crash cash registers after all, even if they are computers. There must have been something about the police computers that made them vulnerable to that evil label."

"Marie, it's the other way around, I think. It seems to me that there was a special program on the Louvre computers which protected them from the square barcode. André was looking for that program."

"A round barcode?"

Robert stared. "Yes–a round barcode."

"A Pi barcode."

"Exactly. A Pi barcode, Apple Pi. So you know about it?"

Robert felt confused. He had assumed that Marie knew nothing about the Apple Pi software, but it seemed that she did. If Ser Aspro had created the "round" barcode to inoculate computers against the square barcode, it seemed quite possible that he had invented the black one as well–he just wanted to be sure that the Louvre computers were safe from it. *I would have sworn, though, that Marie knew nothing about the square barcode, yesterday. She was a little upset by it–or was it just that she didn't expect to see it there and then? And she must be a good actress if she put on all this show of searching the shop for the barcode, if she knew all along that the Louvre had been protected. And now–she just looks tired and pleased with herself.*

"What are you talking about, Robert? Apple pie, apple pie and motherhood." She giggled a little. "No, I didn't mean apple pie, I meant Pi, like in Pi million, our round number, Robert."

She looked up at him with her slightly foggy naked blue eyes and he realized that his suspicions of her were groundless. She had just been thinking of *our round number.*

"Do you have anything with the black barcode, the Arch of Defense one, on it? The police confiscated my copy."

"Yes, I thought of that. I brought you another mousepad, with of course one of our dangerous Leonardo da Vinci codes." She stood up to get her purse, a large one, and brought him another Mona Lisa mousepad in its plastic bag. She explained about the bag reversal, which forced the scanner to include the renegade barcode in its scan of the usual black-on-white label.

He took her elbow and guided her to the worktable. She was surprised to see the antique UV scanner plugged in–"I didn't even know what that thing was, but Ser Aspro told me to bring it home"– and also to see the Apple Pi software and scanner, which she said she had never used, installed on Robert's laptop. She went away into another room and came back with a pair of glasses, rather ugly ones with black rims, on her nose.

He explained about the white-on-white barcodes, which would only scan once.

Once Marie understood, she was excited. She took over selecting an appropriate scanner to use for this experiment, similar to the ones in the Louvre Boutique itself. Since Robert had already copied the *Centre Commercial du Louvre* cash register software onto the laptop, she just had to open it and go through the normal steps of logging in and starting a transaction. Fortunately this "practice" copy did not require access to the Louvre servers, as the cash registers in the store itself did.

Within a few minutes Robert's laptop was, more or less, a Louvre cash register. Marie showed Robert the area of the program interface which emulated the LED readout, which would show the price of the item as it was scanned.

Robert let Marie do the scan. She took the mousepad out of its bag in order to maximize the accuracy of the scan of the square black code. She scanned it and the register program seemed to hesitate. Then the number they were hoping for appeared: 3.141.592,65.

They both took a long drink of beer. Robert was so tired he wanted to weep, and when he looked at Marie he saw that in fact tears were running down her face. Her eyes were blue, blue as Mado's, without the colored contacts.

This would be a good time to give her a hug. A really big hug. In that dress.... and she smells so wonderful, funky, like someone who's been up all night but just naturally smells really good.

But first I just have to try one thing....

Robert took the Apple Pi barcode reader, which Marie had disconnected in order to connect the more normal cash register scanner. He cabled it to Marie's desktop computer and opened the Apple Pi Codes program on that computer.

He took his own *pneu.* He opened the back flap to expose the invisible bull's-eye barcode. He scanned it.

Somewhat to his surprise, Apple Pi did not proclaim, "ALREADY SCANNED."

Instead, the pop-up window showed a few lines of numbers and codes.

When he had scanned the label onto his own laptop computer, the scan had produced a great deal of data–he had seen that there was a scrollbar indicating that the actual file was much larger than would fit in the window. This time, there was much less, and the computer did not shut down. Robert read the window's contents quickly and then, when it didn't close, he opened a Notepad file and made a copy of the contents.

It was a little program, and he understood its meaning instantly. It was an upgrade for an earlier version of the bull's-eye code.

"Your grandfather made sure you were protected," he told Marie, and put his arm around her. "Your computer was already inoculated against that square barcode. It just needed an upgrade. Your grandfather sent you the upgrade on this label.... But you didn't know what it was?"

Marie looked from him to the computer. Then she looked back at him, with a slow anger rising.

"You think I knew anything about this? That's ridiculous. Even that he knew anything about it, that's crazy...."

"Ser Aspro made the white barcode, Marie, I'm sure of it. Or he commissioned it. So that the other barcode couldn't hurt the computers he wanted protected."

Marie looked at him, still angry, and also incredulous.

"Do you understand what he was doing that night, the night he was killed? He was sending out upgrades, patches–literal patches, the white labels which contained the new version of the program that protects cash registers from that–that Fibonacci virus contained in the barcode on the Mona Lisa mousepad. He sent them to you, to me, to your sister, and to at least seventeen other recipients. Anyone who didn't have that patch would be vulnerable, their computer systems would go down when they were exposed to the square label."

Marie leaned heavily against him, shaking.

"No, I don't understand. I don't understand at all."

He realized that she was really crying hard, now. Patting her on the back and keeping her head on his shoulder, he guided her to the couch.

She cried herself to sleep quickly on his shoulder. But by that time he was asleep himself.

FORTY-THREE

...from the very first, [the Golden Section] was the high-est aim and ideal of all figurations and formal relations, whether cosmic or individualizing, organic or inorganic, acoustic or optical. But its most perfect realization was in the human figure.

Adolf Zeising, 1854

Fibonacci and Val Percy made an early start, driving south.

He had slept well enough in the poky little room, and had awak-ened with very little pain in his hand. He was so delighted with the improvement that he would have liked to leave off the bandage altogether, but Val insisted that he keep the wound wrapped up for another day.

It was a lovely June day, the road ahead was pretty, and he felt deliciously alert to enjoy it all.

"It's wonderful to have left Paris! I hate Paris, that city full of holes!"

Val smiled. "Full of holes? What kind of holes? I'm fond of Paris, but–well, there's the hole in the *Arche de la Défense*..."

He twisted in the passenger seat to look at her with his one eye. "That, Madame Val, is not a hole. It is a square. Above ground, too, of course. It is an almost perfect form. Did you know that it would be perfect, absolutely perfect, but they could not make it perfect because of the subway stations underneath? They could not find a place in Paris to build the *Arche de la Défense* that was not so full of holes that it could not be built! Paris is all hollow underneath!" He felt his voice rising and tried to calm himself.

"Yes, yes, you're right," she said, her eyes on the road.

As if I were a child! I am not used to conversation, that's all, so it's a little difficult to explain things correctly. I know perfectly well what I'm talking about.

"As you must know, I am from Edinburgh. That city is built on rock."

"Yes, indeed, and it's a lovely city."

"There is the tunnel they made, when I was little, for the Royal Military Police and the infantry and all to get into the Castle.... but that's just one tunnel. And the one where Burke and Hare brought the dead people they killed. That's an especially bad tunnel."

"Two tunnels, then, a couple of hundred years apart?"

"The thing is, Paris never was built on rock anyway. The city's old name was Lutetia, and do you know what that means?"

"It means something like 'mud flats,' doesn't it?"

"Yes! And they never understood, really, how to build a proper city. Paris is builded on mud and sand. First it was sewers, well, they can't manage without those, I suppose. Then they dug all those subways and they couldn't fill them in afterwards because people got used to them being there. They put up towers and monuments but always underneath they were digging more holes."

"I see what you mean. And there are the archaeological excavations, too."

Ah, she's listening! She does understand. "Exactly. What good does it do to raise pyramids or the beautiful square arch if underneath the ground is full of holes? Napoleon could build the most beautiful monuments and temples, great straight lines and sweeping strong squared arches and long views that do the soul good to see. Why? Because there weren't any holes underneath to worry about, when he was laying his strong foursquare foundations. Even in the Middle Ages, they fortified the Island of the City, that means Citadel, with walls and palaces, and they built Notre Dame with its magnificent square towers. Only afterwards they came along and started digging around underneath the cathedral, trying to find what was buried there, and making parking garages."

"You know, I never thought about the *Île de la Cité* meaning 'citadel.' Of course you're right. It was the first fortress of Paris, before the Louvre."

"Yes, and well built, too. What was underneath? An inferior

civilization. The Romans built on the Left Bank, you know, not on the island. Why do the archaeologists want to dig up what the medieval masons buried? The island was some kind of shabby mess of huts and little buildings, probably round huts. You know, the ancient Parisians were Celts and the Celts are known for round buildings. The Celts, it is well known, are emotional and effeminate and, well, that's why the Romans conquered them. I believe.... well, I don't know if I should tell you this."

"What do you want to tell me that I shouldn't hear?"

"It's because you're not of the Brotherhood."

"That's quite true. However, I am an architect, so maybe I will understand."

"You know, there are Freemasons who do initiate women."

"Yes, I know."

"Well, you should think about it."

"I do, sometimes."

"Well, this is what I was going to say. It is not a secret of the Brotherhood. *That* I would not reveal. It is just my own observation and inference." He felt himself sounding very Scots. "I have not seen the cathedral of Notre Dame in Paris myself. I have only seen pictures of it. The pictures are clear about the design. Two tall square towers, and between them the rose window."

"Yes. Of course, that is the usual design for the western facade of a Gothic church."

"It is the proportions of Notre Dame that interest me. The perfection of the rectangle formed by the towers."

"Yes, of course. An exquisite use of the Divine Proportion. The height of the towers, the fact that they don't taper at all..."

"Yes! It's a fine thing to be speaking to an architect. I see you understand. You could lay a rule across from one tower to the other and walk across it on the level. And the width to the height in every perpendicular is proportional."

"Well said."

"I have studied it, therefore I can say it well. Now, then. The rose window, the circle, is set in a square and it is surrounded by horizontal and vertical lines. The gallery of kings runs below, and above, where there could have been empty space between the towers, there is a row of columns and a parapet so that the horizontal lines continue right across the front. And on either side is a square bay with a window in it. Now, why is that?"

She didn't answer, but seemed to be waiting with interest. She glanced at him encouragingly.

"The lines, the squares, the rectangles, are all there to contain the circle. The Rose Window. In front of the window is the Madonna, the statue of the mother and child. Below, the kings. Above, the little columns all in a row. Above that, the square towers. The Madonna, the mother, and the circle are good, you know. They are necessary. But they must be kept in place."

"Or they will just roll away?" She seemed perfectly serious, and it was the right image.

"Or they will roll away, or fall down, or get lost. You follow me well, Madame Val. Now, then, why did they understand this so well, in that place? Why did they know that the circle must be contained, the round controlled? I have a theory about this."

He drew breath. He had never tried to explain this to anyone. To whom would he have said it all? It took a long time to lay it all out so that his point made sense.

"My theory is that where the Cathedral now stands there was, before the Cathedral, a village of round little huts. Perhaps they were thatched. They were the homes of an inferior people, who needed to be educated spiritually. They did not understand straight lines, squares, the possibility of a true perpendicular. And after their little round houses were leveled to make room for the Cathedral, the builders made them a sermon in stone, a monument to the dangers of roundness, of the circle."

Val said nothing for a while. Then she spoke, slowly. "It's a brilliant theory, Fibonacci."

He felt a sudden, immense pleasure so intense that tears came to his eye.

"Fibonacci, it really is brilliant. In a sense, it is so convincing that I would be ready to make a sketch of that Celtic village of round huts, made of mud and sticks and thatch, and say that your theory proved that such a village had existed."

"Yes, exactly! The Rose Window proves that the round houses were there before, that they were superseded by the superior culture of the masons!"

"Well, it would be proof, sort of. But, Fibonacci, they did make the excavations, and the buildings underneath the Cathedral and the Parvis in front of it, well, they were not a village of round huts. They are Roman stone walls and houses, with rectangle-based floorplans, and heating systems for winter. There was a Merovingian church there, built back in the 700s, not much of a church by Gothic standards but still a nice little basilica-plan building. Basilica plan..." She hesitated.

She doesn't want to insult me by explaining. "Yes, a long rectangular floor plan. I know. Like the Church of the Madeleine in Paris." Tears were rolling down his right cheek, and one tear squeezed out from under his closed left eyelid.

Val turned the car off the main road and found a place where she could pull off the road. He twisted away from her as best he could, but she put her hands on both sides of his face and made him look at her. Then she reached into the back of the car and found a box of tissues which she gave him.

He wiped his face and blew his nose.

"Perhaps the village of round huts was somewhere else. Perhaps it was on the Right Bank. The round window proves that the village was somewhere, or why would they build it like that?"

"Perhaps, Fibonacci. Tell me, Fibonacci, was that eye always closed? Can you remember being able to see out of it?"

"I'm not sure. I don't think so. Maybe. When I was little."

Suddenly he had a strange vision. He seemed to be looking in a mirror at a little boy's face. The little boy had big brown eyes, dark hair, and an earnest expression. He was quite a pretty little boy, a beautiful age, perhaps five or six years old.

That was a strange thing to imagine, or remember, looking in a mirror at a face like that.

FORTY-FOUR

I believe that the automobile is today a fairly exact equivalent of the great Gothic cathedral–I mean, a great creation of the period, passionately designed by unknown artists for consumption as an image by an entire people (whether they use it or not), who partake of it as a perfectly magical object.

Roland Barthes

"What have you been doing?"

Robert Longone opened his eyes to see a face bending over him. *What have I been doing?* he asked himself. He had trouble remembering who this was he was looking at, though the face was very familiar. And the voice.

He sat up. He was on a couch. He had slept on the couch in Marie Navet's apartment. Standing in front of him was the other one, the blonde, Mado Navet.

What *had* he been doing?

Where was Marie?

"Sssh. Marie is asleep." Mado, reading his mind, pointed to the bedroom. "She was at the Louvre practically all night, doing the special inventory looking for the black barcodes. But everything's all right now. Did she tell you about it, or did you just sleep right through it all?"

Robert stood up, stretched his arms over his head, and remembered.

"She told me. I did sleep through a lot of it, but I was awake when she came home. She found out that the Louvre computers had been inoculated by Ser Aspro's invisible two-dimensional bull's-eye barcode. I mean, she didn't know that's what she found out until we compared notes, but that's what happened."

"Unh. So that explains what we have here." Mado waved at the two computers on the worktable. Robert's own laptop computer was set up as a *Centre Commercial du Louvre* cash register, and displayed the Pi million readout for his purchase of a Mona Lisa mousepad. Marie's desktop computer was set up with the Apple Pi scanner and software, and had the window with the little upgrade program open. Beside it was Robert's *pneu*.

Mado picked up the *pneu*. "Ser Aspro's invisible barcode. So that's what these white labels are? Invisible three-dimensional bullshit barcodes?"

Robert didn't feel up to explaining yet. "Yes, sort of. What time is it? Do you know how to make coffee?"

"It's eleven in the morning. Day after yesterday. I brought croissants and in fact I made the coffee before I woke you up. I remember from yesterday that you are useless without coffee." She smiled. "But very useful with it."

He sat on the couch, exactly as he had done the day before, and ate croissants and drank coffee. He remembered leaving some ham in the refrigerator the night before and he went and got that and ate it too, making a sandwich with one of the croissants. Mado evidently considered this anthropologically interesting. He noticed that the evidence of beer-drinking had been cleared away.

Remembering Mado's story about Jesus and Martha and Mary, the Active and the Contemplative Life, from the day before, Robert decided Mado made a good Martha after all.

He explained about the invisible barcodes and made her recite "invisible two-dimensional bull's-eye barcode" twice.

Marie appeared, clutching a robe over her dress from the day before as if it were a nightgown. In fact, it had served as a night-gown, and must have been uncomfortable. The skirt was much less bouffant this morning than it had been yesterday afternoon. Robert noticed she was still wearing nylon stockings, and there was a hole where the big toe of her right foot poked out..

Mado went over and gave her a hug. A stream of French congratulations, narration, and explanation ensued. The twins disappeared into the bedroom and then there were comings and goings between the bedroom and the bathroom. A shower was being taken. He decided not to save the rest of the coffee for Marie. After all, she knew how to make more.

Mado was groomed first, and came to sit with Robert in the living room after changing her clothes. She explained to him, "I spent the night with Madame Rosamonde. Ser Aspro's secretary, you know. I don't think you met her, but she's pretty smart. In fact, she runs the whole shop, officially. Anyway, she put me to bed early and stayed away from the *Centre Commercial* grand investigative inventory. She still feels pretty bad about Ser Aspro. But also, she said that last night was Marie's show. Besides, if Ser Aspro was dead and Marie had been up all night, who would be opening the *Centre Commercial* this morning?"

"Who?" asked Robert politely.

"She would. And me, too. I really don't know much about the Boutique and all but she told me what to do. Some of it was just setting up a temporary office for her, because even if they would let her use her office on the mezzanine she didn't want to go up there. Maybe next week, she said. Anyway, we got everything going quite well, and we both made a little speech to the department heads and clerks before the shop opened to the public."

"Sounds like a lot of work, actually."

"Marie was really glad to hear it. Idiot, she went to bed and forgot all about opening the *Centre* this morning!"

"Maybe she knew you would be there."

"Why? I was never there before."

Marie joined them. Today she had her red hair in a simple ponytail. Her eyes were blue—evidently she did own some clear contact lenses. She wore little makeup and Robert noticed a few freckles. Robert looked at Mado, whose hair was slicked back again, and wondered if she would let the natural red color grow out now that her grandfather was dead.

More coffee was made and Mado brought out one more croissant she had saved for Marie. ("Eat it. It's our genetic destiny to have a little fat on our bones.") Then Mado stood and posed to make a dramatic announcement.

"Last night Marie solved the problem of the black codes. Robert found the white, I mean invisible codes. Well, I solved some codes, too!"

Robert applauded. Marie looked at him crushingly. Mado bowed and continued.

"The one code you didn't really solve yet is the one on the outside of the *pneus*. Robert found out what it says but we don't know what the letters and numbers mean, right?"

"Correct," said Robert. Marie nodded.

"Well, of course I copied them all down and I showed them to Madame Rosamonde. She said she thought Ser Aspro had a database with codes like that, five letters and five numbers, on his computer that was stolen."

"If it was stolen by the murderer, he may have it now."

"Oh. Well, I don't know. But anyway, that computer gets backed up every single night and it was last backed up on Sunday night. And Madame Rosamonde has been helping the police retrieve the data. And so she had the jolly little database with our *pneu* codes in it! What do you think of that!"

Robert applauded again, but he was thinking, *I want a look at Ser Aspro's copy of Apple Pi. He must have a backup of the earlier version of this bull's-eye barcode. That would tell me a lot about this project. What would be really interesting would be if he had the prototype of the square black-on-black barcode.*

Marie said, "So what is the message? Is there a message?"

"Yes, of course! You remember the three codes." Mado showed them a bit of pink notepaper on which she had written them.

> Marie: VZBPF50018
> Mado: STBSM50018
> Robert: BWRLT01010

"Now, my children, what do you think the one that starts with VZ refers to?"

Marie sighed and looked at the code. "Vézelay?" she said.

"Well, yes, in fact. We decided that the initials are for 'Vézelay Basilica Poquette-Filiposi' Because in the database that code points to Monseigneur Poquette-Filiposi, who is the pastor at the Basilica of Marie-Madeleine at Vézelay."

"And the second one? I can't figure that out at all," said Marie generously.

"It's for the Basilica in Saint-Maximin-la-Sainte-Baume, and I know you know it. That is the church that has a body of Mary Magdalen." The twins for a moment seemed to mirror each other, staring in amazement into each other's blue eyes.

"And the numbers?" asked Robert.

"The 50018? Oh, yes. Madame Rosamonde figured that out all by herself. She said Ser Aspro loved to make jokes like that. All the other addresses in the database seemed to be coded with serial numbers—is that the right way to say it? She explained it to me. The first label generated for that address is 00001, the second is 00002, and so on. She thought that probably he had sent all the addresses in the database about ten letters each."

"And how many addresses are there? Do you have them?" asked Robert.

"Yeah, she gave me a copy. There were only seventeen. And that includes the two she used for us, Vézelay and Sainte-Baume."

"I am pretty sure he printed up twenty of the invisible bull's-eye labels," said Robert, remembering the empty label sheet. "Twenty or a multiple of twenty. That would mean seventeen to the regular addresses, and three to us, but using the same codes. Except for the numerical part. Which Madame Rosamonde interpreted for us.....?"

"Well, she said, the 500 is the Roman numeral. And 18 is the number of another letter of the alphabet."

"D. S.? D stands for 500 in the Roman alphabet, S is the eighteenth letter of the alphabet. So what?" Robert asked. Both the girls were laughing.

"I drive a Citroën DS," explained Marie. "A restored one. It's an old car but a great one, a classic. Older than I am, in fact. Ser Aspro gave it to me for my twenty-first birthday."

"So what's the joke?"

"Well, when you say DS in French, it's the same as saying *déesse*, which means 'goddess.'"

Robert sat for a few minutes, lost in thought. "He sent you messages telling you that you are goddesses and that you should go to these Mary Magdalen churches, wherever they are. Is that right?"

They shrugged and nodded.

Mado looked a bit troubled. "Do you think that's what it means? That I'm a goddess too?" It wasn't clear whom she was asking.

Marie explained to Robert, "For our twenty-first birthday I got the DS, but Mado got a Citroën 2CV–a *deux chevaux*, two horses, car. It is also a classic. In fact 2CV is really a much more classic car than the DS, and it was from the same year as mine, and also beautifully restored. But it is not a luxury car. It is more like a Volkswagen Beetle."

"In fact," Mado put in, "it makes the little Beetles look like a luxury car."

"That's horrible! How did that make you feel? How did that make you both feel?" said Robert. He thought of the car envy of his own youth, and how his parents had carefully bought him and Nell the same Toyota model when they learned to drive–each car was about ten years old at the time of purchase, but they were the same model, to be fair. And how he had felt about friends who got new cars or actual classic cars to drive. It sounded like Marie had been given a Jaguar and Mado a clunker. A goddess-car and a two-horse car.

The two women stared at him as if they didn't know what he thought they should feel. Robert decided to say something kinder to the memory of their grandfather.

"Well, I think Mado is a goddess. You're both goddesses. To my mind, that is the message of the barcodes. Ser Aspro wanted you to know that."

They all sat silent for a moment.

"What about my barcode from Ser Aspro?" Robert finally asked. "Was that in the database? What am I supposed to do?"

"I'm so sorry," said Mado. "Your code was not in the database. We did a search for it in all the files retrieved from the tape and we could not find anything like it. I can't tell you what to do."

FORTY-FIVE

I shall be a fugitive and a vagabond in the earth; and it shall come to pass, that every one that findeth me shall slay me.

Genesis 4

Fibonacci felt frightened and helpless. And hot. Val Percy had stopped for gas at a huge station on an island in the highway. They had been lucky–they were the only occupants of that particular self-service bay, so there was no-one else to see Fibonacci.

But then it seemed that she needed to use the facilities. She drove over to the restaurant-shops-restroom building, and chose the very last parking-place. Fibonacci protested anyway.

"If someone parks next to us, they'll be sure to see me."

"I don't think that will happen. Most people wouldn't want to walk so far. Especially if they felt the way I do right now."

"You could have used the bushes on the roadside, where I did!"

"Oh, for heaven's sake! How have you lived like this all your life! Let people see you. You're not all that ugly!"

She slammed the car door and headed for the big red-and-white building.

Fibonacci had forgotten that Val Percy didn't know about the murder. She had no idea why he was a fugitive. She was just doing what the Doctor had asked her to do.

And doing it better than I did. I shot the old man. I should not have even brought the loaded gun, then I could not have shot him. An empty gun would have been as good at scaring off anyone I met, like that old man.

Or as useless.

But my hand is almost all better now.

If the gun hadn't been loaded, I wouldn't be a marked man now. The police must know who I am. They will have my DNA from all the blood I left in the office, if nothing else. I've kept out of the criminal databases, but the Children's Hospital would know who that DNA belonged to, probably. And they don't need DNA. I saw the surveillance camera.

If I hadn't shot the old man, I would be..... going home to Edinburgh, to the Doctor, maybe?

But then I wouldn't have met Val Percy.

She finally admitted I'm ugly. Not all that ugly, but ugly.

"Och!" he gurgled aloud. A car had pulled up beside Val's.

It parked in the space on the driver's side. He wasn't sure whether to try to duck down or simply to stay very still so that no eye would be attracted by his movement. He couldn't see anything on that side, but they would be able to see his profile.

Two car doors opened and banged shut, and he heard footsteps and chatter moving away towards the building.

Now if only she'll hurry back. We have to be gone before they return. When they come back, they won't be in such a hurry as they were the first time....

He closed his good eye and prayed to God that Val would come back quickly, immediately, or at least before the occupants of the car next to theirs.

He hadn't prayed since the night he went to the *Centre Commercial du Louvre* offices. Then he had prayed to do his task well, to find and bring back the secrets the Doctor wanted. That prayer was confident, happy. Easy, he had thought, for God to answer.

A key crunched in the door and it opened. Fibonacci opened his eye and smiled at Val. She slid into the driver's seat, flinging into his lap a pile of magazines and newspapers before fastening her seatbelt and starting the car.

She didn't speak until they were back on the highway. Then she said, "So, Fibonacci, can you read?"

Her voice was so harsh that he twisted around to be able to see her with his good eye. She didn't look at him. It was an insulting question, but perhaps she had forgotten a word.

"I can read French pretty well. Better than speaking it."

He stood the pile of reading matter she had thrown at him on end, so that he could see what was there. He selected a glossy large-format magazine and leafed quickly through it to see if there was anything about Princess Diana. True, it was still only June, and he couldn't really expect anything until the August issues ran stories in honor of the anniversary of her death. But sometimes her sons would be in the news and there would be a picture, even a sidebar, about her.

Sure enough, there was an article about Prince William and his girlfriend. But the other photo was of Charles and that drudge, Camilla. He scanned the article for the inevitable reference to William's mother.

He felt, rather than saw, Val glance at him. "Did you find something interesting?"

"Well, yes. I don't know if you are interested in Diana. The Princess of Wales, you know? Actually this is about her son, one of her sons. But I'm interested in her, so I'd like to see what they say about her."

"You are reading an article about *Princess Diana*?" Val sounded extremely angry. He kept his finger in the page and twisted around to see her face. The rest of the pile of periodicals slid off his knees. There wasn't much space for them to slide into, so they spread out over his legs and feet as well as the car floor.

Val frowned rather horribly. She said nothing for a while. Then there was an exit and she left the highway. She found a little parking place off the road and stopped the car. Fibonacci had not taken his eye off her, though it hurt his back to stay twisted. When she turned to face him, he saw that tears were pouring down her face.

"Look! Look!" she almost screeched through her tears.

Fibonacci looked down at the array of front pages spread over his lap and legs. His own face stared up at him, in black and white and colored tinting, over and over. *Oh, yes, security cameras.*

FORTY-SIX

This result is too beautiful to be false; it is more important to have beauty in one's equations than to have them fit the experiment.

Paul Dirac, 1963

Robert Longone had taken a half an hour to untangle the mingled drives of his and Marie Navet's computers. Now each was back to where it had started, except that he decided to retain two of the more interesting barcode scanning programs, including Apple Pi, on his own computer. He would have to uninstall them, or purchase a license, before the next time Harvard Business School ran an audit of professors' computers, but until then they were worth examining.

Next he checked his email. The message from his colleague Lindy Teabag was still in the Inbox. In the past couple of decades, Teabag had become the great international expert on medical barcoding, the use of barcodes to identify not only pharmaceuticals but also blood, tissue, and other personal samples. He had pushed hard for the adoption of labeling standards after the HIV debacles of the early 1990s, and was on committees of both the United Nations and the European Union health organizations. Robert had no idea what city he considered his home town. He seemed to belong to the world. He and Robert had always hit it off well, though they saw each other rarely.

These two-way barcodes are just up Teabag's alley. I know he's been working on unconventional applications. Heck, he might be able to figure out how to scan the square barcode without crashing a computer. He doesn't call himself Lucky Lindy for nothing.

He sent Teabag a reply asking to set up a meeting as soon as possible.

Then, stimulated by the prospect of talking this over with someone who could really grasp the details, he removed the barcode label from the new Mona Lisa mousepad and examined it with a magnifying glass. He scanned an image of it and used a photo-treatment program on Marie's computer to blow it up to a giant size, and made a couple of printouts. He was able to get it up to about 4 inches square with crisp detail. *Lindy will be able to make something of this.*

The invisible barcode posed different problems. He wondered if it would be possible somehow to tint the label paper so as to bring the bull's-eye image out in contrast, but he was afraid to try. After all, the only three copies they had were on the three *pneus*, which still had sentimental value, especially for the girls. With a scissors Robert cut the big white label carefully from his own *pneu*, since he wanted to keep as much as possible of the blue envelope as a souvenir. He would give the label itself to the police, who probably could assemble the right gadgets to analyze it. For now, he rigged up the old UV reader so that it could stand by itself and allow him to use the magnifying glass on the now-visible barcode.

The white code had its own surprises to offer. Under the magnifying glass, Robert found it was not exactly a perfect bull's-eye, that is, a series of concentric circles. The central pattern of very fine concentric lines was in the shape of a superellipse, that odd compromise between a circle and a rectangle invented by the Danish mathematician Piet Hein. This central section would provide the orientation the barcode reader needed to read the label both vertically and horizontally. The outer lines were thicker and mottled with the "second dimension" of the message. There was no doubt that only an Apple Pi barcode reader would be able to scan this type of label. That meant that all Ser Aspro's correspondents to whom he had sent a label must have Apple Pi readers and probably software, too.

Why a bull's-eye with a superellipse in the center? Why not just make the whole thing a superellipse? It's a circle built to fight a square, but inside the circle is a rectangular circle... and the Pi challenging the Fibonacci numbers.... two different infinite series. Pi implodes into tinier and tinier decimals, the Fibonacci sequence explodes into bigger and bigger. There is a kind of beauty here too, but it's more eccentric. Eccentric concentric. Riddles inside riddles. But riddles are supposed to have answers.

Thinking about Aspro's seventeen correspondents, he turned to the little database Madame Rosamonde had given Mado Navet. This database had certainly been used to generate the blue barcodes on the address side of the *pneus*. The database had probably been used routinely to print the addresses on envelopes, with the little dark-blue barcode included as a guarantee of authenticity. Each of the seventeen database items included a personal name, full address, phone, fax, and a couple of different types of email and website addresses–one, he thought, belonged to a French internet system that had been implemented before the current system had become a world standard. There was space for a few notes, too.

Marie Navet had found a map of Europe for him, and he had located all the seventeen addresses. Not that he would need a map for most of them, he realized quickly.

The British Museum Shop in London, England.

The Tate Museum Shop, also in London.

Rijksmuseum Winkel, Amsterdam.

Galleria degli Uffizi, Riproduzioni, Florence, Italy.

The Vatican Library Collections, Rome, Italy. This one had a longish note about someone named Boyle. A quick Google search made it clear that, since Leonard Boyle had retired from a position as head of the Vatican Library in 1998, the database was probably at least that old.

MuseumsShop, Nationalgalerie, Berlin.

Gipsformerei, Berlin. He had to google that one, and found it was a store full of reproductions of objects in German museums.

The rest of the list included the shops in the Hermitage in St. Petersburg, Russia, and of museums in Copenhagen, Stockholm, Madrid, Barcelona, Athens, and Prague.

The only French addresses were the Orsay Museum right here in Paris, and the two churches somewhere to the south.

Robert made up a quick form for printing out all the information, and got a copy of it. He showed it to Marie and Mado.

"It's very odd. These are the most important museums in Europe. All the big state-owned collections. Except for the two Basilicas of Mary Magdalen," said Marie.

"Unh," grunted Mado, craning to look at the list. "This list is where Ser Aspro sent the invisible two-dimensional bull's-eye barcodes, right? Besides us. To protect against the square black label. Is it an attack on the museums?"

"Yes.... by distributing a few black barcodes on the items on display, whoever wants to can bring down the computer systems." Marie said this slowly, frowning at Robert. *She knows I think the man who invented the inoculation might have invented the virus in the first place. It would make sense that Aspro would want to protect the museums even if the rest of the world came crashing down.*

Marie went on, looking at Robert, "If Ser Aspro sent these white labels to the museums, it must be because he knew the museums, and only the museums, would be under attack."

Yes, ma'am. I'll bite. "What do the museum computers do, anyway?" asked Robert. "Inventory?"

"Yes, but more climate control, lighting control, security."

"I can't believe someone would come up with this barcode just to try to destroy these great museums," said Robert. He knew he sounded the naive American, but he couldn't help it. "Why would anyone want to destroy–well, not the art, but the computer systems that take care of the art?"

Mado replied darkly, "Art makes some people crazy, you know. Some people hate the idea of beauty and want to mar it. And some just hate the privileged quality of art, the fact that it was usually made for rich people."

"Perhaps they are trying out the museums first," said Marie. "After all, these are all national museums. We are a bit of the French government, even though we are just a little bit. After they shut us down, the next move might be to get the black bar codes to scan on identity papers. You could shut down the police."

Mado had been ignoring the tension between Robert and Marie. Robert was pretty sure that Marie had not told her that he was worried about Ser Aspro's role in all this. But now Mado said, "In fact, we *know* that Ser Aspro foresaw a bigger threat. That's why he sent us the mysterious envelopes. That's why he sent me Professor

Longone's visiting card. He knew that we would need help to understand what was happening, and what should be our next move. We have to find out who needs protecting, and protect them. Or find out who is attacking, and stop them."

Robert and Marie looked at Mado and then at each other. It was a very good interpretation of the role of the three blue *pneus.* Ser Aspro would not have invited a complete stranger, a university professor, an expert, to look into the labels with his granddaughters if the labels would prove him a villain. *My role is to prove Aspro a hero.*

"I think we need to talk to *Capitaine* Bulle," said Marie. "He knows about the black barcodes but not about the white ones, or about the database of museums. We need to get this information out to the police and the museums in the different countries. Presumably all the museum contacts understand how to use the invisible codes."

Robert commented, "But in order to scan them they need the Apple Pi barcode reader. I've been looking for the company on the Internet but couldn't find much. It may be based in Finland."

"If you haven't heard of it, it must be pretty obscure.... I wonder how Ser Aspro found out about them...." said Mado.

"And he may not have actually seen the black barcodes at all until I scanned Robert's Mona Lisa mousepad!" Marie went on, "If we understand the situation, that was actually the first time one of these had turned up in the Louvre–that's why it rang up Pi million, as a kind of signal that my cash register had been attacked–"

"–and that the defense system, the program on the two-dimensional barcode, had succeeded in fending off the attack," said Robert. "I think I can guess what your grandfather was doing, working late at the Louvre Monday night. He may never have seen the black bar code before, but he had some idea of how how it might affect the cash register, since he was able to prepare a defensive program. He had installed his program, it worked, but it also collected more information on the way the black code would crash a vulnerable machine. Perhaps his program made a report of some kind which we haven't found. With this information, he was able to produce an updated version of the two-dimensional barcode, which he printed up and sent out in the mail. Probably he also spread the news about the square enemy barcode and told them what to look out for."

"Yes!" Marie exclaimed. "He asked me if I had noticed anything about the item I scanned and I told him about the square barcode, and what you said about it, Robert. He made me repeat it a couple of times. I gave him your card, and he was very interested. Then, a little while later, I noticed him down in the shop, looking through the merchandise. Of course he does that all the time.... I mean, he used to do it. He must have been looking for some more of the black barcodes."

"We should do something about this, or ask Captain Bulle to do something. Contact these museum people, find out if they have had problems with their cash registers...." Robert hesitated.

Just then the doorbell buzzed.

Marie smiled. "Perhaps that's our *Capitaine* Bulle now. On a social call, so he doesn't just break in." She spoke into the intercom at the outer door. *"Bon soir. Vous voulez entrer? Vous me direz votre nom, s'il vous plaît?"*

The voice that emerged from the intercom was rich, hearty, and British, though speaking very good French.

"Madame, je vous en prie. Je m'appelle Linden Teabag. Je suis un ami de Robert Longone. Je le cherche. Hoy, Robert Longone, are you there? It's Lindy!"

FORTY-SEVEN

"Lucky Lindy," up in the sky, fair or windy, he's flying high.

L. Wolfe Gilbert

"Delighted to meet you, young ladies. Please call me Lindy. Lucky Lindy, you know. Though he also was unlucky in his time."

The twins seemed slightly overwhelmed by Teabag. Marie had addressed him as Professor Teabag without hesitation. It was clear to Robert that their excellent education had not included the tidbit of Charles Lindbergh's famous Atlantic flight, or at least not the tidbit of his American nickname. They both looked blank and smiled. Robert, who had heard the line about unlucky Lindy before, smiled too.

Teabag was an overwhelming character for most people. He appeared to be about sixty, but Robert suspected, given his long career, that he was a decade older. He was tall and stout, but not fat, with a tremendous head of white hair and strong features. He dressed extremely well, to Robert's eyes, looking amazingly British in tweeds that fit his generous waistline perfectly. He seemed to be wearing suspenders. He spoke with a glorious plummy British accent which was entertainment in itself.

"Robert, my dear friend, I think we might invite these charming young women—and you are sisters, then?—to accompany us?"

"Lindy, I don't think these *charming young women* would be interested in listening to us talk about barcodes and radio frequency id or how the checksum digit is calculated... and I had hoped to pick your brains about some of the problems raised at the Conference last week...."

Marie had become quite alert at the word "barcodes" and was furiously signaling to Robert that she *was* interested. Mado's feathers were clearly ruffled at the men's dismissal of the "charming young women."

"Perhaps we could have our chat over drinks, Robert, and return and pick them up for dinner? My treat." Lindy seemed quite taken by the twins, though oblivious to their possible interest in being treated as intellectual equals. Robert took his shoulder and turned him a little away from the twins.

"Lindy, their grandfather just died. They're in mourning." Lindy raised his great tufted eyebrows skeptically. The twins were certainly not dressed in black. "They've also had an exhausting couple of days, and now they have to plan the funeral." Robert could feel the women's reactions to this truthful if somewhat slanted version of their situation. He tried to telegraph to them the problem.

You do not want to come to dinner with two barcode specialists. And I won't get anything serious out of Lindy if you're with us. He wouldn't consider it polite to talk shop in front of you, even if it turns out it's Ser Aspro's own Louvre shop barcodes we're talking about.

Besides which, Robert did not want any casual remarks dropped in Lindy's presence about the Personal Sampler. That little gadget was actually a beta version of a diagnostic tool being developed by a medical engineering group. Robert was sure they would not want someone like Lindy, with his contacts in the industry, to see this until it was on the market.

Then, almost with the back of his neck, he felt them relax. They did understand.

So he and Teabag went forth into the late June afternoon. It was too early for dinner in Paris, though Robert felt it would have been thinkable in Boston. Teabag hailed a cab and they ended up in an area new to Robert, in the biggest café he had ever seen in his life. They sat at a table under an awning. Robert nursed a beer and wished for peanuts, while Teabag drank a glass of red wine and no doubt wished for something specific, scones or biscuits or whatever the Brits liked, to go with it.

Robert had decided to save the discussion of the strange

barcodes until later, so he began by talking about one of the conference papers that had concerned him. He wasn't surprised to find that Lindy was ecstatic about the spread of radio-frequency identification technology.

"Robert, there are so many problems that it solves. In particular, when dealing with individual items, unique items. It's something of a scandal that the Vatican Library should be the first important user — of course I would prefer it were one of the great British libraries. But those Romans have shown foresight. I have been working myself on miniaturized two-dimensional barcodes, but a computer chip is really what we need for medical samples."

"Miniaturized 2D? That sounds close to a chip already. Nearly as hard to decode, too. But isn't that overkill for medical purposes?"

"Of course, now we simply use a code that is a serial number, and the number has to be matched up both with the patient's name and with the results of the analysis. At most, the name and date might get onto the barcode, but really with those linear codes that's all you can include. My idea is to add a dimension and code in not only the name and date but the patient's history. And then the lab would add a second label to the first, with the actual analysis. The vials or dishes would be stored until the patient and doctor had gone over the results."

"So instead of going into a database, the information would be barcoded right on the test tube?"

"Yes. It's possible now, technologically. And the computer chip ID is even more attractive–tiny, unambiguous, easier to make and attach. It's also less potentially invasive in terms of the reading process itself."

"I hadn't thought of that. Of course you can't use a laser barcode reader on a test-tube full of blood...."

"Oh, it depends on when it's being scanned. In general, no. And of course RFI would be far more flexible. The point is, people reject the idea of intensive identification. They just don't like it. It's too personal. The argument is that if you include all this information about the patient and then add the actual analysis, it's a violation of privacy. But, my dear fellow, think how it improves accuracy! And accountability! Once the lab puts its label on the vial, the lab has guaranteed the analysis. If the analysis is mistaken, the lab can be held liable."

"Sounds like a good way of getting business for the lawyers."

"Well, of course, in your country you have no National Health, everything is personal between the doctor and the patient, so indeed your American *lawyers*, as you call them, might sue the labs. That is not what I am after, however. It is the possibility of truth."

"Truth?" Robert was looking into the bottom of his empty glass.

"Truth, the whole truth. As complete and exact a correspondence as possible between the numerical barcode and the object it labels."

"Linden, I think that's a dream. Even DNA...." He thought of Marie and Mado, so different in real life, nearly identical in the Personal Sampler.

"DNA! Yes, that's what we have to aim for. A barcode or a radio chip that contains the entire DNA sequence.... but of course that will not come in my lifetime. Perhaps it will come in yours, Robert."

FORTY-EIGHT

We, Hermia, like two artificial gods,
Have with our needles created both one flower,
Both on one Sampler, sitting on one cushion,
Both warbling of one song, both in one key,
As if our hands, our sides, voices and minds,
Had been incorporate.

Shakespeare

The girls were alone in Marie's apartment.

They were glad to get rid of the men. Mado contacted Captain Bulle and brought him up to date, using her cell phone, while Marie called the director of the *Musée d'Orsay* shop, whom she knew personally, and the two English museum shops, which were still open. The museum shop directors were full of expressions of sorrow and sympathy about Ser Aspro's death. They were less willing to discuss the mystery of the barcodes, but all three confirmed that Aspro had corresponded with them and that they had followed his instructions.

The twins went out for a quick meal at a little restaurant on the corner and compared notes.

"The only shop director who would really talk to me was *Monsieur le Directeur* Dandin, from the *Musée d'Orsay*. Well, I don't blame them. He's the only one who really knows that I am who I say I am. He said that he thought Ser Aspro was a bit silly, with all this mystification, but he always did what he said, just in case. 'Where Art is concerned, we have to watch out for madmen,' he said. I guess that's true–one madman can knock a hand off Michelangelo's *Pietà* or slash a Picasso."

"Did he have this Apple Pi stuff Robert says you need?"

"Yes. The others wouldn't tell me when I asked. All the same, I assume they have it too. Monsieur Dandin said Ser Aspro sent the equipment and software in the year 2000, and that's when he started using the invisible two-dimensional barcodes. Before that he just used regular black and white ones."

"The year 2000? *Before* the year 2000? And the attack didn't come until this week? No wonder they thought Ser Aspro was a bit *dingue*. How could he have known four years ago that this would happen?"

"He wasn't daft. He knew a lot, you know, Mado. And he turned out to be right. There was a barcode attack, right where he expected it, and he had the protective shield to keep it from hurting us."

"Now it sounds like science fiction, Marie. The problem is, he really is dead. No barcode did that."

"I know, I know, even though I didn't see the body when it was warm and bloody like you did, Mado. But we need to keep a focus here. What about our *Capitaine* Bulle?"

"Well, first of all, from what he said, I *don't* think they have found the assassin. I don't understand how a man who looks like that could just disappear."

Marie was quiet for a moment. "They'll find him. Soon. Was the *Capitaine* interested in the barcodes and museum information?"

"Oh, he was pleased. That cute cop who was working with you last night, Laurent, had already told him about the black bar codes and the Pi million thing. *Capitaine* Bulle was delighted to have more explanation. I read him off the list of museums. He didn't say what he would do about it, but he said we didn't need to worry about it ourselves. I assume this is where Europol comes in handy."

"Oh, I'm so glad. I really didn't want to try to call all those other directors of museum stores tomorrow. There are other things to think about... the funeral."

"You know that the funeral is to be next Tuesday? Tuesday is the only good day because the store will be closed anyway. Besides, a lot of the curators and department heads who would normally be working at the Louvre Museum want to come to pay their respects.

So the funeral is to be Tuesday, in Notre Dame, with the choir and everything."

"I discussed it a little bit with Madame Rosamonde on the telephone yesterday. So she has made the arrangements? Notre Dame? At what time?"

"Seven o'clock in the morning. Before the tourist crush. They won't close the cathedral but we do get the main nave. Pretty good for old Ser Aspro."

"He was very well respected. You know, he and Mitterand...."

"We know, we know, Marie."

"Mado, darling, about the cars, the DS...."

Mado smiled. "Marie, of course Robert was right. It was an insult for Ser Aspro to give you the DS and me the 2CV. A cruel insult, and it hurt me. On the other hand, like so much Ser Aspro did, there was a lot of insight behind the gesture. I love my little car and I have a lot of fun with it. I'd much rather have it than your big old heavy DS. So I shall just have to be a déesse, a goddess, in a 2CV."

Marie laughed. They finished their coffee and walked back to her apartment.

FORTY-NINE

You could say that hackers are White Hats, crackers are Black Hats.

www.itsecurity.com/dictionary/black.htm

Lindy appeared to be very comfortable in this part of Paris and, as dusk began to fall, he led Robert to a restaurant in which theirs were the only English-speaking voices. Although it was clear that Robert was paying his own way, he let Lindy order for him. The prices were very high for Robert's blood, and he hoped he would have a fat royalty check in September when the Visa bill came due. They had soup right away, and for a while both men were occupied. When the plates were removed and their wine-glasses refilled, Lindy became talkative again.

"I've been thinking about those those charming young ladies, the blonde girl and the redhead, whom I invited to dinner. You said that their grandfather just died. Now, tell me, are these the granddaughters of the late *Directeur du Centre Commercial du Louvre*? Of Monseiur Aspro?"

"Yes. We met by accident, the day before the murder." Robert didn't really want to talk about the twins.

"The *murder*. I suppose the police have confirmed that it was a murder? There can be no question?

Robert didn't answer. *I saw the body. It was murder.*

"It's difficult to believe such a thing could have happened, especially to that particular gentleman. Did you know Monsieur Aspro?"

"No, did you?" Robert felt genuinely curious. He would like an independent view of Ser Aspro. What kind of man was the grand-father of goddesses?

"Once, yes. Some years ago–eight or nine years ago, I think. He was in London. A remarkable personality. You know he built up the whole commercial enterprise of the Louvre himself? When he arrived, it consisted of one postcard stand next to the ticket desk. I disagreed intensely with his goals, to tell the truth. Yet I respected his intelligence and his passion. He was a strategist. If you showed him a game he would play it. He would master it. He could have been a great man.... Well, of course in the eyes of some he *was* great. In his own eyes, certainly. I suppose in his granddaughters' eyes."

"I guess so. I don't know if he was the best grandfather in the world. A player of games? That makes some sense. He was a pe-culiar guy. Used some obsolete technologies, like pneumatic tubes for letters, if you can believe it. I suppose the way some men have model train sets. Obsessed with binaries... and interested in bar-codes, too, oddly enough."

"Ah? Binaries and barcodes? Tell me now!"

Robert did not however tell him now, since their main courses had arrived. Teabag had some kind of sliced red meat with a dark sauce, while the waiter put down a dish of white chunky stuff in front of Robert. Wisely, he tasted it–it was delicious–before asking Teabag what it was. *Rabbit. Well, there's a first time for everything.* There was a long pause for some serious eating.

Robert did not want to discuss the strange theory of the binary goddess as applied to the twins. However, before his dish was emp-ty he began speaking, eager to explain the situation to a friend.

"Ser Aspro and the barcodes. He seems to have had the tech-nology to produce some very unusual barcodes. Two-dimensional bull's-eye barcodes using invisible ink."

"Ah? And what were these invisible two-dimensional bull's-eye barcodes good for?"

"Lindy, actually, what we need to do is sit down with one of these barcodes of his and see if we can break it down. I have the software that generated it. What we don't have is a reader that will tell us what it says. I think it has a program coded in it, but the pro-gram *becomes invisible* once the barcode is read into a computer."

Teabag nodded, as if this made sense. He was, in a surprisingly refined way, using a bit of bread to mop up the last of his meat sauce.

"There are two barcodes, actually, the invisible one, white on white, that's Ser Aspro's code, and the other practically invisible one, black on black. The black one isn't literally invisible. You can read it with a conventional barcode reader. But all the examples we've found were printed in matte black on a reflective label–you remember, that stuff 3-M was hawking in New York, I think that was in 2000, millennial tape, that turns white so the scanner can read it–it's hard to see when applied to black surfaces if you don't know how to look for it."

"The black one. The white one. It all sounds like a cowboy movie, with black hats and white hats."

"You are so right. The black codes are the bad guys. We scanned one and it crashed two computers. Then the police did it again, just to make sure."

Teabag grinned, with a kind of childish pleasure at such destruction. It was infectious–Robert found himself grinning, too.

"Yeah, it made a fool out of us. You were talking about playing games. That black barcode activated some kind of program that filled the screen with the Fibonacci sequence until the system wiped out. Makes no sense at all. I have no clue about the symbology involved because I can't scan it.... any more than I can scan the invisible white barcode. The other thing it does is ring up Pi million."

"Pi million? You mean Pi times a million? That seems innocent enough. This is the white barcode, now, not the black one?"

"Nope. It's the black one. You get a readout of Pi million when you scan the black barcode into a cash register that has been inoculated, protected, by having the white bar code scanned."

Finally Teabag was impressed.

"This is remarkable! A fairy tale, Robert! Where are these marvelous barcodes that cannot be scanned? I would like a good look at them, my dear fellow."

"I... I have a copy of the white one myself. Come to think of it, I have a copy of the black one, too. But they're back at Marie Navet's apartment."

"Oh." Something in this syllable implied that, although it was possible to think dishonorable thoughts about Marie Navet and

Robert, Linden Teabag would not do so.

"Yes. I mean, she put me up last night. On her couch. I couldn't find a hotel room, and, well, she wasn't there most of the night herself so she let me borrow the apartment. The night before...." *The night before I spent with her sister on a medieval garbage heap in the Louvre.* "I do need to find a hotel for tonight, I guess. But all my things are at her apartment."

"No doubt, no doubt, my dear fellow." Teabag folded his napkin beside his plate and called for the check. Checks, in fact, separate. He waved off the waiter's suggestions for coffee and dessert. "But when can I see these magic cowboy barcodes?"

Robert looked at his watch. It wasn't ten o'clock yet. "I really don't know how late Marie is likely to stay up tonight, after all. She was up all night last night–at the Louvre, working on finding the black barcodes. Let me give her a call and see whether we would be welcome."

FIFTY

...the love
Which teacheth thee that thou and I am one:
Shall we be sunder'd? shall we part, sweet girl?
Shakespeare

"Now, Marie, you must tell me—what happened last night?"

"Oh, Mado, it was wild! First we were looking at the Mona Lisa mousepads, of course, and then Madame Encre, you know, the head of the stationery department, noticed that the bar codes on the packages that had the black bar code were reversed, I mean...."

"Not that! Not what happened at the Louvre! What happened here! Robert told me he woke up when you came home."

"He didn't wake up then. He was already awake. He was working on the invisible barcodes. We figured out that Ser Aspro must have protected all the cash registers in the Louvre! But then...."

Marie stopped, looking distressed.

"Then?"

"Last night we didn't check the cash registers inside the museum itself. All those points of sale in the exhibits, with postcards and catalogues. What if Ser Aspro hadn't managed to protect those computers? Oh, Mado!"

"Marie, this morning Madame Rosamonde and I took care of it. Do you think we would have let anyone use a cash register that wasn't checked first? Your cute cop, Brigadier Laurent, was still there. He showed us how to check them and stayed there while we did it."

"My God, I'm so glad! I just slept through it all."

"So, what happened last night?"

"Well, that's all. Robert and I found out how the thing worked and then... then... oh...."

"Oh, what? You fell into each other's arms and...."

"We did, I think. I don't remember very well. We were drinking beer. We saw that it worked, that it protected the computers. Even mine was already protected, Ser Aspro had done that. I think I was crying... and then... I woke up on the couch. I was lying on top of Robert and I went into my bedroom because... he wasn't a very comfortable mattress."

"Kind of lumpy?" Mado grinned lewdly. "But did you....?"

"No. I would know if we had... you know. I am still a virgin. Intact."

"Lucky you. Do you wish you had?"

"No. But maybe some other time. I mean, I don't think it would have been right. I was too tired to concentrate...."

"Marie, I tell you, it's not something you concentrate on. It's a lot more fun if you don't."

They sat quiet for a moment.

"So, then." Mado began again. "What about the Mary Magdalen barcodes?"

"You mean the ones for Vézelay and Sainte-Baume? Why do you think he put them on our *pneus*? Was it another sort of joke, like the 50018 that means DS, *déesse*, goddess?"

"Unh. That's possible, of course. You are Marie, I am Madeleine. Together we make up the binary of the goddess, Mary Magdalen."

"Actually when you say it like that it sounds disgusting. It's gross. Mary Magdalen was a woman, not some goddess."

"Yes, but we are trying to think like Ser Aspro, aren't we? He might have just thought it was a lovely compliment to us, to send us these stupid little puzzles that have to do with the two great basilicas of Mary Magdalen."

"Have you ever been to either of those churches?"

"Me? No. I thought about visiting Saint-Maximin, when I was on that dig in Provence, but I never went there."

"Me neither. I wonder why they are in his database with all the great national museums of Europe."

Mado got up and went over to get Robert's printout of Ser Aspro's database of museum addresses. They stared at it. The two basilicas did not belong on the list, it was obvious. There was a little note on the Vézelay one, the word "yes" and a February date.

Marie said, "Ser Aspro was sending the good barcodes, or upgrades of them, to all these museums, or rather, the museum stores that sell merchandise based on what is in the museums. That much we are pretty sure of. So he thought all these museums might be attacked by whoever is using the square bar code. Why did he think that? Why would anyone want to shut down all the museum stores of Europe?"

Mado sighed. "Maybe they were just starting with museums and they were going to move on to supermarkets and department stores. Or the government, like you said. Maybe they don't like the euro and they want to disable the European Union economy. Maybe they want everyone to go back to barter or writing the prices of the items on the bag and adding them up on the spot. They still do that in some markets in Provence, and of course in Africa and Greece."

"And you think that Ser Aspro believed that if he stopped them at this early stage they would give up?"

"Not really."

"Even if this does mean there is an attack by barcode on museums, it doesn't explain why anyone would attack these two churches of Mary Magdalen. They may have postcard shops or something like that, but so do a lot of other churches. And they are not even the only churches of Mary Magdalen. We have the church of the Madeleine right here in Paris, but it's not in the database."

"Well, there is one thing those two churches have that no other church of Mary Magdalen has. Her body!"

"Oh, well, yes. You're right. Although I don't know what Vézelay did with their body when the one in St-Maximin-la-Sainte-Baume was decreed to be the true body of Mary Magdalen."

"Maybe they still have it, tucked away in a corner. Maybe the Monsignor with the hyphenated name keeps it under his bed!"

They both giggled.

"Marie," said Mado, "You need a vacation. We need a vacation, you and I."

"Mado, I think that after the funeral, after the new *Directeur ad interim* of the *Centre Commercial du Louvre* has been selected, then perhaps...."

"The funeral's not for a week and Rosamonde is in charge, and the *Pompes Funèbres*, the undertakers, are all busy with it. All we have to do is get a black dress and show up."

"Are you suggesting we should leave Paris *now*?"

"Now listen: who is in Paris right at this moment but was supposed to have left Paris yesterday, to fly home to Boston? And so far he has not made a reservation to go home, but I don't think he knew Ser Aspro so well that he wants to stay for his funeral."

"You mean... we need to keep him interested if we want him to stick around?"

"Marie, he's interested! He's interested in you and also, I think, in me. He's so interested he's confused. He might be so confused he goes home, unless we give him something to think about until he gets... unconfused."

"And he *is* really good at thinking about barcodes and databases."

FIFTY-ONE

Jesus said to her, "Woman, why are you weeping? Whom do you seek?" He asked the reason for her sorrow, to intensify her desire, so that she would burn more ardently with love as she named him whom she sought. She, thinking he was a gardener ... perhaps was not in error ... for was he not a spiritual gardener, who planted the vigorous seed of virtue in her breast through love?

Gregory the Great

Fibonacci savored the odors of the hills in the faint last light of day.

"At least you have electricity," said Val Percy. "I hope I can get my car back down that road in the dark. Or I should call it a driveway, since it seems to end here. And it has only the one lane. I have got to figure out how to make a turn, because I can't back out all that way."

She set down the bags of groceries she had picked up at the next to the last town—she had seen from the map that the last town was only a village. She came outside to stand beside Fibonacci, and looked at him in the dark.

"You like this, don't you?"

"Aye. I can see...." With an arm he swept the horizon. "I can see anyone coming, I can see where I am. And it smells so sweet."

"It does." They just stood for a moment, enjoying it. "But who is likely to be coming here, Fibonacci? How would you even get to the village if you needed help? There's not even a bicycle."

"I can't ride a bicycle anyway," he said gently.

Val envisaged that ill-proportioned, asymmetrical body on a bike. "No, I guess not. But can you walk that far, either? It's almost six kilometers, five point eight to be exact, each way. More than three and a half miles, that is."

He didn't reply.

"Someone in the area knows you're here, at least. The bed seems to have been aired and someone brought you some sheets."

"Yes, I suppose I will be taken care of."

I was going to offer to make the bed, but I can't stand this. "I will be taken care of." Who is he that people should take care of him? A king? A baby? And what will become of him here? Did he come here to die?

Tears began to roll down Val's cheeks. She was on Fibonacci's blind side, and it would have been too dark for him to see her face anyway, but she felt stupid and ashamed of the tears. She went inside so that if she made some horrible crying noise or had to wipe her nose he wouldn't know.

She wiped her nose. The toilet paper provided by the mysterious person who was "taking care of" Fibonacci was country style, rough and coarse, but she had bought some softer rolls among the groceries. She looked around. Two rooms, really one room with a partition, in a stone-built hut. She had seen an outhouse dark against the dark blue sky as she drove up. There was a tiny wood stove, barely big enough to heat water for washing, and a table and chairs. No refrigerator, no sink. There must be a pump somewhere outside, too. The mattress on the bed was rather horrible, but she could smell that it had been out in the sun today.

She made the bed after all, then took her keys and went out to her car.

"Good-bye, then, Fibonacci."

"Good-bye, Val, Madame Val. Thank you very much for all you have done for me. You've been extraordinarily good to me."

She shut the car door, turned on the headlights, and made a three-point turn. Fibonacci listened to the car bumping slowly down the drive for a moment. Then he went inside.

He found his cell phone and plugged in the charger to the only outlet, which was part of the ceiling socket which also held an electric bulb.

Val had left the pile of magazines and newspapers on the table.

Fibonacci thought of looking for the one that mentioned Princess Diana again, but instead he found himself spreading out the newspapers. His picture was in all of them, but he found himself drawn to the articles with images of *Monsieur l'ancien Directeur* Aspro. Evidently the dead man was mourned by the nation. Fibonacci had not realized before this that he had killed such an important man. Most of the photographs of Monsieur Aspro showed him quite a bit younger, handsome in a big-nosed skinny French way. One of them was a British paper, with an article not on the front page but on page 4. Fibonacci read it.

He pushed the newspapers aside to make a space on the table. He got out his marbles and let them roll in this space.

He should feel safe in this house. He did feel safe. The Doctor would take care of him.

At the same time, he felt sad and lost.

He had killed that old man, and Val Percy hated him, just for that one thing.

She had not minded his ugliness. She had taken care of his hand and examined him with less disgust than he had seen in some nurses.

She had listened to his theories about the cathedral of Notre Dame with such attention, and commented on them so usefully. He knew now that the theory was not valid, and why. That was a useful thing to know. But she had not laughed at him or implied that it was undignified to have held an invalid theory.

But when she found out he had killed the old man, she had not been able to look at him. He knew what revulsion was, and he had felt it in her.

He had wanted to tell her "He kicked me! You saw what he did to my hand! I didn't mean to do it! The gun went off by itself!"

But what good would it do? It would be like telling the boys in school, "It's not my fault I look this way."

And it *was* his fault he had shot the old man. He should not have brought a loaded gun if he didn't expect to kill anyone. He should have run away when he saw that there was someone in the Louvre office, instead of staring stupidly at him trying to decide whether or not to go in. He should have hidden until the old man went away.

If he had simply not pointed the gun at the old man. That's why he got kicked.

Fibonacci selected a marble with an orange cat's-eye. He wondered if the wooden table top was clean, or full of germs that would have transferred to the marble. Val was right. If he got sick, he could die up here and no-one would find him for a long time.

He put the marble in his mouth and let it warm, the saliva cushioning it. It was important to warm it. A cold marble would constrict the throat muscles.

He heard a noise outside. There was some light, which disappeared, and then a car door opening and shutting. He turned to face the door, frightened. *I will not threaten this person. I will not hurt them even if they hurt me.* But it was not an enemy who appeared in the door.

Val had returned.

"Fibonacci, I couldn't leave you here. I know that you're fine, but I keep thinking...." When he didn't answer, she said, "Fibonacci, what's wrong with you?"

He spat out the marble into his hand and showed it to her. She stared at him. She took in the marbles spilling from their bag on the table, and the newspapers with the face of old Aspro staring up.

"All right," she said, sitting down in the other chair. "Tell me about it."

FIFTY-TWO

The history of the "Mona Lisa," for instance, encompasses the kind and number of its copies made in the 17th, 18th, and 19th centuries.

Walter Benjamin

"My dear young ladies, you are too kind, letting me have my little peek at this mystery of Robert's," said Lindy Teabag, the medical symbologist. "Robert, do show me these exciting barcodes so that we can leave these young women to their night's rest."

"We believe our grandfather sent us a message in the barcodes," said Marie.

"Well! A message for *you*? Robert? You didn't tell me....."

"Marie is talking about a different set of barcodes. The ones she mentioned pose no problem in scanning and we have located the relevant database. They do seem to have a personal message of some kind, but... your special expertise would probably be wasted trying to figure it out."

"Oh," said Marie, "it's the black and white barcodes you're interested in."

"The invisible two-dimensional bull's-eye barcode?" said Mado. "And then the other one–the black one that looks like the *Arche de la Défense*. Those are the ones you're interested in, eh?"

"They are a real technological puzzle," said Robert. "The personal ones are more of a...." He sought the right word. *Psychological? Family?*

"A moral puzzle, just like our grandfather Ser Aspro," said Marie.

The sisters seemed quiet, subdued. Marie told Robert and Lindy to make themselves at home. Then the two women sat on the sofa, very quiet, occasionally exchanging a remark in French.

It was a little bit like an eighth-grade dance, boys on one side of the room and girls on the other. Boys' team against girls' team, Robert thought, rather glad all of a sudden to have a fellow male, and a fellow scientist, beside him.

Robert had decided against using Marie's computer. He trusted Teabag's professionalism, but it would be better to avoid the possibility of impropriety in looking at her private files, or even at the *Centre Commercial* files on her hard drive. *Maybe I also feel as though it gives me an edge, to have seen the files the way Ser Aspro gave them to her....*

He showed Teabag the black barcode and the blow-ups he had made of it. He examined them with great interest and took one of the printouts.

"This is the one that flushes the computer while displaying the Fibonacci numbers?"

"That's the one. I think it's rather a beautiful thing, don't you?"

Lindy snorted. "Handsome is as handsome does, you know. Beautiful but deadly to the computer that scans it."

Robert showed him the Mona Lisa mousepad and explained how the label had been invisible on the back, and had been scanned along with the normal price code.

Lindy picked up the mousepad with distaste, turning it over once or twice. "What a nasty thing. A cheap souvenir and overpriced probably at that. I wonder what Leonardo himself would think, to see his masterpiece turned into a badly colored print and coated with silicone for a mouse to run over.."

Robert flushed. "Ouch! You have a point, Linden. But remember that the person who buys the souvenir–in this case, me–buys it because they just got to look at the real thing. It's a way of remembering...."

"It's a way of preventing yourself from remembering. It stands between you and the memory of the painting. Every time you see the mousepad, you remember the last time you saw it on your desk. You congratulate yourself for having seen the original, but you have forgotten it. You pay for the mousepad the way you might pay for a whore in order to forget your wife."

Robert saw no point in continuing the topic. He rose and walked around the table to get rid of the anger and embarrassment he felt. They were irrelevant to the problem, after all.

"I suppose," he said finally, "that the real Leonardo da Vinci would be more interested in the mouse and the computer attached to it than in the mousepad."

Teabag smiled. Evidently he regretted his outburst. "Quite right. Or this barcode, perhaps. Beauty and technology combined." He passed his forefinger along the top, left to right, then right to left along the middle section, then back to the right. "I think that it must be one continuous barcode, not three separate ones. It has to contain quite a bit of data. Of course, from what you say, this barcode had to be read by an ordinary cash register scanner, set up to handle linear barcodes. And it has to key into some basic program on such a computer in such a way as to trigger the crash."

"And find the network ports and get out on them to locate other local computers, including servers."

"Hmm. So it must be exploiting some weakness common to the cash registers, servers, and so on. Do you know what we need on our team? A good hacker."

Robert laughed. He felt better now. "You know, I have an ex-student who could probably give us some good ideas. Perhaps I'll shoot him an email. If I just tell him what happened, and give him an idea of the size of the code we are looking at, he might be able to make a guess."

"Hard to tell the size of it, though. I would estimate about 400 bars...?"

"That's what I'd make it. Now that I think of it, though, it might be better, since this happened in France, to see if the police here have any good computer security geeks. I worked with one of them recently–yesterday?–anyway, he was quite competent. There may be a French angle to the coding."

"Do you think so? This originated in France, then?"

"Well.... You know, Lindy, I had been assuming that. Because everyone thinks it looks like the Arch of Defense. But you're right–it could have come from anywhere in the European Union, I guess. The network of museums...."

That's more than I meant to say.

"Network of museums? I am guessing that, since this barcode was found on a Mona Lisa mousepad, undoubtedly from Monsieur Aspro's Louvre Boutique, that it was meant to take down the cash registers there. Were other museum shops involved?"

"We think so. I'm not really at liberty to discuss it."

"Quite right. Now, how about Monsieur Aspro's own barcode? Presumably it provides a patch for whatever vulnerability was targeted."

"Yes, and a counter-joke. Instead of a stream of Fibonacci numbers, the cash register is programmed ring up Pi million."

Lindy laughed. "You know, it really is funny, after all. Delightful!"

Robert showed Lindy a printout of the upgrade script, his UV setup for looking at the label, and the Apple Pi software on his laptop, along with its barcode reader. Lindy spent a long time examining the pattern under the UV light, and then even longer playing with the Apple Pi. In fact, he created a barcode which resembled Ser Aspro's in pattern and density.

"Robert, it's just immense, the amount of data he could get onto a barcode of this type. He could do just about what he wanted. I suppose he had this Apple Pi installed on all his cash registers, to read in the barcode."

Robert sighed. "Actually, when you point that out, it seems like an insane amount of trouble to go to. Inventing a barcode to stealth-crash cash registers makes sense. Creating a barcode to deliver a patch to computers in your own store, a barcode which requires special software and hardware to read, seems a bit silly. Why not just deliver the patch to the computers on a floppy or CD, or via the network?"

"I told you, Monsieur Aspro was a remarkable man. He had his own sense of proportion, a somewhat skewed sense, I thought. But I suppose it seemed the right thing to do, to him."

The women had arisen and come within hearing distance. Lindy lowered his voice on the last sentence.

"So, did you find out who's attacking the great museums of Europe?" asked Mado, indiscreetly.

Lindy raised his eyebrows at Robert.

"We were working on how, not who," Robert said.

"Or why?" asked Marie. "I'd like to know why. What's the point of crashing museum computers?"

"So in fact it is museums, several museums, that are being attacked? Not just the *Centre Commercial*?"

"Ser Aspro sent these white labels to seventeen museums. Well, to the directors of the museum shops, actually," Marie said.

"Seventeen museum *shops*." Lindy smiled at Marie in a condescending way, as if he were not merely repeating what she had just said.

"Actually," Mado said, "fifteen major European museums and two basilicas of Marie Madeleine, one in Provence and one in Burgundy."

"Do these basilicas have shops, too?"

"I don't know. Maybe a postcard stand or something," shrugged Mado. "The barcodes he sent us, the personal messages, sort of, had the Basilica codes on them."

"How lovely. So your grandfather was in communication with the shops of fifteen great national museums, shops like his own *Centre Commercial*. I don't think you can call this an attack on museums, can you?"

"But the *Centre Commercial* is part of the Louvre," said Marie, and then stopped.

"Are the computer systems linked? If so, of course the barcode would be an excellent way to access the Louvre museum systems."

"No, I... I know that the physical plant systems are completely separate. There might be a sharing of networks at some point, though. If our points of sale inside the museum use their system...." Marie hesitated. "It's worth looking into. I can find out, easily. Or maybe it's a question for Captain Bulle."

"What you're saying," Mado said to Lindy, "is that this barcode is not an attack on the museums, or on the government, or on anything at all except the shops that sell merchandise related to museums."

Robert thought, *This is beyond me. I'm tired, folks. You're tired. Go home, go to bed.*

"Linden, in medical symbology the puzzles you solve are usually life and death. This one... well, I doubt we will see any more deaths from it." Robert patted him on the shoulder. "Maybe we just need to sleep on it and come back to it tomorrow."

Marie ignored him. "Of course, Ser Aspro knew all these other museum shop directors quite well. They all worked with the same artisans, and would selectively display each other's reproductions, and so on. It was kind of a club. Perhaps he contacted them, and them first, because they would trust him."

"Marie, you know that Ser Aspro loved his store. He felt that museum stores had a mission, sort of, that they were a very special part of the museums. Maybe this really was somehow an attack just on museum stores, not on museums." Mado's face was a combination of defensive and tired. Marie nodded at her wordlessly, mirroring her expression.

Lindy looked at them rather sadly. "I think... I think that we should all go visit the Basilicas of Mary Magdalen. Perhaps we will find the solution to the barcode problem there. You said your grandfather gave you each a barcode for one of the basilicas. Now you need to discover what quest he set for you. It's the old pilgrim route, isn't it? You should take up your staff and scrip."

Robert had no clue as to what a staff and scrip might be, but it seemed to make sense to the twins.

"We shall," said Marie. "Certainly we shall do that. But not until after the funeral." She did not seem to be inviting the men along.

"Well, then. I will leave you now. Thanks for your hospitality. Robert, may I take this copy of the invisible barcode?"

Oh, well, the police can use one of the other two.

Mado spoke up suddenly. "Would you mind taking me home? I mean, to my friend's, where I'm spending the night. It's in the sixteenth *arrondissement*. I have a cab, and you can have it after I get home. Is that out of your way?"

"My dear, how delightful! How could it be out of my way? I will be glad to share your cab. Otherwise I'd have to wait for my own."

He shook Marie's hand and pressed Robert's.

"I'll see you all tomorrow, then."

FIFTY-THREE

These heretics say…that the Christ who was born in terrestrial and visible Bethlehem, and crucified in Jerusalem, was evil, and that Mary Magdalen was his concubine, and was the woman taken in adultery of whom the Gospel speaks. But the good Christ, they say, never ate or drank, nor took on a fleshly body, nor ever was in this world at all.…

Peter of les Vaux de Cernay, History of the Albigensians

Fibonacci's telephone was ringing. It drew him out of a dreamless sleep into a strange place. It took him a moment to scan the room with his single eye and remember it.

It looked different with the daylight streaming in through a couple of small windows. The aged linoleum floor and white walls were clean. The wonderful forest or herb smells of last night seemed to be all around, as if the sun was baking the countryside into a great fragrant pie. He smiled as he saw that he had forgotten to close the house door last night. *That's how safe I feel here.*

By the time he was thinking this, he had answered the telephone. It was, of course, the Doctor.

"Fibonacci Fibonacci, is that you, laddie?"

"Aye, sir. I'm here."

"You are there. Tell me where you are and what it is like."

"It's a little stone house in the hills. There are plants around that smell wonderful. Better than the heather. Lavender, perhaps. Have you ever been here, sir?"

"No, Fibonacci, I have not. And you have a way to keep your cell phone charged?"

"Yes, there's an outlet."

"Ah, yes, very useful indeed. Listen to me, now."

"Yes, I'll listen. I do like this place."

"I am so glad, my boy. But listen now. I have terrible news. The police do have your picture. A strong likeness, from a videocamera. Everyone in France, everyone in Europe knows what you look like."

"I know. That old man I killed, Monsieur Aspro, he was quite an important person, the Director."

"You have seen the newspapers, then?"

"Yes, I got them yesterday. Your friend bought them for me. Even the *Guardian*, so I could read about him. I wish I hadn't killed him. I've thought about how it happened, and I never will let myself do anything like that again. Never."

"Ah. Now, you're a good lad. You're too hard on yourself..... Blind men should not be made to judge colors. Now, then. I am going to send you by express mail some photographs. The postman is one of ours, one of the outer Brotherhood. He knows nothing of our larger goals, but he knows you are a Brother and he will not give you away. His wife owns the cottage you are living in."

"That's fine, now! So I'll see them sometimes?"

"Indeed. You will see the postman today, in fact. I want you to take these photographs and study them. I want you to be able to recognize these three people. And there will be a package.... don't open the package yet, lad. Just the envelope with the photographs. The package you must keep to open later."

"I will not open the package. I will open the envelope and study it to be able to recognize those people."

"Wait for my next call, then, Fibonacci Fibonacci. And mind you, a misty morning may be a clear day. "

"I will, sir."

He sat in the chair after hanging up and, without thinking much about it, caught the marbles still rolling around on the table and put them back into their bag. Then he tidied up the pile of papers and magazines, setting them on the floor by the stove. He didn't intend to use them for kindling until he had looked through them again, though. He found the grocery bag and rooted out a loaf of bread and a packet of butter. He saw no way to make coffee or tea, unless he lit the stove, so he would make do with a bottle of *limonade* and the bread and butter.

He felt quite odd. There were some aches in unusual places, perhaps from sleeping in the new bed. That was to be expected. But there was also a sense of elation. Perhaps it was just the Doctor's approval and his evident plans for another project in which he, Fibonacci, would have a part.

"I bought teabags. If we start the fire we could make tea."

Fibonacci looked up in astonishment from the groceries.

Val Percy was standing by the door, or rather doorway, for there was no actual door, into the bedroom area. She was wearing nothing at all. The darkness of her pubic hair against her white skin shining in the morning light amazed him. For a long moment he just examined her as if she were a statue or a photograph, a guide to what a naked woman looks like.

Then it swept over him. Last night he had told her a great deal, he had wept, he had repented. Yes, and he still repented killing the old man Aspro. But afterwards something quite terrible had happened, in the bed. The same thing had happened to him when he was alone, quite a few times in fact. But with the woman it had been both terrible and... something else.

"Ya hoor! Cunt! Wanton minky tail! Filthy cunt!"

She disappeared and came out again wrapped in the bedsheet.

"Fibonacci–what happened with us–"

He had control of himself now. "I'm sorry for calling you those names." He added, reasonably, "But you are a married woman, are you not?"

"Actually, I'm divorced."

"There is no divorce in Heaven."

FIFTY-FOUR

Then Mary stood up, greeted them all, and said to her brethren, "Do not weep and do not grieve nor be irresolute, for His grace will be entirely with you and will protect you. But rather, let us praise His greatness, for He has prepared us and made us into Men."

Gospel of Mary Magdalen

Robert dreamed that he was using a handheld instrument on a woman's body. Sometimes he was quite clear that he was using a barcode scanner and that he was looking for a tattooed barcode, perhaps on the underside of a breast, which seemed to him an ideally discreet placement for such a marking. At other moments the object in his hand was his Personal Sampler. The woman he was searching had a stable but seemingly infinite body, with a continual supply of lovely small breasts and gently curving bellies to explore, but no very definite face. Her hair, including the hair of her pudendum, did change, now wavy red, now sleek short blonde, now dark and curly and wild. Finally he found the barcode tattoo, a rather conventional product code with numbers underneath. In his dream he was not sure whether it was EAN-13 or an American UPC. When he aimed his instrument at it to scan it, the barcode changed into a circular glyph and the item in his hand became a two-tone blue pneumatic cylinder. Nevertheless it seemed to him that he was passing a laser beam over the barcode, and as he did so the tattooed skin burned and opened into a bleeding wound.

Robert sat up, shaking himself out of this nightmare. He was in his underwear on Marie Navet's living-room sofa. He had a light blanket which he clutched over himself, feeling frightened and somehow exposed, though the apartment was very quiet. After a few minutes he felt calm enough to go get himself a drink of water in the kitchen and to try to remember the good reasons he had for being on Marie's couch.

The night before, after Mado and Teabag left, Marie had told him that the sisters were in fact planning a trip to the two Basilicas, immediately, and that they did want Robert to come along, if he could spare the time.

"It's as if that man read my mind!" she had said.

Robert had wandered over to the worktable. "Either that, or he saw the railroad reservations you were making." Marie's computer was logged into the SNCF, the French railway system. "But he can't have actually seen where you were going, unless he has superb eyesight. Much less that you made three reservations."

"Will you come, Robert dear? You've been our guardian angel in this disastrous mess so far."

He had laughed. *Flattery will get you everywhere.* "A lousy angel, Marie. But I'll come, just to see what happens. I'd like to meet a couple of Ser Aspro's correspondents. Let's see, there's Monsignor Poquette-Filiposi in Vézelay, and Father Pater at Saint-Maximin."

A lousy angel.

He looked at his watch now—it was a little after six a.m. He stretched and went as quietly as he could into the W.C. and the separate bathtub room to perform a few morning rituals. He had showered last night before going to bed, so as to leave the facilities open for Marie in the morning. When he emerged, dressed, he found that Marie was puttering around the kitchen making coffee. She told him Mado was on her way with croissants.

He had nothing to do, really, except fold his blanket up and sit back down on the couch.

He drank his first cup of coffee and then, when Mado arrived, ate his first croissant, saying little except "thank-you." The sisters spoke and laughed or sighed in French. Watching them, he thought of what their grandfather had been trying to do.

Teabag had said, the night before, *Aspro was a remarkable man. He had his own sense of proportion, a somewhat skewed sense. But it seemed the right thing to do, to him.* He was talking about barcodes, but maybe it was true of the twins, too.

One reason Robert had not married was because he had, during his college years, dated a couple of single mothers of girls. This had made the problem of raising children seem confoundingly impossible. Obviously, these women had had bad relationships with the girls' fathers, and they were mighty concerned that their daughters should grow up to be happier than they were. One of them had been a virgin more or less date-raped by a man who had, however, married her for about a year when he found out she was pregnant. *Her daughter* was going to be brought up to know about birth-control and to make her own choices about sex, as early as she wanted. The other woman had, herself, been raised with a great deal of sexual freedom and choice, and her resolution was that *her daughter* was going to stay away from men at least until she was twenty. "We can't compete with you men, you know. Screwing the maximum number of guys is stupid. Teen-age girls just get exploited if they try to pretend they can do what they want."

So Robert had understood that child-raising nowadays, in a world without the pressure of local community standards, involves a vast dilemma. One wants to raise one's child to be as happy as possible, but how? Is sexual freedom or total sexual restraint the answer? A deluxe car that gets the kid safely from one place to another, or a clunker that teaches responsibility, planning, and skills? Tattoos and punk hair or young-adult tidiness? What kind of fences do you make the kid jump over, if any, to train him or her for life? What kind of room to rebel do you build in?

He already had a satisfying full-time job. He had decided to avoid fatherhood.

Aspro had apparently embraced these problems. He seemed to have found a special solution for the twins. He had seen to it that they were both well-educated, provided with a variety of friends in older generations–Madame Rosamonde, Captain Bulle, and the contacts that enabled Marie to intern in the US and Mado to go on important digs. They were prepared for a responsible, productive life that would use their special gifts.

One of them had been raised to be the conventional good girl, the other to be the conventional bad girl–the virgin and the whore, sacred and profane love, the female "beanery" as defined and ide-alized by men. But because they were so close and loved each other so much, each understood vicariously the other's life. They talked about it all the time. They shared their experiences. They healed each other's wounds and gave each other courage.

The binary theory might say that they were complementary halves, meaningless without each other, who together made up one perfect woman.

In fact, what they were was a community of two wonderful women.

FIFTY-FIVE

Year of Christ 48. Jews of Jerusalem, deeply offended by Blessed Lazarus, Magdalen, Martha, Marcella, Maximian, Joseph of Arimathea, and several others, put them in a ship without oars, sails, or rudder, and sent them into exile. God carried them over the vast sea, and they landed safe at the port of Marseilles.

Flavius Lucius Dexter,
Chronicle of All Kinds of History, ca. 430

The reservations were for an express train leaving a little before 8 in the morning. It would have them in Aix-en-Provence in a mere three hours or so. There they would rent a car. They had chosen this train because it would get them quite close to their first destination. They would return via Burgundy and Vézelay, home of the second body of Mary Magdalene, in the car, if it turned out that Father Pater at Sainte-Baume could not answer their questions.

Robert and Marie met Mado at the station and they settled into their first-class seats (all seats on the TGV express train were first-class). They had three out of a set of four facing each other. Robert sat opposite the twins.

Mado told them that Linden Teabag had dropped her off from the taxi "like a gentleman" last night. This startled Robert. He had been working hard at being gentlemanly, himself, to these very young ladies. It hadn't occurred to him that a man Lindy's age could be anything but a gentleman, but apparently it had occurred to Mado.

"As you know," she told Robert, "I'm quite good at keeping a man at a distance when I want to."

This must be a reference to their night in the Louvre garbage dump. *Is she trying to make me jealous?* "Well, that was a first date. I never make a pass on a first date."

Mado rolled her eyes, but had no chance to reply.

A loud voice hailed them. "I say, Robert! Robert Longone! Is that you?"

It was Teabag.

Either he had actually managed to read, from a distant angle, Marie's computer screen with the reservations displayed, the night before, or he had simply guessed that this train would be their best choice. At any rate, he was clearly planning to tag along. He explained that his seat was elsewhere but that the train was not full, and he'd prefer to sit with them if possible. He took the seat next to Robert, considerably narrowing the amount of elbow room available to Robert even in these deluxe seats.

Boys' team against the girls', thought Robert. *Scientists against the art and lit. types. Though I suspect Lindy is an art and lit. type too.*

"Why, my dear Marie and Mado! You two look like twins."

They were all a little startled. Marie and Mado did look more alike this morning than Robert had seen them yet, except on the screen of the Personal Sampler. They both wore white skirts and colored sweater sets, a cardigan over a simple round-necked sweater. Mado's was a sort of greeny-blue and Marie's was pink. They had brought hats, too, which they had not yet removed, and these hid the difference in hair color, accentuating the identical eyes and skin. Mado promptly stood and removed both their hats to a rack overhead.

"Yes, thank you, I'm very pleased to be told I look as young as Marie," Mado replied promptly.

"You're not that much older, old lady," commented Marie.

Five minutes older? thought Robert. *They enjoy teasing Lindy. Odd that he knew old Aspro so well but never knew his granddaughters are twins. I suppose they had other things to talk about. Come to think of it, I have no idea whether there is a Mrs. Lindy and young Lindys ... probably not. He's handsome enough to have attracted a mate, though. But so am I, and look at me....*

The train began to move. When it had reached a steady speed,

Lindy produced an amazing little set of porcelain coffee cups and a large thermos of strong coffee. He poured a cup for each of them, offering sugar as well. Robert took two lumps and began to relax.

"Now," said Robert gamely, "Tell me all about the two bodies of Mary Magdalen."

Mado made a hooting noise. "You really want to listen to Marie go on for three hours? She won't have finished until we get there."

"Mado, I think you may have a few contributions to make. Archaeology, which is your field, is really more important here than art history, which is mine." Marie spread her skirt, crossed her ankles, and seemed to take up a story-telling pose. For Lindy's benefit, she began with a review of yesterday's lesson.

"As I told Robert already, the minimal interpretation, which I prefer, of the New Testament presents us with a Mary Magdalen who is a rich widow. She is not only a disciple of Jesus Christ who follows him around but a financial supporter of his mission. She was an important figure, perhaps the most important woman in the gospels, and all the Evangelists, the gospel authors, knew her name. For that very reason, I dismiss the idea that she is the same woman as the anonymous repentant sinner with nice hair who anointed Jesus's feet, or the same as Mary of Bethany, who has her own character as the sister of Lazarus."

"Let Pope Gregory try to get more *ex cathedra* than that!" exclaimed Mado. Then, for Lindy, she added, "Pope Gregory is the one who said all these women were the same, but Marie sounds just like a Pope, doesn't she?"

Marie continued. "The facts will bear this interpretation."

Mado complained, "*Chère* Marie, the poor little facts will bear any interpretation at all! All women named Mary are the same, Mary Magdalen was from the Moon maybe, that idea that Plantard fellow had that Mary Magdalen was his great-grandmama!"

Lindy, who had half-closed his eyes, opened them. "Plantard.... Pierre Plantard, you mean? I know of him. A madman of a particularly unpleasant kind. He thought everything in France was a conspiracy of Jews and Freemasons."

Both girls nodded approvingly at this put-down. *Score one for the barcode team*, thought Robert, mentally giving Lindy a high-five.

"Ser Aspro knew him," Marie noted. "Back in the 1950s I think,

Ser Aspro helped get Plantard put in prison for fraud. After that, Plantard started cooking up that Priory of Sion nonsense."

"Nonsense, yes, but...." Lindy paused and seemed to be considering whether he should go on. "He attacked the Freemasons–quite a traditional political ploy in France, you know–but at the same time he borrowed the idea and structures of the Brotherhood, secrecy, initiation, oaths, and so on. His Priory of Sion was a travesty of the Masonic order–a pack of lies, or if you prefer we can call them the fantasies of a madman, pretending to be a secret Truth."

"Unh." Mado nodded. "It's a common kind of madness. Everybody has the fantasy that they are special, that they are secretly the heir to some wonderful title or ancestry or fortune. Right?"

Marie nodded, Robert smiled, but Lindy looked rather stern and cleared his throat.

Mado continued, "But we grow out of it. This Pierre Plantard just kept growing into it. First he was related to De Gaulle, right after the War when De Gaulle was practically king. Then he was the direct descendent of Mary Magdalen and Jesus. Finally he said he was the lost heir to the Merovingians and ought by right to be king of France. Ugh! Those Merovingians were a nasty bunch anyway, good riddance. I think he should have decided to be the lost heir of the Carolingians, or the Capets, or the House of Valois, or the Bourbons...."

"Mado, you know perfectly well that there are plenty of people in France who are related to all those royal lines. I wouldn't want to have any of them for a king, though."

"Marie, you *don't* in fact know perfectly well, but probably you and I are descended from every one of those royal lines. The population geneticists claim that anyone alive however many hundred years ago either has no descendants at all or else has contributed genes to every one now alive."

"Not really sound biology, my dear child, and you overstate it, but there is some truth to a version of what you say," Lindy commented. "There are no doubt pockets of fairly pure inbreeding even in Europe. But one might posit with reason that the equation would work for royal houses of Europe and modern Parisians–or Americans. That is to say, if Dagobert the Merovingian, or Charlemagne, has any descendants at all, you are all probably among them."

"What about you? Are all the British inbred?" Robert couldn't resist a small dig.

"Oh, most of the British would be descendants, too," Lindy said, noncommittal.

Marie was smiling with a ridiculously naughty look at Mado. "But then, Mado, if Marie Madeleine–I mean, Mary Magdalene did have a child, we are her descendants!"

Mado laughed. "Yes–if she came sailing to Marseilles as the story says, and if she had a baby, and if that baby has descendants...."

"Then we are all cousins in Mary Magdalen," said Robert. The girls grinned.

"Yes, well, if that story happens to be true. And the story that she had a child is not in any of the recorded traditions at all, alas." Marie went back to her lecturing mode. "After the Gospel period, there are *numerous* traditions about what Mary Magdalen did. One is the Gnostic tradition, represented by some gospels and Acts of the Apostles that didn't make it into the Bible."

"Marie, I wouldn't call that Gospel of Mary Magdalen a Gnostic text. I would call it *mystical*. The idea that love, of a sexual kind described as desire expressed by kisses, between Jesus and Mary or Jesus and his disciples, is a metaphor for union with the divine.... You get that mysticism all over the Mediterranean, in the Song of Songs in the Jewish Bible, in Arabic mystical poetry, in Spanish mystics like Saint Theresa and John of the Cross. The lover and beloved in those poems are always a little bit sexual, a whole lot mystical."

"So how is that not Gnostic?"

"The Gnostics were into binaries, not oneness. Mysticism is, you are me, I am you, we are all God. Gnosticism is bad guys and good guys, and the good guys trying to get power over the bad ones. Look at the Acts of Saint Thecla. Now there's a Gnostic gospel for you. Anybody who tries to touch the virgin gets eaten by sea lions or turned to stone or something. When Saint Thecla was about eighty, and living in a cave in the hills, a couple of locals heard that she was still a virgin and decided to rape her. So she just tunneled out the back of the cave, through the mountain, and came out on the other side."

Lindy Teabag laughed. "Saint Thecla? Is she thus the patron saint of the subway systems of the world?"

Mado snorted with laughter. *Two points for the barcode team? But Lindy is scoring them all.*

Marie tried to get her audience back. "So, the first tradition is a tradition that we have in early Christian *mystical* writings, in which Mary Magdalen is an important interpreter of Jesus's teachings, on the *mystical* side. And that is really a long tradition, too. Think of your Georges de la Tour coffee mug, Robert, where she is staring at a candle in a mirror...."

Lindy sat up straight and ran his hand through his thick white hair. Suddenly he seemed twice as large as he was. *Like a cat with its hair on end*, thought Robert.

"The Georges de la Tour coffee mug? A *coffee mug* with Georges de la Tour's painting of Mary Magdalen pasted on it?"

"Printed on it, under the glaze, using a waterslide process." Marie looked at him with narrowed eyes, a bit like a cat herself. "Not something we could have done properly even a few years ago, technologically. They are a popular item, especially with Americans, who often collect coffee mugs. The warm colors and candlelight probably make it particularly attractive."

"And the skull helps them remember not to drink too much caffeine, in case it kills them?" Lindy's voice almost squeaked with fury.

"And the candle in the mirror reminds them that a replica, a reflection, can double the light of the original." To his own surprise, Robert had said this. Both twins looked at him with amazement. *Score one for me!*

But at which end of the court?

Lindy, however, had a comeback. "You are describing a painting of the Magdalen by Georges de la Tour which is in the Metropolitan Museum in New York City. In the Louvre painting, there is no mirror."

"But I'm sure that my coffee mug...."

Marie touched his knee. "Actually, Robert, that mug does show the New York Magdalen. We order these mugs from a very important workshop, a company that does work for many museums. Well, they got confused and used the wrong image. So the shop at the Metropolitan Museum right now has a stock of Louvre Magdalen bookmarks, and we have the Met Magdalen mugs."

Robert stared at her. "So the picture I saw in the museum is not the same as the one on the mug I bought right afterwards? No wonder you were glad someone was dumb enough to buy one."

"Well... in a way, yes." *Honesty is the best policy, Miss blue-eyed virgin.* "But I did explain to you that there were other paintings of Mary Magdalen by Georges de la Tour. You would have gone to New York to see their version, wouldn't you?" Robert shrugged–yes, he had thought he might do that. "And the Met painting on your coffee mug, with the candle and the mirror, gave you such a beautiful insight, Robert, into the beauty of reproduced beauty."

Lindy made a deep noise of disgust and closed his eyes completely, settling back into his seat with his arms folded in the posture of one who is determined to doze off..

Marie, after a pause and glance at him, went back to her story.. "Besides this mystical Magdalen, there are various stories about her martyrdom and death. According to one of them, she accompanied the apostle James and his mother Mary to Spain, and died there. According to another one, she became the companion of the Virgin Mary and the apostle John and went to Greece and died there. Her body ended up in Constantinople. There is a tradition that she went to Rome and preached Christ to the Emperor himself. Something about an egg...."

"Like Christopher Columbus?" asked Robert helpfully.

"Undoubtedly," said Marie a bit sarcastically. "The tradition I want to focus on is the one where she comes to Provence and dies there, of course. That's why we're going there. The story is that a group of disciples of Jesus were packed into a boat in the Holy Land, a boat without rudder or sail like you find in the fairy tales. They ended up landing in the South of France, at a place now called *Les Trois Saintes Marie sur Mer*, 'the three holy Marys by the sea.' So the boat contained three women named Mary, supposedly including Mary Magdalen. Other passengers were Lazarus and his sister Martha. I think myself that these three Marys did *not* include the Magdalen. If Mary Salomé and Mary the mother of James and John were there, that makes two. The third would have to be Mary of Bethany, sister of Lazarus and Martha, because they were in the boat. If Mary of Bethany was not the same woman as Mary Magdalen, there isn't room in that tradition for our girl."

"Marie, just a minute." Mado interrupted again. "I actually visited the church of the Saintes-Maries, when I was working on that dig, you remember? Well, I'll tell you why there are three Marys. That part of France was the *Provincia*, the Province of Rome. It was full of Greek settlements when there was a sort of Greek empire, and then the Romans took it over on their first wave of expansion from the Italian peninsula. I know you know this, but maybe Robert doesn't."

Robert nodded a bit numbly. Gnostics, mystics, Saint Thecla, three Marys none of whom was the one they were supposed to be discussing. And now the Roman Empire. It was a bit much.

"Good. O.K., now the Roman soldiers worshiped a lot of different gods. Basically, you could pour a little wine on a rock and worship it if you felt like it. But a big favorite was the *Matrones*, the Three Mothers. They were painted or sculpted as three identical women holding loaves of bread. Nice for soldiers far from home. This triple goddess was really important in the more Celtic areas, Brittany and England. It's hard to say whether the Brits had their own triple-goddess tradition or they got it from the occupying Romans. Anyway, obviously the tradition of the Three Marys was a replacement for a strong cult of the *Matrones*. I'll bet anything that if you excavated under the church you'd find some kind of temple or house dedicated to the *Matrones*."

"Virgin, mother, and crone?" said Lindy, his eyes still closed.

"No, not these ladies. They are all identical, in a row, in the carvings that have survived. They were triplets, not three different aspects of Woman."

"So..." Robert was trying to get a handle on this. "You are telling me, Mado, that this very old Christian church of the Three Marys is actually a *pagan temple*?"

"Not exactly." It was Marie who answered. "It's a Christian church, in which most of the prayers are to the one God and to Jesus, not to the three women. The old temple would have been just for the *Matrones*. And what you prayed for would be somewhat different, too–for eternal life, and for personal virtue, as well as for daily bread."

"Also," said Mado, "An odd thing happened. Instead of three similar or identical Maries, the three women actually revered in the church are two Maries and Sarah the Egyptian. The two Maries are depicted in a sculpture in a boat, which is carried to the sea in an annual festival. But Sarah is the patron saint of all the *gitanes*, the gypsies, of Europe. Her statue is separate, and it's black, like an African princess. And that statue gets carried to the sea every year in a separate festival. So instead of three *Matrones*, you actually have two similar Maries, plus one quite different."

"Mado, that's fascinating!" said Marie.

Lindy gave a tiny snore.

FIFTY-SIX

They hunted till darkness came on,
But they found not a button, or feather, or mark,
By which they could tell that they stood on the ground
Where the Baker had met with the Snark.

Lewis Carroll

Captain Bulle had been very optimistic when the day began. The newspapers and television had done a marvelous job of publicizing the bizarre appearance of the murderer. A doctor affiliated with the police had confirmed that the strange face and twisted body were no disguise, and had added the name of the illness from which the man suffered, based on the blood he left behind. Europol was looking through hospital records for such a man with this particular disease. So far the shooter seemed to have stayed hidden from them, but they would find out soon enough who he was.

The mystery of the *pneus* was a side-show, but Bulle felt it was important. Ser Aspro had risked his life–had given his life–to prevent the hunchback from learning about his computer activities. Therefore, they must have something to do with the attack. All this business of invisible white and invisible black barcodes made no sense to him. However, the forensics team had confirmed that the printer Ser Aspro was using that night–Madame Rosamonde's printer, in fact–had had a special cartridge of ink installed. The ink was invisible except under UV light, but legible by barcode scanners.

The database of museum shops was another interesting line for investigation, though he hesitated after all to involve Europol on this aspect, which might prove trivial. *Monsieur le Directeur des Boutiques du Musée d'Orsay* Dandin, however, had been very co-operative and had provided them with the Apple Pi hardware and software, and with copies of some of Ser Aspro's famous barcodes. Monsieur Dandin had received Ser Aspro's posthumous barcode on Tuesday, the day after the murder.

Ingénieur André was at work down at the Louvre Boutique, trying to restore the contents of the stolen computer drive from the tape back-ups. He hoped to locate any records or correspondence related to the mysterious barcodes or the plot against museum shops, if indeed there was such a plot.

But by mid-morning, nothing seemed to be happening. Captain Bulle had emailed the American professor, Robert Longone, to ask for his help, but he had not replied. Hospital records had yielded nothing. And the only sightings of the deformed assassin were all too easily dismissed by a quick investigation.

FIFTY-SEVEN

Magdalen, leaving her sister and the others, climbed a steep hill, not more than two miles from the town of Aix, and never after left it, praying there in a cave horrible in its darkness but adorable in its horribleness, for thirty years, turning her mind always to heavenly things, without any food brought her by mortals, and then she died.

Sermon on the feast of Mary Magdalen, 12th century

"O.K, we are done with the Three Marys. Now we just have to tell you about Sainte-Baume and Vézelay."

"Like you asked in the first place," said Mado with a grin.

"This story can fit either with the Three Marys story or the one about Mary Magdalen going to Rome. It begins when Mary Magdalen arrives in Provence along with a Christian man named Maximin. Kind of a Roman name, so maybe she picked him up in Rome while she was converting the Emperor Tiberias. But other traditions say he was the man born blind that Jesus cured in the Gospels. That's lovely, and it doesn't really matter. Now, according to this tradition, they preached as a team and converted a lot of people in the old Roman province, including the king of Marseilles. Maximin became the first bishop in the area. Then Mary Magdalen wanted to retire. If she really was a mystic, that makes a lot of sense."

"Or if she wanted to repent her sins," said Robert, remembering the paintings of a naked woman in a cave, with red hair and tears running down her face, from Ser Aspro's collection.

"Yes, of course, that's the usual way of interpreting it, that she was a repentant whore or adulteress. Anyway, she is supposed to have fasted and prayed and finally died in a cave in the mountains of Sainte-Baume, and St. Maximin buried her there."

Lindy snored, quite loudly. Marie lowered her voice a little, so as not to disturb his rest, but she would have to raise it again when he snored.

"Well, the records are minimal, but it looks like her body and Maximin's were considered worth the visit by pilgrims after Christianity became legal in the fourth century. People would visit the area to pray. Hermits would go live in the hills near where she had died, that sort of thing. Then we have a dark period, when the Roman Empire was shutting down and, after that, Islam got going. The coast of Provence was a very desirable stretch of real estate. We don't have a lot of records for the period. But then, around the ninth century, Mary Magdalen's body turns up in Vézelay."

"Vézelay is off the main roads now, but in Roman times it was an important place, with baths," said Mado.

"Yes, well, eventually Mary Magdalen's body became the treasure of Vézelay, maybe around 850, maybe later. According to one story, a monk named Badillon brought the body there, either from Jerusalem or by digging it up in Sainte-Baume! The pope declared that, wherever it came from, this was the authentic actual body of Mary Magdalen. Then the monks at Vézelay got going on building a church worthy of her. If we get there you'll see—it's absolutely amazing. The masterpiece of Romanesque sculpture. Although I've never been there."

"So if we get there we'll all see," said Robert. "One body of Mary Magdalen down, one to go. Where did the other one come from?"

"Well, Vézelay, being on the main pilgrim road a lot of people took through Burgundy to get to St. James of Compostella in Spain, had five stars as a must-see church. It didn't seem right that Sainte-Baume, where she had lived and died, was not getting much pilgrim business out of her. The count of Provence around the end of the 13th century decided to do some digging, and he found a lovely old sarcophagus which very obviously, to him, contained the body of Mary Magdalen, hidden from the Saracens back 500 years or so earlier."

"Body number two!" said Robert, to show he was listening. Teabag snored a bit louder.

"Right. So Charles of Provence built a terrific Gothic basilica to house the relics, and the town put itself right back on the pilgrim map." She glanced at Robert, hesitated, and couldn't resist adding for his edification, "Gothic is the architectural style that comes after Romanesque, which is what the Vézelay church was."

"But what about the Vézelay body?"

"You can imagine, the monks at Vézelay were not happy about this development. They had the authorized body, and now Saint-Maximin was saying it had the true body. So for a few years there were claims and counter-claims. The king of France said that Vézelay had the real body. The Pope said that it was Saint-Maximin. Finally the Saint-Maximin folks got very nice and sent a bit of *their* body–a small bit–to Vézelay. But they kept the most interesting parts. I believe the skull is on permanent display in Saint-Maximin."

Lindy Teabag started awake and opened his eyes. The train was slowing down.

FIFTY-EIGHT

"Now," said sir Percival's sister, "fair knights, I see well that this gentlewoman is good as dead without help. Therefore, have my blood drawn."

Thomas Malory

It had been a long morning for Val Percy.

Fibonacci ignored her. She got dressed. She had brought a couple of changes of clothes in the car, but this was the last.

She made a fire in the little stove, using wood from a pile near the house. Someone had set lavender twigs there for kindling, and they gave off a rich aroma.

She went out to the pump and figured out how to make it give water. She filled the one trustworthy-looking pot in the house with water, boiled it, and made tea for both of them. Fibonacci took his, sugared it, and drank it without speaking.

She used the rest of the hot water to clean herself up, and then heated another potful for laundry, since she had found a tin tub in a corner. She washed Fibonacci's underwear as well as her own, spreading the items to dry on a lavender bush near the house. Fibonacci had comments on this.

"Bugs and birds will get them dirty."

"Then I'll wash those items again."

"It's not good for the bush, I think."

"There are a lot of lavender bushes to make up for one that is damaged by our laundry. Besides, in this bright sun things will dry very fast."

He went back to sitting at the table, doing nothing.

Val Percy had certainly not intended to become intimate with Fibonacci, and she hadn't enjoyed it, either.

Am I some kind of pervert, who gets turned on by cripples? Why am I still here?

No, I was not turned on by him.

But I must have been or I wouldn't have done it. I wouldn't still be here thinking that one more night might somehow be... enough.

Val had heard Fibonacci's confession the night before. He had carefully not revealed to her what he was looking for in the *Centre Commercial du Louvre*, or who had sent him, and she had respected that. Her ex-husband was a Freemason (which was how she had gotten into this mess), so she knew enough not to press for details. But he had told her about the old man, the kicking, the anger and fear and claustrophobia. At the end, he had been sobbing in her arms, saying over and over again that he wished he had not done it.

At some point they had moved over to the bed. She had thought he would go to sleep, but instead she felt his arousal. And, from whatever motives, she had done something about it.

He was worse than the teen-age boy who had been her first sexual experience. There was no tenderness, and no sense that he realized he was grasping another human being. At least it was over quickly.

And now he's acting just like a teenager, ignoring me. A fucked woman doesn't exist. No more than yesterday's garbage.

All the same, she prowled around, fixing things up, putting the groceries on shelves. At one point, after going outside to collect the laundry, she returned to find Fibonacci working at the stove.

"I banked the fire," he said.

I have no idea what that means, but I guess it's a good thing. Keeping the fire going but not hot? This boy knows some things, really. Maybe he'll be O.K. if I leave him. But she didn't leave.

Towards noon Fibonacci became restless. They ate in silence, and then he said, "If you're going to stay here, would you move your car around behind the house?"

Looking at him, she realized that he did want her to stay. He *expected* her to stay, expected darkness to bring a repetition of last night's interesting experiment. Perhaps that was why she wanted to stay, just because he wanted her to. *I should have had a kid. That would be easier than this.*

"Is anyone coming to visit today?"

"Yes, the postman. The phone call.... I was told about it. There will be a letter and a package for me."

He looked into her eyes with his single one, for the first time all day. "My mobile phone is charged. Do you want to charge yours? Isn't there someone you should call?"

"Not really. I could call my ex-husband to tell him that the mission is accomplished."

"If you are divorced, why did he ask you to drive me? Why did you agree to do it? You told me the Doctor asked *him* to do it, not you."

"He and I are still friends. We don't hate each other. He doesn't ask me for help very often. Actually, it sounded pleasant, like a vacation, to drive from Paris to Provence."

"What a pity you ended up with me," said Fibonacci, and went back to staring at the table.

There's hope for him, she thought as she went out to drive the car around to the back of the house.

FIFTY-NINE

While the Beaver confessed, with affectionate looks
More eloquent even than tears,
It had learned in ten minutes far more than all books
Would have taught it in seventy years.

Lewis Carroll

Madame Rosamonde had taken her lunch hour early, to pay a call on Captain Bulle.

"*Monsieur le Directeur* Aspro's assassin was a one-eyed deformed hunchback," she announced.

"That's true," said the Captain thoughtfully.

"And you have not been able to locate him in two days."

"My dear lady, do you have any information about him?"

"My dear *Capitaine*, do *you* have any information *whatsoever* about him?"

Captain Bulle began to be a little bit *fâché*. This woman was irritating.

"We have our sources, Madame. We have leads."

"Do you? His picture has been in all the newspapers. Has anyone seen him?"

"I can't discuss that." *Plenty of people think they've seen him....*

"Well, where? Because I hope he is not after the girls."

"The girls? The Misses Navet? Why would he be after them?"

"Well, they went off to Provence with that American, Longone. And with this other man, a big old man, Teabag."

Bulle laughed at the name. "Teabag?"

"Yes, Mado telephoned me from the train station in Aix-la-Provence. They are going to rent a car and drive somewhere. I wrote it down. And it's in *Monsieur le Directeur* Aspro's database, too. Saint-Maximin. And this American is with them, and a Mr. Linden Teabag. I saw him from the window last night, when he brought Mado to my apartment. A large old man, he was."

"They should have told me where they were going. Ah, yes, Linden Teabag."

"Is he a criminal?"

"No, I doubt it. But I recall discussing linden tea, *les infusions de tilleul*, with someone recently. Perhaps I will have linden tea this afternoon."

Yes, "linden teabag" had been the topic of a difficult or unpleasant conversation in the past day or two. He would have to look over recent cases and see if he could remember why the phrase seemed so important.

SIXTY

....a compaignye,
Of sondry folk by aventure yfalle
In felaweshipe, and pilgrimes were they alle,
That toward Caunterbury wolden ryde.

Chaucer

Their rental car was waiting for them at the Aix-en-Provence station. Marie had managed to contact the priest at Saint-Maximin, Father Pater, to arrange a meeting for two o'clock. They bought a picnic lunch and set off. The twins sat in the front, with Marie at the wheel, the men in the back. In about an hour the car had climbed into the fragrant hills and rounding a curve they could see the huge Basilica of Mary Magdalen rising up like a beautifully carved rock from the red-tiled roofs of the town. They stopped by the road and sat admiring the view for a while, and ate their lunch, then continued on into the town.

There was still a good half-hour before their appointment. Marie parked the car just off the square in front of the Basilica. The front of the church was surprisingly hideous. It rose in a high windowless wall, between two huge niches. A great bare area of smooth cement over the door stood out in a general wall of rough stone. It was as if the rose window had been cemented over. The Basilica looked like some desolate warehouse in a part of Boston that had been productive a hundred years ago, Robert thought, and was waiting now for gentrification. But it had been built before Columbus discovered America.

"I wonder if it was stripped of the marble façade and statuary during the Terror," said Marie, adding for Robert's benefit, "What you call the French Revolution."

"Or the Counts of Provence decided they had better things to spend their money on than a marble façade," sighed Mado. "That's probably it–look, the side doors did get finished and they have lovely marble carvings all around."

They went inside.

It was cool in the church, and before his eyes became accustomed to it Robert had an illusion of having walked into another world, a giant dark forest with light coming down from far above. Then he saw that the forests were tall columns which branched out halfway up to form huge archways, and then again at a great height in interlacing pointed patterns on the roof. The light came through the clear glass of many windows, a row on each side above the high archways, with more rows visible lower down in the walls behind these archways, and then a semicircular array at the far end, where the altar must be, with a great gold sunburst in front of it. The lowest window seemed to be some twelve or fifteen feet off the floor.

"We should look in the Crypt," said Marie, whispering. "Perhaps I'll have time to explain the architecture to you after we meet with Father Pater. I believe there's a remarkable Retable of the Passion."

Robert quietly hoped there would not be time for a lecture on the Retable of the Passion, whatever that was.

They walked to the front of the church, following Marie through a kind of wooden fence with gates which enclosed the altar area. The altar itself looked like a beautiful coffin, and above it was a picture, hard to make out in the light. Robert gazed up at the altar's gigantic gold decoration. This turned out to be a mass of plump naked bodies and clouds writhing around a stained-glass image of a dove through which light poured.

Robert noticed that both Marie and Mado bent one knee quickly before passing in front of the altar, and did something with their hands in front of their faces. The sign of the Cross? Teabag seemed irritated by this.

The Crypt which Marie had mentioned turned out to be the basement under the altar itself. There was a stone staircase in the floor, going down, with a wrought-iron railing around the opening, and a closed gate. Mado unhooked the gate and scampered down.

Marie followed, eagerly. Teabag hesitated, then muttered to Robert, "I'll stay up here. I'll keep a lookout for the priest. I've seen enough crypts, anyway."

Robert walked slowly down into the Crypt, through a wrought-iron door that made him feel as if he were entering an underground dungeon.

The stone room was brightly but erratically lit with candles and red lamps, like hurricane lamps with red chimneys. It was shadowy and a little smoky and, Robert thought, certainly had potential as a fire hazard.

In the flickering light Robert saw the two women standing in front of a small image of a person–man or woman, he wasn't sure–in a glass box. He didn't want to interrupt their lively whispers.

He looked around at the other things in the Crypt: marble boxes, tombs of some kind he supposed, some carved, some plain. Each of these had a metal stand in front of it with spikes for tall white candles, of the sort he considered appropriate for a dinner-table. There were long sticks of wood and a few matches, and stores of extra candles on a lower shelf of the stand. A slot in the front of the stand had a hand-printed label taped on it, "Offerte" and Robert got the idea that one was supposed to pay for each candle before lighting it. Larger candles stood around in glass chimneys, some clear, some colored, some set on the floor, some on stands like tall candlesticks.

There were descriptive paragraphs, also handwritten, posted near each of the marble boxes. He took the time to find the name of the person buried inside, looking through the French text for capital letters. He was surprised to see dolphins and a merman carved on one of the boxes.

Finally Mado called his name softly, and he went over to look at the thing in the glass case. It was not after all a human figure, not exactly. It was a skull held up by four golden angels. The "body" of this strange doll was a glass tube holding something that looked like a flap of old leather.

"That's supposed to be Marie Madeleine's skin where Jesus touched her after the Resurrection," whispered Mado. "The Gospel says he told her not to touch, 'Noli me tangere,' 'Don't touch,' but the story here is that *he* touched *her*."

Robert felt quite disgusted by the whole thing for a moment. Superstition and nonsense! They couldn't even get the story straight! No wonder Teabag had wanted to stay above!

He turned to the women to say something, but found that they were intertwined, arms around each other, touching hands, and looking for once completely like twins. They glowed. For them, he realized, coming here together was, as Teabag had said, a real quest–something they had wanted to do for a long, long time, but which had been difficult for them to undertake. He himself felt no desire to kneel to the bones of Mary Magdalen, but he felt included in the power of their desire.

Mary Magdalen, Marie Madeleine, Marie and Mado, two women, a pair of double women. No wonder I can't manage to make a pass at one of them. How could I choose...? He looked at the skull again to distract himself.

My Georges de la Tour coffee mug started all this. That beautiful image of a woman with long dark hair staring at a candle and holding a skull. The artist made something I would call real. But for Marie and Mado, this is the reality.

One skull's worth of possible reality.

Suddenly he remembered that he had brought along the Personal Sampler.

Wouldn't I like to get a chance at that noli-me-tangere skin! I wonder what this Mary Magdalen really looked like!

SIXTY-ONE

How Badillon broke open the tomb of the Magdalen and how he pulled out her blessed body which was lying inside.

Wauquelin, Girart de Rousillon

Father Pater turned out to be much more helpful than Robert had expected. He was a tall, completely bald man of about forty, wearing a black and white robe which Marie whispered to him was a Dominican habit. Robert had noticed some black-and-white cloth insignia in the Church. So whatever Dominicans were, they seemed to be black and white.

Unfortunately, Father Pater didn't speak English, so Robert couldn't actually understand his explanations. Teabag, whose French was excellent, had to represent the barcode team.

They were meeting in a kind of shop near the basilica entrance, in a sort of porch area walled off between the outside doors and the actual church. There was a big old wooden desk, and on it sat a computer, which evidently served as cash register and probably as the home of the parish records, too. Robert hung back, excluded by the language barrier, and examined the merchandise.

There were a great many large candles for sale, with a choice of handsome glass holders and even some of the tall candlestick-type holders. But there was quite a bit of other merchandise. There were postcards of the church and of the skull thing in the Crypt, and also of various artistic Mary Magdalens–Robert recognized some of the ladies in Ser Aspro's collection. There was also a small display of rolled-up fake parchments with ribbons and plastic disks hanging from them. Robert gathered that these were copies of the Papal bull that had established the church, or perhaps certified the remains of Mary Magdalen. Reading the French words BULLE PAPALE reminded him of *Capitaine* Bulle, and he wondered if Ser Aspro's murderer had been apprehended by the police yet.

There were a lot of rosaries, some in packets and some hanging from the wall, some with large tags showing the Pope's face. Robert assumed the last group must have been blessed by the Pope. There was a rack of books, some of them hymnals or mass-books in pamphlet form, about a dozen different books about St. Mary Magdalen and one very thin little one about her friend St. Maximin.

So far as he could tell, the only items which had barcodes were the ones that had come from the manufacturer with the barcodes printed on them–the books, and oddly enough some of the rosaries which had explanatory tags attached to them. A few of the candles and holders were in barcoded packaging, but many were not. *Not much room here for a black-on-black barcode. Of course you'd only need one....*

Mado came over to him. "Robert, it turns out that Ser Aspro has been corresponding with Father Pater for at least seven years. The only other person he knows about on Ser Aspro's list is Monsignor Poquette-Filiposi in Vézelay. Father Pater never did understand this project of Ser Aspro's at all. He said he used to get barcodes from Ser Aspro, and he even got the special barcode reader a couple of years ago, but he hasn't gotten any more recently."

Mado skipped back to the group. Robert saw the priest fumbling around in a desk drawer. He pulled out an Apple Pi scanner, like the one Marie had at her apartment. Robert joined them and was handed the scanner, along with a CD. He was allowed to examine the CD's contents in the computer and found that it was, essentially, a pirated copy of the Apple Pi software. *I hope that when Ser Aspro sent the software to the Vatican Museum, he at least gave them a legal, licensed copy. Unless the Pope doesn't subscribe to international copyright law....*

Mado whispered in his ear, "Father Pater didn't know what the Apple Pi barcodes were until Linden showed him the one you gave him. He just thought the invisible two-dimensional bull's-eye barcodes were blank labels. Apparently Ser Aspro sent him letters explaining what to do with them, but it was too confusing. He hasn't tried to scan one of Ser Aspro's barcodes for a long time."

But he did try it once upon a time? The computer was a Pentium I running Windows 98, and it did have a barcode wand attached. *They probably just use the barcodes for re-ordering books and such.* It had a 28.8 modem and, so far as Robert could tell, was not on a network with any other computers.

Mado whispered again, "He found the letters. He's giving them all to Lindy! So now you two can figure out what it's all about, maybe."

Robert did not have too much trouble finding what he wanted on the basilica computer. In the Program Files was a folder called "Aspro." It had a 1999 date, and contained a program called boutique.exe. There was a floppy disk already in the drive, containing one file, apparently a sermon. Robert copied the contents of the floppy to a folder on the desktop, then copied boutique.exe onto the floppy. Surreptitiously he ejected the floppy and put it in his pocket.

Robert stood up. Lindy was thanking the priest effusively, and clutching quite a stack of envelopes. Robert saw Marie reach out towards the envelopes as if she would like to have them. *After all, they are letters from her grandfather, even though he probably printed them out in sets of seventeen.* Lindy stepped out of the church into the bright sun outside, as if to escape any second thoughts on the part of the twins or Father Pater.

Robert looked forward to sitting down with Teabag and going over the evolution of Ser Aspro's protective barcodes.

Aspro had evidently taken some time to work out a way of loading a program onto a computer via a barcode. His early efforts, including the one that Father Pater had actually scanned onto the drive of the basilica computer, had been relatively straightforward. Later, he got fancy, hiding the program so that, for example, Robert had not been able to find it on Marie's computer once it had been installed. Once they knew what the program looked like and what it did, they would be able to identify it even in its more sophisticated forms. Not only that–they could understand the nature of the code it was designed to combat: the square black barcode, the one that wiped computers clean.

The program on the floppy in his pocket, boutique.exe, was probably the clue to the whole scheme. *Lindy will be a happy man when I hand him this diskette.*

Patting his pocket, Robert remembered the Personal Sampler. He asked Marie to put the question to Father Pater: could he, might he, use it on one of the relics, in the interests of science? Wouldn't it be wonderful for Father Pater and the other people who cared about the skull to know what the person it came from looked like? *Of course, maybe that skull belonged to a man... Then it would be science versus religion. Holy Genetics, Batman, I'm just curious as heck.*

Father Pater's bald head turned bright red. He stared at Robert but spoke in a low, tense voice to Marie. She listened respectfully to quite a long speech. When the flow of French eloquence stopped, she looked up at Robert and simply shook her head "No." Father Pater, taking the cue from her, glared at him and also shook his head.

Outside the basilica, the four travelers looked at each other.

"What next?" asked Robert. He wanted very badly to get to a computer and look at how boutique.exe had been compiled.

"Well, it isn't three o'clock yet," said Marie.

"I have a proposal," said Lindy. "I suggest that we all go visit the Grotto of Mary Magdalen in the Sainte-Baume mountains. I believe it is a beautiful place, and the Dominicans run a hostel there. We could spend the night. I understand that you want to go on to Vézelay, but since our young ladies Marie and Madeleine seem to be on a pilgrimage to the various sites associated with their name-saint, I think they should not miss this opportunity."

"Any more relics, skulls or skin or anything?" asked Robert. Perhaps at the Grotto it would be easier to slip the Personal Sampler up to a bit of bone.

"Yes, I think so," said Marie. "It's a bone that's supposed to have come from the same body as the skull we just saw. Saved from the Protestants at some point, I think, or maybe from the Terror, the French Revolution. The family that saved it decided to donate it to the Grotto."

"I think we should do it," said Mado. "This is the place where Mary Magdalen is supposed to have lived for about seventy years all by herself, crying and growing her hair out really long, until she died, right? I want to see that. Who knows, maybe there's a tunnel in the back, where St. Thecla came to visit."

SIXTY-TWO

Indeed it was called the tree of the knowledge of good and evil ... because it brought man this: that he knew what good he had lost, and what evil he had gotten, and the difference between the good of obedience and the evil of disobedience.

Commentary on Lactantius

The postman came at around two in the afternoon. Val, without being asked, hid in the bedroom. The postman was full of questions and conversation, but all in a French that sounded half Italian with a good spike of Spanish. He gave Fibonacci some eggs along with the two packages. They heard his noisy truck rattling away down the "driveway" for a long time.

"Did you understand what he said?" asked Fibonacci when Val came out of the sleeping area.

"Not much," she admitted. "I think he was talking about the Brotherhood—I heard the word *fraternité* or maybe *fraternita*."

Fibonacci was opening the envelope. It was a large manilla envelope, and inside were three color photographs and a large-scale map. He had set the larger package aside, on the floor by the door

As Fibonacci bent over the photographs, Val couldn't resist looking at the map. It was a map of part of Provence, identical to one she had been given when she undertook her task as Fibonacci's chauffeur. Since the stone hut was on an unmarked drive off a tiny road through a village too small to figure on most maps, she had needed to study it carefully before undertaking the last part of the trip. She easily found Fibonacci's house on the new map. In fact it was marked with an X, just as on the map she had used yesterday. This time, however, a further itinerary was marked in ink. Farther south, into the mountains, to the Massif Sainte-Baume.

Suddenly Fibonacci sprang up from his seat and went over to the pile of newspapers and magazines on the floor by the stove. He began scrabbling through them. Then he dragged the whole pile towards the doorway, so that he could see better in the light.

Val bent over him. "Fibonacci, what is it? Can I help, or...?" *Or is it a secret of the Brotherhood, and I have already violated that by even looking at your map.*

Fibonacci sat back on his heels, pointing to the heavily pictorial front page of a small-format newspaper, a scandal sheet. His own face, captured by a security camera, stared up in the center, with Ser Aspro's official photo in an insert. A smaller insert showed two young women, arms around each other's waists, looking very much alike except that one was blonde and wore glasses. Val bent over the pictures. Then, with a flash of understanding, she went back to the table and looked at the photographs from the envelope.

The same two girls stared up at her, along with an unknown man. The blonde girl looked somewhat tackier than in the newspaper photo, her hair sticking straight up in a punk style, and studs in various parts of her face. There was writing in ink on this photo, and Val bent close to read it.

"No jewelry. Hair may be slicked down smooth. Glasses–yes."

The man's photograph had writing on it, too: simply "No beard." The man in the picture had a goatee.

The third photo, of the other woman in the newspaper, had no notes. She was a striking redhead.

Fibonacci came back to Val and took her hand, so that she looked up into his eye.

"What shall I do? They are Ser Aspro's granddaughters. What do you think the Doctor wants me to do?"

"Does he want you to help them in some way, to make up for what you did?"

"No. How could I help them, anyway, except by turning myself in?"

"Fibonacci, maybe it's just a warning. Perhaps they are traveling in this area and you need to avoid them."

But then why the map with a route marked which leads from here to Sainte-Baume?

"Val, I told him that I was sorry I killed Monsieur Aspro. That I would never do anything like that again. But I did do it. What if...."

He looked fearfully at the second package.

"Fibonacci, I don't think the Doctor would ask you to do anything wrong. Well, of course he asked you to burglarize the *Centre Commercial*, but perhaps they had something of his that you had to get back... or something. He brought you to this nice place...."

Fibonacci looked at her. "*You* brought me to this nice place."

"Yes, but...."

He knelt down by the second package and began to unwrap it. Val shuddered, realizing from his hesitation that he was violating the command of the Doctor. That was probably worse for him than having killed a man. He would be expelled from the Brotherhood. And the Doctor was his father, to be obeyed twice over.

The package contained a gun and a letter.

SIXTY-THREE

It is as sad that you had the bad luck not to learn about the Grail—what they do with it and to whom it is carried—as that your mother is dead.

Chrétien de Troyes

Lindy Teabag, who had a cell phone with him and had apparently made a note of the hostel telephone number, called and made reservations for them to spend the night. Apparently there was a good restaurant, too, and tonight, he said, he would treat them all to dinner.

Marie drove slowly on the winding road up into the mountains. They stopped twice to admire the view, the second time, at Lindy's suggestion, for a "high tea" (as he called it) at a café perched over a valley. With help from the café owner, a relaxed woman, they made out, in the distance, the hostel towards which they were driving. The Grotto was hidden by a shoulder of the mountain.

The café was almost empty–it was far too late for lunch and early for dinner. Lindy went out to the parking area to make a telephone call, and Robert and the Navet sisters sat quietly admiring the view. They became aware of a discussion at another table, between a man and a woman speaking American English.

"Well, that was all very nice, this grotto and shrine, but it doesn't have anything to do with the real Mary Magdalen," said the man. "It's all in this book, if you'd just read it."

"Well, I tried to, Howie, but it didn't make any sense to me," said the woman. "Even the title. Of course the holy Grail has to do

with holy blood—anybody my age who was raised Catholic under-
stands that. It's the cup of the Last Supper, and Jesus changed the
wine to his own blood. I don't see why they have to go making up
a big secret mystery about it."

"Jane, you didn't read far enough. The Holy Grail is not the
cup of the Last Supper. That was just a story for simple people, to
keep the power in the hands of the Church. As you say, growing up
Catholic it all made sense to you—you were brainwashed! The point
is that the word Sangreal itself doesn't really mean 'holy grail' or
'holy blood' either. It means '*royal* blood.' That's the royal blood of
Jesus and Mary Magdalen, passed down through their children."

"So—Christianity is a crock. I could figure that out for myself.
Your Knights Templar strike me as good evidence for the idea that
Catholicism was on the wrong track all along—crusades and build-
ing churches in other people's holy places, military monks and sex-
ual abuse and stuff. I just don't see why it matters if there was a real
Jesus who got married and had children, then."

Marie had twice turned right around to stare at the couple rather rudely. She had been making some notes in a notebook taken
from her purse. Now she got up and went over to their table.

"Excuse me, but I couldn't help overhearing," she said. "I did a
special subject on the Grail legends for my degree. I've always been
interested in medieval literature. I just want to show you something."

Robert and Mado got up to see what she was showing them. On
the notebook page she had written two phrases:

SANCTUS GRADALIS (HOLY GRAIL)
SANGUIS REGALIS (ROYAL BLOOD)

"These are the Latin words for Holy Grail and Royal Blood," she
explained. "In the various regions where Latin was the basis of the
vernacular—I mean, in Italy, France, Spain, Portugal in particular—
these words got worn down in different ways. They lost syllables or
letters. But there was never a place or time when they both would
have been spelled or pronounced as if they were the same phrase.
For example, when the word Grail first appears in Old French, it

has the form—" and she block-printed below the other words:

GRAAL

"You see, it lost the *d* between the two *a*'s, and also the ending *-is*. But it was a perfectly good word in Old French. It could mean a big dish in which a course of a dinner was served, or a book containing psalms the priest recites during Mass as he climbs the altar steps. The Latin word *gradalis* had to do with steps or sequences, you see, like the English word *grade*. The very first author who tells about the holy Grail, in the 12th century, was Chrétien de Troyes, and he specifies that it is an uncovered jeweled dish. However, his grail contains not meat or fish but a Eucharistic host. Beside it is carried a spear whose tip drips blood."

"The Lance of Longinus!" exclaimed the man, Howie.

Mado put in, "You mean the story about the blind Roman soldier, Longinus, who pierced the side of Jesus on the Cross? And then when the blood dripped on him he could see? The part about the piercing is in the Gospels, at least, but Longinus is kind of one of those legends that's too good to be true."

"Oddly enough," said Marie, "in Chrétien's Grail story, the spear does *not* appear to be the spear of Longinus. It seems more likely that it was the spear which hurt the old king, Perceval's grandfather. In a Welsh version, the grail dish holds the severed head of one of Perceval's relatives, whom he must avenge. So the grail and the spear seem to have to do with a personal quest for righting family wrongs, in that story at least. Unfortunately Chrétien didn't really finish the story so we don't get to see that happen."

"And how does this author spell '*Holy Grail*'? You didn't tell us that," Howie asked.

"He doesn't. I think at some point he says the grail, G-R-A-A-L, is a holy object, *saint* in French, like your word "saint." But he does not refer to it as *the* Holy Grail at all. It's just a grail that happens to be special and mysterious. So there's not much room to confuse it with Holy Blood."

"Where does this word 'sangreal' that is supposed to mean 'royal blood' come from, then?" asked Jane.

"I don't know, actually. It's not French. Various French writers developed the idea of the Holy Grail and tied it into the Joseph of Arimathea legend, another popular one like the Lance of Longinus. Instead of a dish it became the cup of the Last Supper. I think that had to do with a new interest in the Mass, in the physics of transubstantiation."

"You lost me," said Robert, speaking for the American audience in general.

"Well, the way the bread and wine actually got turned into Jesus's body and blood during Mass, when the priest repeated the words of the Last Supper, 'This is my body.' It was a big philosophical problem in the 13th century, to explain why it still looked and tasted like bread and wine but was really flesh and blood. Making the cup Jesus used into a magic vessel must have seemed obvious, so they sort of took over Chrétien de Troyes's Grail and made it into this very important sacred object. Probably they wanted to get some Crusading adventure in there, too, but they couldn't because King Arthur was supposed to have lived before Mohammed did. Now, since the Last Supper took place in Jerusalem, the Grail of course came from there. Their new hero, the virgin knight Galahad instead of Perceval with all his family ties, well, Galahad has to go back to the Holy Land with the Grail and become a king there."

"You're telling me that people just made all that up, about the Grail? That there never was a Holy Grail, a cup of the Last Supper? Some medieval author just thought it all up? That's stupid! Of course there was a cup!" Howie obviously felt his criticism was devastating, but Marie seemed serene.

"Well, now. The Gospels say Jesus took a cup to bless at the Last Supper, but you don't get stories about it until more than a thousand years later, and even then I don't think any church or king ever claimed to have the actual cup, the relic itself. The Cross, the Crown of Thorns, clothing of Christ and Mary, images of them, yes... Such things were kept in churches and there were stories about how they were discovered and preserved. But not for this cup. So it is the perfect thing to put into a story, because it didn't have its own story yet. Besides, your book, here, seems to have made its story up out of nothing, too, all this royal blood story that is easily dismissed by anyone who has studied the languages. In all languages it's clear that the Grail is a particular thing, and its being holy is taken care of by a completely separate word, the adjective that means holy. In French the adjective holy, 'saint,' always had the -t- in it, like Sainte-Baume, where we are going, and not like *sang*, blood." She got out her pen again and flipped to a new piece of paper.

GRÂL (GERMAN)
SAINT GRAAL or SAINT GREAL (FRENCH)
SAN GRADALE or SANTO GRADALE (ITALIAN)
SANTO GRIAL (SPANISH)
HOLY GRAIL, GRAYLE (ENGLISH)

"See? Nothing that looks like 'royal blood.' That would be *sangre real* in Spanish, or *sangue regale* in Italian, or *sang royale* in French."

By this time Lindy Teabag had returned and was looking over her shoulder. He saw the book the man was clutching. He gave one of his less polite opinions.

"That rubbish! Marie, my dear, it's foolish to try to explain this sort of thing to people who read such filthy nonsense. *Sangreal* is in fact a British form–I mean English. In the 15th century Sir Thomas Malory seems to have created the word, though he also calls the object in question the Holy Grayle, just as you wrote it down."[2]

"Ah, Malory! The great English translator of the French prose romances. Some say his is the best version of all." Marie answered as if it were an exam question. Robert thought, *she didn't read that one for her special subject, did she?*

"So you're saying the one-word form Sangreal is much later than the two-word Holy Grail form? 15th-century English instead of–?" Jane asked

"12th-century French, or 13th-century French, German, Italian, or Spanish," said Marie.

"Why did the English writer make it into one word, not even an English word?"

---

[2] Lindy is not quite accurate. The one-word form (which can be broken in two as either "Holy Grail" or "Blood Royal" in a kind of pseudo-French), does appear first in 15th-century English works, but the earliest of these is Henry Lovelich's *Merlin*; the Stanzaic *Morte Arthur* ("Sangrail") and Malory's *Mort D'Arthur* ("Sankgreal") picked up on the term, a little later in the same century.

Lindy answered, "I suppose the idea of Arthur's knights chasing around after a mysterious object called the Grail, however holy, seemed too modest, so he gave it this fancy English name that looks Italian or Spanish. Probably Malory did mean to make a pun on 'royal blood.' After all, the cup was supposed to have been used by Joseph of Arimathea to catch the blood of 'Jesus of Nazareth, King of the Jews,' as he hung on the Cross under that inscription. It's a perfectly transparent little multi-language joke, very much in the late-medieval taste. One can hardly say it hides some dark secret about Jesus's sex life."

"Then how do you explain how this guy Bérenger Saunière got rich?" asked Howie, tapping his book. "This guy lived back a hundred years ago, he was poor, and then he found out these secrets and got rich. The money must have come from somewhere."

Teabag snorted. Marie and Mado giggled. Jane sucked in her cheeks and looked from one person to the other, as if to say, *See what I have to live with?*

Boy, that is one book I can ignore in the airport racks. Robert, brought sharply back from the world of Marie's careful explanations, recognized in Howie a type he met all too often at all levels in his profession: the guy who sincerely believed that getting rich was the result of a bargain with God or the Devil. Whereas Robert knew from observation that people got rich because they cared about money. His own lack of this passion was what kept him in the classroom, and relatively poor. He said gently, half to himself and half to Howie and Jane, "Show me the money."

They went back to their table and each threw a few coins down, to pay for their tea, and left.

SIXTY-FOUR

…a cult nut insisting you could read Proust as anagrams predicting the end of the world during the Administration of Mr. Reagan.

Veronica Geng, "Love Trouble is My Business"

The hostel turned out to be a large complex of rambling buildings, rather simple in construction but attractively clean-looking. The huge parking lot had several tour buses and vans, some commercial, some with emblems of various Catholic societies. There was one pink SUV with a wonderful curvy fat female outline painted on it, with huge breasts and hips and a tiny head.

The place was run by nuns, wearing grey habits instead of the Dominican black-and-white, but there seemed to be plenty of Dominicans around, too. Flocks of wizened little nuns clattered together cheerfully in the corners of the big airy reception hall. Some individual pilgrims, women and men, too, sat looking worried but hopeful in chairs—or wheelchairs—by themselves. Two groups of six or eight middle-aged women on "goddess pilgrimages" (one group had identical pink scarves, the other purple tote bags) made quite a bit of noise as they discussed their day's doings. There was also a large troop of children, about eleven or twelve years old, all dressed in some kind of blue and white uniform. They were in the charge of black-gowned priests, who did a pretty good job of keeping them from leaping around the room.

The nun who checked them in smiled and told them that, as had been requested, the party had two private rooms–that is to say, one for the men and one for the women. Apparently these were in separate buildings. She gave them each a little map and explained that the Grotto itself, the cave in the mountains where Mary Magdalene had lived, would be closing its doors for the evening fairly soon.

"She says it's too late to walk up, but we can drive if we want to see it tonight," Marie translated. "There's a sung service, vespers, beginning in a little while."

They stepped outside and looked up at the Grotto. It hung over the valley, above the trees, like an abandoned building fastened to the cliff face. The sunset lit it up. It was, of course, not abandoned at all. Robert decided there was something about the narrow windows and the irregular angles of the walls that made it look empty.

"It's quite a hike," said Linden Teabag, examining the xeroxed map. "From this plan I would say several miles uphill. To be frank, that is not what I want this evening, though I would love to do it tomorrow morning when I'm fresh. Apparently it's quite lovely, through the woods."

Mado stretched her arms over her head. Marie, who had been driving all afternoon, yawned and stretched. "Well, we could drive up and take a peek, and then make the climb tomorrow."

"You young folks are marvelous. Such energy. Do you know what I want? What I need? A little nap. In an hour or two we can drive back to the village for dinner. Right now.... Robert, shall we see what our digs are like? Got your bag?"

Robert had brought his suitcase, though he had left the carryon with the fragile items packed in it in Marie Navet's apartment. Since Marie had unlocked the car trunk, he opened the suitcase without removing it and pulled out a few things. He was running low on clean clothes. He stuffed a pair of briefs into his pocket, hoping that he would not find later that the Personal Sampler had collected data from it. He got out his dopp kit and a fairly clean but very wrinkled shirt, for tomorrow. A bit of bright blue caught his eye, and he remembered the book he had been reading before all this began–Swann's Way. Captain Bulle had told him something about it–that it held some clue to Ser Aspro's pneu. Robert pulled out the book and found tucked in its pages that little square of cardboard Ser Aspro had enclosed in the pneu. Yes, Captain Bulle had put it there, saying there was a clue to it in the book itself.

He still had the *pneu* in his jacket pocket, though it was almost in two pieces, from having the white barcode label cut off. He brought it, and the book with its boxtop bookmark, along into the hostel.

To Robert's disgust, the "digs" consisted of a small room with a sink, one chair, and a bunkbed. Any showers or toilets were in a room somewhere down the hall. The one nice point was a big window with heavy folding wooden shutters. Lindy Teabag immediately claimed the top bunk, and Robert wondered if the springs would hold him–he was a big man. Robert did not look forward to sleeping underneath an insufficiently supported Teabag.

"What a day, eh, old chap? We have a complete set of old Aspro's barcodes! There's no question. We'll track down the programs now. Maybe we can convince the women to head straight back to Paris tomorrow. Marie has that useful collection of scanners and software." Teabag climbed up onto the bunk. It creaked mightily.

"Lindy, I had forgotten. I *have* Aspro's program."

"What?"

"I think so. An old, probably very beta, version. It's called boutique.exe, it has the right kind of date for one of Ser Aspro's early attempts, and I got it off Father Pater's hard drive." Robert handed the diskette to Teabag.

"Robert, you are a clever man, aren't you? Sitting over in a corner by yourself. I didn't expect this."

"All we need is a computer to sit down and take a good look at it. I wish I had brought my laptop along."

"Me, too." Teabag slipped the diskette into his shirt pocket and patted it. He lay back down and smiled at the ceiling. "Now, Robert, you and the young ladies.... Mademoiselle Marie Navet is very lovely, very intelligent too, I find. Her sister, now, looks more... *accessible*." He gave some kind of snort. Robert remembered that Mado had emphasized that Lindy had been *like* a gentleman–not that he was one, but like one–in the taxi last night. "I suppose I may congratulate you on having done something worth regretting with one of them."

"No, I haven't, and if I had I wouldn't discuss it."

"Good for you. A gentleman's reply. I shouldn't have asked."

Locker-room talk. Part of being on the same team?

Something worth regretting.... Should I regret not having done anything worth regretting? Should I be sorry for hiding evidence from the police and stealing Father Pater's little program? Robert was not given to regretting his own actions. Up until now, it seemed as if the only thing he had ever really regretted was being born too late to vote for Ronald Reagan–but all that was water under the bridge, and this evening his task was to read some Proust.

It was still light enough to read by the window. Robert found he had forgotten the plot of the opening section he had read a few nights ago, so he would have to start over from the beginning. He was also motivated to reread it because Captain Bulle had mentioned a scene which he did recall. It involved drinking tea. He looked at the pages which he had gotten through before, trying to find the part about the tea.

"*Swann's Way*, eh, Robert? Proust. I didn't think you were the type." Lindy was still awake.

Robert sighed. "Probably I'm not. I just bought it to have something from a bookstore in Paris called Shakespeare and Company."

"Excellent! But I wouldn't really have thought you were the Shakespeare and Company type, either. Hemingway, Joyce, that sort of thing?"

"Hemingway, *Old Man and the Sea* and that other novel. Of course. And James Joyce–that's who that was, yes, they had photos on the wall in the bookstore. I remember reading a story by Joyce, about a party in Ireland. Something about a woman with red hair, washing it and drying it in front of the fire. But the reason I wanted to go to Shakespeare and Company in particular was because of *Highlander*."

Lindy propped himself up, looking puzzled and concerned. "The Highlander? Who–which Highlander?"

"It was a TV show. A movie spinoff. You must have heard of the movies, but I don't know if the TV show was on in your country. An action series, about a kind of secret society of immortal men, and women too, who would try to kill each other with swords."

"Hmpf! And how did you get to be one of these secret society members?"

"Oh, you were born that way. The hero was born in Scotland in, well, medieval times, I think. So he was called the Highlander."

Lindy was listening but it took Robert a moment to come back to why he was talking about the TV series. "Oh, yeah. So the Highlander lived on a houseboat on the Seine River in Paris, one of those barges. And he stayed close to a certain church on the banks of the Seine, because the immortals were safe from each other on holy ground. They wouldn't try to kill each other near a church. And there were some episodes with that bookstore, Shakespeare and Company, in them. The owner got killed, I think. Anyway, it was all there, when I went looking for it, right there in Paris, not just the bookstore but the church, too. I went inside. It was just like in the show."

Lindy lay back down. The springs creaked. "Well, Robert, enjoy your book. When you get to the part about the linden teabag, think of me."

"About the what? *You're* in this book?"

"No, no, of course, not having been born yet when it was written, no. But also, yes. That is, the narrator dunks a cookie, a kind of cookie called a madeleine in fact, just like our little friend Mado, about whom you have nothing at all to reproach yourself. He dips it into a cup of tea, and that tea is made from the dried leaves and flowers of the *tilleul*, a tree called in English the lime-tree or the linden tree. True, the infusion his mother gives him is probably made from loose vegetable matter, but nowadays you can purchase linden teabags in the shops. That's what they call them, linden teabags. So I *am* in the book, you might say." His voice trailed off.

Robert turned the pages of his book until he found the part about the madeleine cookies and the tea, but the translator called it "lime-flower tea." Robert was pretty sure that was what Captain Bulle had called it, too.

Bulle had been talking about the little bit of cardboard which Ser Aspro had sent Robert, in his *pneu*, the night the old man was killed. Robert was holding that boxtop in his fingers now—he was using it for a bookmark. Evidently it was from a box of linden teabags. He peered more closely at the faint green tracery of flowers and leaves.

Was the message of the teabag boxtop sent to Robert by Ser Aspro something like: "Find Linden Teabag. He will help you"?

Robert glanced up at Lindy. A hearty snore came from the bunk.

He could see the old man's big, competent hand, relaxed at the edge of the mattress. His shirt front, its pocket full of Ser Aspro's old letters and his program disk, rose and fell gently. Of course. Lindy and Aspro knew each other–they were friends. Aspro would know to turn to him for help on barcode matters.

Something nagged at him, though. He put the book down and thought about the boxtop and the *pneu* in which it had arrived at the *Hôtel du Prieuré*.

He went quietly over to where he had piled his things on his bunk, and got the *pneu*. He looked again at the blue barcode under his name on the front of the envelope. The letters and numbers of the message had not been printed below the code, but the sight of it was enough to remind him of the message Ser Aspro had encoded for him.

BWRLT01010
BEWARE LINDEN TEABAG. X X

X marks the spot. Not for treasure, but for danger.

SIXTY-FIVE

Spreading throughout Europe from the end of the sixteenth century ... the celestial [and terrestrial] spheres
soon found a place in libraries and collectors' cabinets.
Symbols rather than scientific objects....

Louvre online boutique

Robert watched Marie and Mado Navet walking towards him
across the field of wildflowers. The sun was at their backs, not setting yet, although some parts of the valley were already in shadow.
From where he stood, at the beginning of the woodland path to the
Grotto, they were just two moving silhouettes.

Lime-flower tea, linden teabags. As he gazed into the setting
sun at the two dark shifting blurs, he thought of the *camera obscura*
Marie had described to him when they first met–a pinpoint hole in
the wall which enables one to see what is on the other side, only
upside-down. He saw a little boy named Marcel Proust dipping
some kind of cookie called a Magdalene into a cup of lime-flower
tea. He saw old Ser Aspro in his office, excitedly composing a secret
message to a barcode expert he had never met, a man he had heard
of only a few hours earlier–a message which that man had taken
a good long time to decode. He saw Ser Aspro dead, his shattered
leg, his granddaughter crying on his breast. He saw that the two
women coming towards him were wearing hats. Their shapes were
clearer now, but of course he could not know which was which.

He had summoned them with a note. He had left Teabag snor-
ing in a partly darkened room (Robert had closed the heavy wood

shutters as far as he could without making a sound). He had had a pleasant but strange conversation with the little nun at the reception desk. He gathered that it was impossible for him to enter the building where the twins were housed. However, it was possible to send them a note. He did so, asking them to meet him at a distance from the hostel.

If Teabag woke up, it would be better that he couldn't find them. And they would be able to tell him that they had simply decided to explore the Grotto path a bit.

As the women approached, Robert turned away from them and headed up the path, assuming they would follow him into the privacy of the forest. After a while the path became a kind of stairway, made of timbers and impacted earth. It was shady in the woods, though still pretty hot, and there was a wonderful smell of earth and pine needles. Occasionally a bird would sing, but otherwise it was very still, until a gaggle of nuns came swooping down the path, presumably having enjoyed the final service of the day at the Grotto. Robert stood aside to let them pass, and when they were gone he found that the twins had caught up to him.

They had taken off their cardigans. The sweaters underneath were sleeveless.

Robert found himself unable to take another step.

The women kept walking for a few yards, and he stared in stupefaction as the twin pairs of shoulders, with twin pairs of tattoos, swung along up the path ahead of him, in and out of the light from the low sun across the valley.

I had forgotten. Mado has those circular tattoos—and I did see Marie's, only I forgot. I saw one of them when I first went to her apartment. But I had forgotten it.

Then Mado stopped and looked back at him. Marie stopped, too, a bit farther along.

"What's the matter, Robert? Is this far enough?"

"Marie, I know what it is!" Mado laughed and slapped her right shoulder. "He knew I was tattooed, but he didn't know about you!"

"I did know... sort of." Robert took a few long strides to catch up, and grabbed one of Mado's arms so that she wouldn't get away. Marie came back down to their level, smiling.

"Oh, yes, the tattoos." They moved helpfully into a patch of golden sunlight so that he could examine their shoulders.

Each twin had an exquisite circle tattooed on each shoulder. Mado's was a map, or rather a double map, one circle for each hemisphere of the globe. Each continent had its name written in a tiny script. Some areas, such as the north of Russia, were not defined by lines but left open. There was a tiny ship sailing in the Atlantic. The Equator was clearly marked, and some lines of longitude sketched in.

Marie's tattoos also appeared to be two hemispheres, with an Equator and a number of other geographical lines marked. However, instead of continents her maps were filled with figures which Robert quickly identified as constellations and signs of the horoscope. With the vanity which astrology inevitably inspires, he looked for his own sign, Leo.

"These are very beautiful."

"Ser Aspro would not have made anything ugly," said Marie, a little grimly.

"Ser Aspro made these?"

"Of course he didn't tattoo them himself, but he paid for them. And he chose the designs."

"Actually, he got the Louvre Museum to lend him the originals. He said he was going to see about getting replicas made. What, on those little plates that protect furniture?"

"Coasters. Actually, the Museum Shop does carry paperweights in the form of Celestial and Terrestrial Spheres. But they aren't as pretty as these designs."

Robert said slowly, "Yes, I saw them in the shop. Terrestrial Orb, Celestial Orb. But I didn't want to be buying too many things, and it seemed like they belonged together. I didn't want to break up the set."

Mado laughed as if he had made some wonderful joke. Marie smiled and shrugged.

Robert continued, "Your grandfather had you tattooed with matching tattoos? Marie got the Celestial Sphere, meaning the stars, the sky, Heaven. Madeleine got the Terrestrial?"

"Meaning earth, dirt, whatever. Oh, Robert, don't look like that! Dirt, earth, full of history, good for digging in! We told you that Ser

Aspro had certain ideas about us... sacred love and profane love, virgin and whore, heavenly and earthly...."

"Right, and Citroën DS and Citroën 2CV. I understand. Were the tattoos also a birthday present?"

"Yes. For our sixteenth birthday."

"We loved it, didn't we, Marie? It seemed truly, do you say in English 'cool'? Very cool to have tattoos from our grandfather. And such beautiful tattoos."

"I don't think we really understood, when we were sixteen, what he was getting at. He was saying to us, 'You two are the same, but also different. Never forget that.'"

"As if we could. *I* liked it when he said I should bleach my hair. He seemed so cool."

Marie said, "Well, you do look good as a blonde, Mado. At least, when you wear it in a simple hairdo like that...."

Robert wanted to put his arms around both of them and give them a big hug. However, as he thought about this "twin sandwich" another element in his emotions surfaced.

"Thanks for showing me the tattoos," he said, wrenching himself from the hug and the visions it inspired. "But I do have something else to discuss. I think I figured out your grandfather's message for me."

SIXTY-SIX

The simultaneous contemplation of paintings by a large public, such as developed in the nineteenth century, is an early symptom of the crisis of painting.... The change that has come about is an expression of the particular conflict in which painting was implicated by the mechanical reproducibility of paintings.

Walter Benjamin

They found a place a bit off the pathway with a stone bench. The sun was strong there and they could see each other fairly well, though the shadows were also sharp.

Robert explained about the boxtop and the coded message. They agreed that it was a warning about Teabag.

"Do you think Mr. Teabag knew that you were involved with us, Mado and me, and so with Ser Aspro?"

"He was really insistent about meeting up with me in Paris. And he responded very fast when I said we should get together. I don't even remember giving him your apartment address, but he knew where to show up."

"And he just invited himself along on this trip."

"And he took Father Pater's letters from Ser Aspro. All of them." Marie looked quite sad. "Robert, do you think he will be able to figure out the program on the Apple Pi barcode labels?"

"I'm sure of it, since I gave him a copy of the early version of the program myself. I copied it from Father Pater's hard drive. And he would have a huge advantage if...."

"If?"

"If he is responsible for the square black barcode. If he knows how the black code works, he will know what to look for in the white-on-white one which Ser Aspro designed to combat it."

"If, for example, he designed that black barcode himself," said Mado.

Marie was fierce. "Why would Linden Teabag want to hurt museums? I mean, museum stores?" Then she paused. All three of them realized *why*, but Mado finally said it.

"He hates museum reproductions. He hates copies of art objects. He hates the idea of people living surrounded by useful things with pictures of famous paintings on them."

"But," said Robert, "that's really just an intellectual position. It's philosophical, sort of. Surely nobody would try to halt an important form of commerce because of an *intellectual preference*."

The two girls stared at him as if he were a child who had used a dirty word without knowing what it meant.

Mado patted his knee. "Dear Robert, I'm afraid the world is just so much nastier a place than you know." She wasn't smiling, though.

Marie reached out to touch her sister's shoulder.

The tatoos are, of course, museum reproductions. I wonder how they would affect Lindy? Would they raise the stakes of regrettability?

Robert tried not to let himself be distracted. He had been thinking about this since he realized what Aspro's teabag boxtop meant. "Actually, I don't think it was quite like that. Lindy told me that he had met Ser Aspro a long time ago, and obviously Aspro knew who Lindy is. Aspro has been planning his barcode defense for at least eight years, right? Seven or eight. The program I copied off Father Pater's computer was about five years old. So here's the scenario: Lindy meets Ser Aspro and tells him, I hate your type of business and I could stop it dead with a barcode. Maybe he tells him a little bit about what this barcode would do. Aspro sees it as a challenge...."

"Yes, he would do that," said Mado. "He would go right ahead and figure out how Linden Teabag could do what he threatened."

"And how it could be counteracted. But of course using another barcode," said Marie.

"I can see it," said Robert. "For him merely to write, or have someone else write, a protective program and install it on the cash registers would have been cheating. Using a baseball bat in a tennis match." He paused. "And I suppose that if Lindy Teabag found out he was playing that game, he would have to see whether or not he actually could write such a code...."

At that moment, a woman came out of the gloom of the forest path into their little clearing. She was tall and slender, with short dark hair. She walked right up to them and looked at their faces carefully. The sun was setting now. Robert couldn't quite see her own face in the uncertain light, but her voice was certainly deeply worried when she spoke. She said in French,

"Can you tell me who you are? I'm sorry, but this is a difficult matter. It's important...." *It's a matter of life and death,* thought Val Percy. "I can start by introducing myself. Val Percy. I'm English."

Robert hesitated, but Mado spoke up, in English. "I am Madeleine Navet and this is my sister Marie. The gentleman with us is Robert Longone, a professor of Symbology at Harvard Business School in America. Can we help you?"

Val smiled, encouraged. "You are very kind. I need to talk to you. Actually... if I could speak to you, Professor Longone, privately?"

They didn't answer.

"I do understand that I have interrupted a private conversation among the three of you. I feel, though, that it is great good luck for all of us that I found you here. I will be glad to walk away, out of earshot of your voices, while you finish your discussion. I only ask a moment of Professor Longone's time."

Without waiting for an answer, she did walk away, back into the forest. She was wearing a white jacket. When they could no longer see it glimmering among the trees, Marie whispered, "What do you think? Do you know her, Robert?"

They all agreed that they had never met this woman. She might be an associate of Teabag's, but what point would she have in meeting them in this way?

That brought them back to the Teabag situation. They agreed that they would go out to dinner that night and climb to the Grotto the next day, as planned, but that the three of them would stick together and try also to keep an eye on Teabag himself. Robert resolved not to let Teabag near a computer until their return to Paris, and to try if at all possible to get the barcodes and diskette back.

They all walked back to the forest path. Val Percy was waiting above them, at a bend in the rising stairway. Mado and Marie said good-bye, and left Robert to climb up to speak with the dark woman.

SIXTY-SEVEN

I feel trembling in myself something which moves and wants to rise to the surface, something that has come away from its anchor in the depths. I don't know what it is, but it is coming up slowly. I feel resistance and I hear the noise as it travels great distances. This throbbing within me must be the image, the visual memory....

Marcel Proust

When Robert reached Val Percy on the woodland staircase, she held out her hand to him. To his surprise, her first words were, "You know Dr. Teabag of Edinburgh? I couldn't help hearing the three of you mentioning his name."

"Linden Teabag, the renowned medical symbologist? I suppose he must have an M.D. I didn't realize he was from Scotland."

"Yes. That's the man. I didn't understand that you knew him personally."

"There wouldn't be two men named Linden Teabag, would there?"

"I want to warn you. Well, to tell you....."

Robert became aware of another person on the pathway, or next to it. *Just a dark shape in the darkness. It moved a little.*

"Fibonacci?" said Val Percy softly.

"The Fibonacci sequence is a series of numbers in which each term is the sum of the two previous terms," Robert answered.

Val Percy put her hand on his arm. Her dark eyes gleamed as she leaned close to him. She whispered, "I didn't want to speak to those women. Fibonacci killed their grandfather, after all."

"Fibonacci?" Robert felt as if he'd fallen down Alice's rabbit hole again, but a lot deeper and without his Alice.

"Yes. Fibonacci is a man, and I'm sure that the women, and you too, know what he looks like. You would recognize him quite easily."

"The one-eyed hunchback? You're saying his name is Fibonacci? Tom, Dick, Harry, Fibonacci? Fibonacci *what?*"

A soft male voice said in the shadows, "Fibonacci Fibonacci."

Adrenalin surged through Robert. *Fibonacci, like the code on the black square barcode that produced the Fibonacci sequence on the computers before shutting them down. If Linden Teabag did write that code, did he name it somehow after this creature? Does he know this Fibonacci, this murderer?*

"The murderer, the man who killed Ser Aspro, is here? I am going right back to the hostel...." Robert patted his pockets to see whether he had brought a cell phone. No, just the Personal Sampler.

"Please," said the voice, and the hideous creature stepped out onto the path. "I did do it. I'm sorry. Please do call the police. But listen first."

Robert paused. He was already a few yards away, down the path. Val, standing now beside the hunchback, spoke first.

"Dr. Teabag asked Fibonacci to burgle the *Centre Commercial du Louvre.* He didn't expect to find anyone there. Monsieur Aspro defended himself against the intruder. He hurt Fibonacci's hand, quite badly–I saw it the next day. Then Fibonacci shot him. But now–"

"Are you friends with those two girls?" asked Fibonacci. "The granddaughters of the old man? I am sorry, please tell them, and I don't want to hurt them."

"You *are not* going to hurt them *at all,*" said Val Percy. She seemed to be trying to reinforce this concept for him.

"You're damn well not going to hurt them," said Robert at the same moment, feeling a John Wayne rush. He touched the Personal Sampler in his pocket as if it were a gun.

"No," said the monster. "I am not going to hurt them. But he wants me to kill all of you. In cold blood. He didn't even tell me why."

Robert felt a shiver in the warm darkness.

After a moment he walked back up and peered into Fibonacci's face. One brown eye stared back at him. He could see the eyelashes of the other eyelid, swollen closed under some kind of tumor that reached up through the eyebrow and forehead.

Robert looked from one of them to the other.

"Linden Teabag, my colleague, told you to kill me, and also my friends the Navet sisters?" Both nodded. "And you have no idea at all why?"

Val said, "Well, presumably it has something to do with what went on at the Louvre the other night. He did explain some of that to Fibonacci. The trouble is, Fibonacci can't repeat it without violating his oaths."

Robert waited. Fibonacci seemed to be waiting, too.

Val said, "Well, I'll have to explain. Being a woman, I'm not allowed to take these oaths. Dr. Teabag is an important figure in one of the oldest lodges of the Freemasons."

"*The* oldest lodge," put in Fibonacci.

"He is one of the Masters. Now, the Freemasons are generally a fine organization. They do like secrets and games and, and– *hierarchy*, I guess you'd call it. Higher initiates telling the lower ones what to do. But our lives would be poorer without their ideals, and especially your lives in America, Professor Longone. Your Declaration of Independence and Statue of Liberty are just a couple of Freemason products."

"If you say so," said Robert, thinking uneasily of the weird pyramid on the one-dollar bill. Someone had told him that this was a Masonic symbol. He preferred nice clear symbols like Mary Magdalen's ointment grail.

"Right. Well, the trouble is, Dr. Teabag seems to have gone off on some kind of project of his own, which we don't understand, but which involves theft and, now, murder. He is using Fibonacci here, and other Masonic Brothers, to accomplish this. This is a real abuse of the Masonic oath."

"He's my father," said Fibonacci. "So I owe him obedience as a son."

"He's *your... father*?" Robert could not put together this monster and the tall, elegant symbologist.

"He adopted me. When my mother saw what I looked like, she

didn't want me. My father didn't, either. So the Doctor adopted me."

Val sighed. "Fibonacci, I am not sure that's true. Babies born with neurofibromatosis look normal. Maybe they have a few unusual freckles or birthmarks. You would have been a perfectly nice-looking baby."

"Well, maybe it's not neurofibromatosis. Maybe it's something else. But I always looked like this. The Doctor told me. My mother wouldn't give me milk."

Val didn't reply. Evidently they had been through this before. Robert decided it was his turn.

"Is this neurofibromawhatever a genetic disease?" he asked.

"Yes, it's due to a mutation," said Val.

"Let's look, then." He took his Personal Sampler in one hand and reached for Fibonacci's wrist with the other. Fibonacci was, he found, trembling. His wrist seemed strangely light.

Touch, sample. Save. Image, 10 years old. He showed the little display screen, lit up eerily in the now-dark woods, to the other two.

"Oh," said Val. "Is that what you looked like!"

The boy in the picture had two big, dark eyes. One shoulder was higher than the other, and his forehead had several lumps on it. On his naked body were several birthmarks. Interestingly, both his hands had red x's on them: he was genetically ambidextrous.

Fibonacci began to cry. Val almost absent-mindedly put her arm around him.

"How did you do that?" asked Val.

"It takes his DNA and projects from that what he will look like at ten, twenty, and forty years of age. Shall we look at twenty?" Without waiting for a reply, Robert switched to twenty and, considering Fibonacci's feelings, hit the modesty button.

He looked pretty much the way he did now. The eye was closed, but the back less twisted, the head less lumpy.

Fibonacci stared, then said "Don't keep going!"

"Yes," said Val, "you're right. Please don't show us what he will look like at forty, Professor Longone." *If he lives that long,* was the unspoken thought in the air among all three of them.

"The Doctor lied to me, then. You're right, Val. I looked normal when I was a baby. Or just the birthmarks. That picture showed *exactly* where they are!"

Robert was pleased. "Pretty good. I didn't know they could map the progress of an individual's presentation so accurately. It was just a hunch that this gadget would be able to track the progress of your disease at all, but it seems to have been programmed with that particular mutation."

"Yes," Fibonacci admitted. "I remember now, looking like that. I remember looking in the mirror with two eyes and seeing the tumors and not knowing what they were." He rubbed his hugely lumpy forehead. "I even remember...." He looked so distressed, Robert felt a kind of admiration for him, as he tried to go back in time to recover his past. "I remember now. When I was little, I loved to run so much. And then all of a sudden it became hard to run. The other boys laughed at me. That's when my back began to twist, you see."

Val shook her head sadly.

"And tunnels! I used to love to go into closets and the hole under the basement stairs of the big house when I was little! I even made a foxhole in the yard and he caned me for it. And then he fixed it with stones so it looked nice, though, and made it into a fishpond."

Val said, "And then, Fibonacci, when you became claustrophobic because of your disease, Dr. Teabag filled your head full of ideas about tunnels and digging. He told you they were evil."

"Yes, he told me they were evil. Aren't they?"

Robert looked at his watch, which had a light-up dial. It was nearly eight o'clock. "I need to go back to the hostel, probably. I think I understand some of why Teabag wants to get rid of the three of us. We are the only ones who really understand his attack on the museum shops."

Val gave a little snort of nervous laughter. "He is attacking museum shops? How could he do that? Why?"

"I know it sounds crazy," Robert admitted. "Lindy doesn't like museum reproductions, so he wanted to sabotage the whole business. Being a barcode expert, he planned to do it by a barcode label that would invade and trash all the computers in each store. Ser Aspro, Monsieur Aspro, knew about the sabotage and had figured out a program that would protect the store computers."

"This is ridiculous," said Val.

"It is, but so are one-eyed pyramids. It makes a kind of sense, to me, as a colleague of Teabag's. It's actually an elegant plan, and not likely to be found out. He must have had other conspirators, too, to place the destructive barcode labels on objects in the museum shops."

"I know who," said Fibonacci miserably. "I've been the courier. I brought these packets to certain Brothers in Paris and Madrid and London and Copenhagen, a lot of places. I could write out a list if I had to. Anyway, it was raining in Copenhagen and the package got wet. I wanted to put the stuff in a different envelope, so I opened it. It was sheets of sticky labels. Is that what you mean? They were sort of like barcodes, but beautiful. Like a tiny *Arche de la Défense*."

"That's it!" cried Robert. "This is marvelous! If you turn state's evidence, or whatever they call it in France...."

"The trouble is, I am under oath," said Fibonacci. "I need to speak to the Doctor."

"Tomorrow," said Val. "Dr. Teabag told Fibonacci to wait here on the path tomorrow morning for the three of you and kill you. He didn't even suggest how to make a getaway."

Robert looked at the hunchback. "I suppose..."

"Oh, he told me," said Fibonacci. "He came right out and said it, because he was in such a hurry on the telephone this afternoon. He didn't have time to make it pretty. I killed the old man, so I'm a murderer already. In for a penny, in for a pound. They can't hang you twice. He told me *he* was lucky, really just plain lucky, that I haven't been arrested yet so that I can do this for him. He's right, he has all the luck. But someone that looks like me is not going to stay hidden. I am not likely to be useful much longer. Just for this task."

Robert said slowly, "But you won't do it? You won't kill us?" He saw Val starting to reply, but stopped her with a gesture. He wanted to hear Fibonacci say it.

Fibonacci said, slowly, "No. I will not hurt you. We came here to warn you and to tell you that, when I am... gone, when I am gone he may try to find someone else to do this."

"Thank you. I think it's clear, anyway, that Teabag lied to you about your birth and the nature of your disease. I think you need to ask yourself, to whom do you really owe loyalty? To Teabag, even if he adopted you and is the top Master or whatever, or to the people you've already hurt, the man you killed?"

Fibonacci was listening. He clearly was used to this kind of moral proposal.

Robert continued, "I plan to try to stop this barcode plot, myself, but it will take me a long time. I think I finally understand what is going on, and I can find copies of Ser Aspro's barcodes and understand Teabag's barcodes. But if we don't stop Teabag, someone will have to keep on protecting the museum stores against Teabag, the work Ser Aspro himself was doing."

Robert hesitated. He hadn't really defined his own role in this strange business, yet, even to himself. "Maybe I can do that, with the help of his granddaughters. That's why Teabag wants us dead, so that there will be no-one left who could perform that task. But *you* could do it in a half an hour, simply by naming the names."

Fibonacci sighed. "I would have to name the Doctor's name, too."

SIXTY-EIGHT

Mary "had seven demons" because she was full of every vice. But lo! She sees the stain of her sins, she runs to wash herself at the font of mercy, she is not embarrassed by the citizens seated at their banquet. What then is more surprising, my brothers, Mary coming to Christ, or Christ receiving her?

Gregory the Great

Robert was not in top form the next morning.

The night before, his dinner had been a bit of soup and bread that the nun in the Reception hall scrounged for him. Teabag and the twins, waiting so long for him, had eaten a more substantial version of this supper when it was served, at 8 p.m., instead of going to the restaurant in the next town.

Teabag was furious at him for having spoiled his "dinner party." The twins had explained his absence as due to a desire to climb up and see the sunset from the Grotto itself. Robert played along, implying that on the way down he had lost his way in the dark wood.

Once Robert understood what the sleeping accommodations were like, he made plans. With the help of the nun in the reception hall, he got the loan of a high-quality noise-excluding headset, for a few euros, from a teen-aged boy pilgrim. He pulled his decaying pajamas out of the laundry bag where the police had shoved them a few days earlier when they packed his suitcase at the *Hôtel du Prieuré*, and found a sweater that he hadn't worn at all on the trip so far. After Teabag was asleep again, and the distended cradle of springs above him was rising and falling at a regular rate, Robert moved his blanket and pillow to the concrete floor, used the sweater to cover himself a bit, and prepared to sleep. The headset kept out the snores but let through a few high-pitched creaks from the springs.

Still, he felt very fuzzy after the little coffee-and-rolls breakfast at the hostel.

Teabag had managed to injure his ankle getting out of the top bunk. He would not be able to make the climb. *So that's how he was going to set it up. We would be murdered on the path and he would be down here having another cup of coffee, chatting with the nuns.*

Since the murder attempt was not going to take place at all, Robert decided not to tell the twins about Fibonacci and Val Percy. They didn't ask him about Val until they were on their way, again, to the woodland path. He said he would tell them later, and he had a good excuse. The path was not very private at this hour. The flow seemed to consist of nuns coming down and Goddess-explorers going up. At any rate, they were rarely alone.

They won't enjoy the Grotto if they are thinking about Ser Aspro's murder. And, Robert admitted to himself, *they'll be furious at me for meeting him and not capturing him or alerting the police. But he's such a pitiful fellow.*

The woods were darker and cooler, now, than last night. Although it was after 8 a.m., and near the longest day of the year, the sun had not quite made it over the top of the mountain whose base they were climbing.

They came to the part of the path near which they had had their discussion about the tattoos and Teabag, the night before.

Mado screamed.

Marie screamed, in unison.

What a noise! Robert wished for a split second that he was still wearing the headphones. But there were a lot of things he wished right now.

Fibonacci was standing on the path. Evidently he had been waiting in the clearing. Robert glimpsed Val Percy sitting on the stone bench, behind him.

The twins were raising quite an alarm. They stood quite still and screamed in French. Robert caught a word that was definitely "Assassin!" in French, repeated several times.

Fibonacci stood still, too. He looked reproachfully at Robert. *He thought I would have told them about him. Well, I guess I should have. But I don't know if it will make any difference. What is he doing hanging around here anyway? He wants to apologize in person for killing their grandfather?*

Quite a crowd had gathered, and a couple of young and rather tough-looking nuns had grasped Fibonacci by the arms. Robert thought they were probably twisting the hunchback's bones a bit more than was necessary. He was not resisting at all. It seemed likely to Robert that Fibonacci didn't understand a lot of the French words being yelled at him. But certainly he would get the message.

Val Percy had come out onto the path to stand near Fibonacci, and she was saying something, in French he thought, to one of the nuns holding him. She looked a lot worse than she had the night before. *That woman cares about him. She's broken by this, because she can't do anything at all for him.*

A tall thin man walked up to Fibonacci and spat in his face. Fibonacci closed his open eye, as if he knew that was the thing to do when being spat at. Robert was aware suddenly that Mado's fists were clenching and unclenching, as if she wanted to strike Aspro's murderer.

Val Percy looked desperately at Robert. *This is about to get out of hand! Do something!*

Robert walked towards Fibonacci with his best first-day-of-class authoritative manner. He was tall enough and he liked to stay in shape, so he was the biggest and fittest-looking person in the crowd. Fibonacci, and most of the nuns, seemed quite short beside him. He waved off the nuns and seized Fibonacci's arms himself.

"Now then! Marie, would you please translate for me?" She nodded.

"We have been most fortunate to find the murderer of the great Monsieur Aspro, Director of the *Centre Commercial du Louvre*, here today. Doubtless it is a blessing of Saint Mary Magdalen, whose home for many years all of us have just visited. Or else we plan to visit it."

Marie translated, and Robert found himself hitting his stride. "In this place Mary Magdalen repented her terrible sins for many

years, praying God for mercy. Perhaps this miserable assassin"–
great word–"has come here to ask Mary Magdalen for forgiveness,
or to find in her example the courage to repent his terrible deed."

He paused for translation. Most people seemed to follow this
train of thought, and two of the nuns looked quite gratified by it.
Marie nodded tearfully. Mado looked skeptical, but not so terribly
angry and beside herself as she had at first. Fibonacci did not look
at Robert.

Amazingly, the sun broke out over the top of the cliff behind
them, and suddenly they were bathed in bright light from above.

"This murderer is a sinner. He has come out to meet the very
people he has offended, these beautiful young woman"–he wondered how Marie would translate *that*–"knowing that he would be
recognized and taken into custody. We should allow him the dig-
nity of an escort to the hostel, where the police can be contacted."

Val Percy looked so sad that Robert wondered if she would faint.
But he felt Fibonacci, insofar as his twisted body allowed, standing
up a little straighter.

The people on the path below them began to clear a way so that
Robert could march Fibonacci down the stairlike treads of the path
towards the hostel. He realized almost immediately that this was
going to be difficult, because the hunchback's walking style was eccentric and a little pressure on his arms from Robert threw him off
balance. Robert wondered if he could manage to convey physical
control of his prisoner while holding Fibonacci's hand.

The path below was lined on either side with pilgrims, as far as
Robert could see.

Then he saw a figure striding up the path towards them.

"Robert! Please, you will have to help me!"

It was Lindy Teabag. His ankle had, apparently, healed.

SIXTY-NINE

This is my beloved Son, in whom I am well pleased.
Matthew 17

When Teabag came up to the group, he looked around as if a little startled by the crowd. He seemed at first not to see Fibonacci, who was standing beside Robert. Teabag was panting.

"Robert! I'm so very glad to have found you."

Before Fibonacci killed me, on your orders? thought Robert.

"You can't imagine what has happened. Some policeman is trying to question me. Could you please vouch for me? Tell them that I am an eminent medical symbologist."

Suddenly he saw Fibonacci, who had been quietly looking at him. Teabag's reaction was immediate, and rather magnificently cool, thought Robert.

"Robert! My dear man! You've caught the murderer! Monsieur Aspro can rest easy in his grave." He looked around. "Yes, and Marie and Madeleine, his granddaughters, are here to see it! Marvelous! But... but you must be careful. He may have a gun. Let me check his pockets."

He moved towards Fibonacci, but Val Percy spoke up to prevent him.

"I have the gun, Dr. Teabag. Here it is." She held up a revolver with a silencer on it, and then held it out to him.

He took it from her hand and in the same movement he raised it and fired, at point-blank range, into Fibonacci's face.

Robert had not imagined this move, but his body seemed able to react to it–he lurched between them to protect the little cripple.

There wasn't any noise, and he felt no pain. He looked down into Fibonacci's frightened brown eye, very close. He turned to Teabag, who was looking at the gun in his hand with a kind of crumbling, sagging horror.

"Of course it's not loaded," commented Val Percy.

Robert stepped back from between the two men.

Fibonacci went for Linden Teabag's throat with both hands, screaming. "You're not my father! You lied to me! I wasn't born this way! My mother didn't hate me! You're not my father!"

The crowd around them was pressing close again. However, no-one needed to pull Fibonacci off the man who had just tried to kill him. Linden Teabag was a big, strong man–bigger than Robert–and he detached Fibonacci from his neck with a single gesture. He threw the frail hunchback on the ground and stood over him.

Everyone craned to see the two men. Sympathy seemed to be with the weeping Fibonacci, but Linden Teabag's powerful personality kept anyone from interfering. His face no longer sagged. He was like an angel, blazing with some incomprehensible thought, standing over a defeated demon.

Teabag seemed to have forgotten Robert, the pilgrims, everything except the twisted man on the earth in front of him. He gazed at him as if he were going to hypnotize him.

"Fibonacci, Fibonacci, lad." The plummy British accent was gone. He sounded quite terrifically Scottish. "I *am* your father, my boy. *I am your father.*"

"No! You are not my father! Not really! You told me I was born like this."

"And so you were. Neurofibromatosis is what you have, laddie dear, and it is something you are born with. The prettiest baby with those birthmarks will become–a misshapen monster like you. A good cow may have an ill calf, and so your mother did. And *I* am your father."

"You told me my mother wouldn't nurse me...."

"Aye. Your mother left you, she left *us*, when I told her the diagnosis. I spotted the disease quite early, having an interest in such things at that time. *She* was not interested in such things. She took her departure." He paused, looking down at Fibonacci, who had closed his eye so that his face seemed like an expressionless lump of flesh. "She left me alone to raise my little monster, my malproportioned misbegotten mistake of a son!"

Fibonacci opened his eye again after a moment. He gasped a little, then said fiercely. "But you told me you *chose* me! You told me my parents were, were, I don't know, of the house of Stewart."

"Oh, you believed what you wanted to believe. I did choose you. I could have left you too, the same as your mother did. Blood is thicker than water, for a man like me at least. But you wanted to think you were a prince. What a prince!" His mouth twisted in contempt. Fibonacci stared up at him, immobilized.

"*You* are actually his biological father?" said Val Percy.

"Aye." Teabag looked at her and apparently recognized her for the first time. "Mrs. Percy. I don't know what you are doing in these parts. Your *husband* might be here, I suppose. He was to drive my delightful offspring to a safe place. A safe place." Lindy paused, looking from Fibonacci to Val. "Yes, you are right, Mrs. Percy, you understand me correctly. The only replica of myself, of my genes, in this world, is–*this.*"

Robert was stunned. *Lucky Lindy, unlucky Lindy. A man who loved art and beauty and hated... well, if he didn't hate them when he was younger, certainly now he hates bad reproductions of beautiful things.*

"And you were ready to throw him away? You told him to kill these innocent people, knowing he would be arrested and die in prison, probably rather soon?" Val gestured to the twins and Robert. Marie took Mado's hand and they stared at Val and each other, trying to understand.

Lindy turned on Val, his voice sharp, rational, more English. "He murdered Salvateur Aspro, who was worth more than the whole pack of them. They that dance pay the piper, you know. He is a murderer, he would have been caught. How could he escape? And he would die in a state hospital rather soon anyway. It might as well be a prison hospital." He paused, as if to let his points sink into his audience's minds.

Val gasped out, "*You tried to shoot him!*"

Mado let go of her sister and moved closer to Lindy. She caught Fibonacci's attention, and he stared at her in fascination as she began to tense up and shift her weight. Fibonacci had seen this pose before, in Ser Aspro, just before he shot him.

"Mado, arrête! Non, ma chère, faut pas!" Marie said hoarsely, reaching for her sister's arm to stop whatever Mado was about to do.

A whistle blew below, and a number of uniformed men trotted up the path, surrounding Captain Bulle.

"Ah, Professor Longone," he said. "I decided to follow up this little clue of the teabag box. Lime-flower tea, Linden Teabag.... Old *Monsieur le Directeur* Aspro was just far too clever. And we find Ser Aspro's assassin."

A gendarme was happily putting handcuffs on Fibonacci. Teabag seemed to be edging away.

"I suggest that you detain Dr. Teabag, too, Captain Bulle," said Robert.

Teabag instantly broke away, running into the woods. Three gendarmes moved after him alertly, and Robert started to consider a tackle, something he hadn't practiced since high school. A little black-and-white nun was quicker than any of them, however. She stuck out her foot to trip Teabag and he fell sprawling.

Two of the gendarmes handcuffed Teabag and only then helped him to his feet. The third one helped the nun get up. She had hurt her foot but seemed very pleased with herself, and was quickly surrounded by an admiring group of fans.

Captain Bulle said, "That is the second time that man has run away from us. Do you have some evidence for his complicity in *Monsieur l'ancien Directeur* Aspro's death?"

"I have evidence of his complicity in commercial sabotage, burglary, and attempted murder. This soul"–he indicated Fibonacci, who was on his feet by this time–"killed Ser Aspro all right, but somewhat in self-defense. There are also mitigating medical factors, I think–claustrophobia, for example. But, best of all..."

Robert lifted an eyebrow at Fibonacci.

"Oh, aye, I'll talk all right. I'll name you names. I'll save your precious museum shops." Fibonacci sniffled, unable to wipe his running nose. "I'll do what your man Aspro wanted done."

Bulle said something to the policemen who had hold of Fibonacci. Robert hoped it was advice to handle him gently.

SEVENTY

October 8, Feast of St. Badillon. St. Badillon brought the body believed to be that of St. Mary Magdalen from Gallic Provence to Vézelay church in Burgundy.

Acta Sanctorum

About forty-eight hours later, Robert was walking from their hotel in Vézelay up a narrow medieval street to the Basilica of Marie-Madeleine, St. Mary Magdalen, at the top of the hill.

In those forty-eight hours, Robert had been stuffed with French history, medieval architecture, pagan springs turned into Roman baths before Mary Magdalen was born, and some remarkable food. He would never be the same. He had written down the name of each wine they drank with their meals, since the twins assured him that these wines would be available in Boston, too.

He had even learned what a Retable of the Passion is.

He didn't think he had learned anything new about women in general, but he was beginning to be able to sort out his feelings about these two women in particular. Regrettably, however, nobody had yet done anything to regret.

They had arrived in Vézelay the night before, late, after a multi-course dinner at a multi-starred restaurant in another town. The twins were paying for dinners, and Robert for lunches. He knew this wasn't at all a fair split, but his Visa bill was going to be a monster and he didn't argue with their proposal.

The twins met him in front of the basilica. They had been to Mass, an experience Robert had decided to postpone. However, on

Tuesday he did plan to attend Ser Aspro's funeral, so he would not escape Catholic ritual entirely.

This basilica seemed to Robert even more imposing than the one in Saint-Maximin. It had a square tower on one side, giving it a friendly lopsided look, and where a Gothic church would have a rose window was a huge carved arch-shaped structure, with narrow windows and statues looking down. The smaller arch over the main door was finished with beautiful marble and carvings, but Marie ignored these and led them right inside. "Over-restoration in the 19th century," she muttered.

Inside there was quite a wide sort of porch or entryway, with a second set of three doors. Robert had been coached in advance to admire the *tympanum*, the semi-circular chunk of sculpture over the main door, which was dominated by a huge figure of Christ. He noticed the signs of the zodiac crawling around the edge of the tympanum. It reminded him of Marie's tattoos, but here the signs were interspersed with little images of seasonal agricultural work, so that the terrestrial and the celestial were presented as inseparable. He picked out his own sign, Leo, near the top. The carvings were beautiful but a bit battered. A figure carved on the post separating the two doors, which he thought might have been a Virgin Mary or even Mary Magdalen herself, had been literally de-faced.

"The Terror," muttered Mado, nudging him.

"St. John the Baptist," noted Marie, disillusioning Robert as to the feminine quality of the figure. *How can I tell a man saint from a woman saint? I have to ask Marie every time.*

Inside the church, a straight path of large patches of light lay on the floor in front of them, leading to the altar. As at Saint-Maximin, the windows had clear glass in them, and they made this rather mysterious pattern of light. This church was as huge as Saint-Maximin, or even bigger, but different—the roof was a series of rounded arches, rising from great square columns. *Romanesque, as opposed to Gothic*, he thought, not too confidently.

A few people were sitting quietly in the rows of chairs with padded kneelers up near the altar, but there was no service in progress, just a faint smell of incense from the Mass earlier. A small man in a black cassock came bustling up to them from a side aisle. He greeted Marie and Mado in French.

Oh, no, not again. I hope the priest has an interesting computer for me to play with.

But the little priest turned to Robert, holding out a hand, and speaking in clear English.

"Professor Longone! I am Ser Aspro's friend, Monseigneur Poquette-Filiposi. And your friend, too, I hope. Of course we have heard of your adventures, apprehending that poor cripple who killed Ser Aspro. Such a terrible thing! But the newspapers and the TV say you were right on the spot, protecting these girls."

Robert felt himself blushing. "No, that's not right. I wasn't protecting them..." *I think I was protecting Fibonacci from Mado.*

Mado explained to him that they had made sure Robert hadn't seen any newspapers in the past couple of days. "But we are keeping a collection. Madame Rosamonde is buying a copy of everything for each of us. And taping the TV shows."

Maybe I can find a way to make some money off this notoriety, and pay off my bills for lunches in Burgundy. Exclusive interview with heroic Harvard symbologist.

"Of course," said the priest, "you are interested in this strange correspondence with Ser Aspro, the business of the invisible barcodes."

"Did you actually use these barcodes?" asked Robert.

"Oh, Professor, you will laugh at us here. Ser Aspro used to laugh. We do have a little shop of sorts attached to the church, with books on the architecture and history of the basilica, and rosaries and candles for the devout, and so on." He gestured towards a dark corner of the basilica, near the door, where there seemed to be a little lit-up enclosure. "And postcards. Ser Aspro actually used to insist I keep a good stock of postcards of artists' depictions of the Magdalen, and tell him which sold better, the blondes or the redheads! Can you imagine!"

"Yes, by now I can."

"Well, but we don't have a cash register. We never bought a mechanical cash register, it seemed like a waste, since we sold so little. Someone donated one to us back in the 1950s, but it broke, oh, a long time ago–yes, in '68, along with a lot of other things, the cash register broke. We have a computer for parish business, but it is certainly not in the shop. People just drop the money for the postcards in a box, you know, or if it's a more complicated purchase they have to find someone to help them. We put the items in a paper bag, and then we just write the amounts for the different items on the bag and total it up. Very simple. And ecologically sound, one piece of paper serves as both the bag and the receipt!"

"How about credit cards?"

"Well, you know, there's an ATM right out in the square in front of the basilica. Everybody has an ATM card, these days. So we can ask for cash."

Robert did laugh. Then he asked, "So, Monsignor, tell me, why did Ser Aspro send you these useless barcodes? Father Pater in Saint-Maximin was really puzzled by the whole business, too."

"Oh, yes, Father Pater is quite quite brilliant you know, really a very fine preacher. You'll see, someday he will be famous. But he didn't appreciate Ser Aspro's sense of humor. No blondes and redheads for Father Pater."

Robert laughed again, but pressed his question. The four of them had been walking down the path of light in the center aisle, towards the altar end of the church. The Monsignor and the twins did the little bend-the-knee-wash-the-face mime and they went to the right. Monsignor Poquette-Filiposi opened a door into a small, pleasant room with chairs and a table. It was a high-ceilinged room with neat-looking cabinets and drawers and, unexpectedly, a sink.

"Why did Ser Aspro send us these things? Well, I think it was that.... Well, actually I don't know. But I can tell you what he told me." Monsignor Poquette-Filiposi drew himself up, evidently imitating Ser Aspro. "Monsignor, you have a body of Mary Magdalen. Saint-Maximin has a body of Mary Magdalen. Which is the original and which is the reproduction?"

Marie said, "That makes no sense, does it?"

"Not really, but it does sound like our grandfather," commented Mado.

SEVENTY-ONE

If I've only one life, let me live it as a blonde.
Clairol advertising copywriter Shirley Polykoff

"Another question, since you are doing such a great job filling in the blanks for us," said Robert. "Ser Aspro sent each of his grand-daughters a *pneu* the night he died, with something in it."

He was a bit startled to find himself able to say the word *pneu*.

He had forgotten about this when they visited Father Pater. The question of the barcodes seemed so much more important then, and Linden Teabag had dominated those proceedings. This morning he had asked the girls for their *pneus*, which they had of course brought with them on the trip. He pulled them from his inside breast pocket, and drew from each the little glassine evidence bags with the bits of dead woman in them.

Monsignor Poquette-Filiposi was distressed. "Oh, you mustn't keep them like that! They are quite fragile. I told Aspro, and I sent them to him in special plastic boxes, just for the mail, you know. Glass would be more correct, or porcelain, or gold."

He set them down carefully, peering at them to be sure he could remember which was which, then jumped up and went to a drawer built into the wall. He took from it a couple of tiny clear glass boxes, with gold-colored fittings and some kind of white insert. He took the little envelopes into which the police had put the relics, cut them in half so that it would be easy to get at the contents, and picked up an elegant little tweezers, at least as delicate as the forensic tools of Captain Bulle's policewoman.

"Or do you want lockets? I only have sterling silver, I'm afraid.

Not at all correct for these. Ser Aspro said he might have gold lockets made up. I believe it was to be a birthday present for the two of you." He smiled sympathetically at the twins.

"Monsignor, what we would like to know is, what are these items? Actually, at the police station I confirmed that they are in fact parts of a human body."

"What?" said Mado, jumping out of her chair so energetically that she knocked it over. "You never told us that. Both of them?" She reached out for her own little evidence bag, but Monsignor Poquette-Filiposi would not let her near it. Instead, he finished placing the tiny items in the two tiny boxes, and shut them carefully. Then he handed them to the twins.

"Did you test them with the Personal Sampler, then, Robert?" asked Marie.

"Yes. Captain Bulle was there, I think. The results were quite interesting. But.... Monsignor, I gather that you were Ser Aspro's source for these relics?"

"Indeed I was. He had asked Father Pater for a relic of Mary Magdalen from Saint-Maximin. Of course, that is the authentic body, the official body if you will. Our relics here, which we venerate in processional next month on the Magdalen's feast day, are part of the Saint-Maximin treasure. The relics in the Grotto at Sainte-Baume, which you may have seen"–all three nodded–"those are purported to have come from the Saint-Maximin relics, although their provenance is not as good as ours." He chuckled. "I don't think anyone has been so scientific as to see whether the Sainte-Baume bit of leg is actually missing from the Saint-Maximin skeleton."

"Or DNA testing?" asked Marie, with a glance at Robert.

"What a question! That would be something, now, wouldn't it? Could you get DNA from these old relics?"

"I did," said Robert.

"Not really! And what did you find? That they are the same woman?"

"No...."

"Good! Because if they were, it would mean that I had gotten quite confused. That's why I sent the hair from one and the skin from the other."

"The one and the other....?

"Ah! Do you know the story of the relics of Mary Magdalen at Vézelay? How the monk Badillon went to the Holy Land, some say, and others say it must have been Constantinople or Ephesus, but probably you know just down to Sainte-Baume in Provence or the Three Marys in the Camargue, and brought back for us the body of the saint?" Robert nodded, although he realized that he wasn't sure where Ephesus was. "Well, of course in the 14th century this body, our body, was discredited. But we still have it. You don't throw out a perfectly good saint's body just because the Pope disagrees with you."

Mado snickered.

"Now, my dear, I'm quite serious. Vézelay had been a place of pilgrimage for five hundred years by that time. Pilgrims came here to pray to God in the presence of one whom He had loved so dearly. Down in Provence, they understood this perfectly well and sent us some relics of the new body to make such prayer officially possible again. Let me see, now, that would have been in the thirteenth century that we had to replace the relics. But, you see, a body that has *been Mary Magdalen* for hundreds of thousands of people over many centuries is a sacred object in itself. We still considered it a treasure, our treasure."

Robert felt he was finally getting the hang of the relics-and-pilgrimage business.

"During the Terror, when enlightened men came and smashed our statues, they also smashed the reliquaries. They mixed the Magdalen's skin with dirt and ground the bit of bone to dust. But–they didn't bother so much about the discredited body. They dumped it out of the reliquary and took that away to make war medals out of, but the relics themselves were saved. As to the relics of the official body..."

He shook his head sadly. "The ones that had been destroyed were truly lost. Later on, when things calmed down, we recovered some of the relics from the original gift of Saint-Maximin, in this way. We had given some fragments of the St-Maximin body to the Cathedral at Sens, and they returned a portion of those very fragments to us. So we have a share of a share of a share of the treasure of Saint-Maximin. Besides that, we still have nearly the entirety of our original dear body, everything except of course the parts that were given as relics to the Kings of France, and other distinguished persons who requested them."

The Monsignor leaned towards the twins. "What Ser Aspro wanted was a relic of the Magdalen for each of you, my children, because of your names. One from the Saint-Maximin body, one from ours. I simply provided him with both. Because of our old friendship."

There was a moment of effusive thanks in French.

He smiled at Robert. "That is why I am pleased to hear that they are from two different bodies. I was very, very careful to take samples from each, but I worried that I might have gotten confused. That's why I took the hair from the Saint-Maximin relics, but skin from our own body. It helped me remember which was which. But tell me about your DNA analysis. Are both our Marys women, at least?"

Robert smiled and said yes, but he felt more confused now than he had been. He must be misremembering what he had seen in Captain Bulle's office.

"Come on, Robert, now you have to entertain us with your gadget," said Marie, holding up the tiny box with the relic in it.

Robert pulled the Personal Sampler out of his pocket and explained it to the Monsignor. The little priest was quite excited. He wanted to see the results, not based on the twins' relics, but on the more important relics of the two bodies in his own treasury. "Provided it doesn't damage them, of course. You only take a tiny tiny bit?"

Robert reassured him. Marie said, a little wickedly, "They won't feel a thing."

"Now," he said, as he drew out a key and used it to open a tall door in the wall of the room where they had been sitting, "Don't tell me, yet, Professor, if these women had red hair!"

The room within was full of golden objects, chalices and tall sunbursts and a beautiful tall candlestick. There were several objects of the sort Robert had learned to identify as reliquaries, elaborate gold boxes, usually with a crystal container visible showing a bit of organic matter, sometimes a bone fragment. These often were in the shape of the body part from which the relic had purportedly come–for example, an arm or hand. The priest bent down and brought up a much simpler object, a lovely flat gold box. He opened it, and inside were several odds and ends of hair and bone.

"These are from Saint-Maximin. We have more, in the reliquary on display in the Crypt, but these are kept here, just in case.... The provenance is excellent, unless something happened at Sens during the Terror and they replaced the true relics with substitutes. I don't think so, do you?"

Robert chose a bit of bone and touched the Personal Sampler to it, where the marrow would once have been. Sample. Save. Data, 20 years old.

"No modesty button!" said Mado. "Unless the Monsignor wants to."

They crowded around, gazing at the same woman Robert had seen on Tuesday in Bulle's office, when he tested the relics Ser Aspro had given to the twins

The image was much clearer, with strong features, dark eyes, and thick dark hair. He could see that she had been beautiful.

"Well, she looks Jewish, at least," commented Mado frankly. "Kind of grumpy, though." Robert switched to age 40, and, as he remembered, the woman appeared looking older but more cheerful.

"Neither blonde nor red-haired. Poor Ser Aspro! He would have been disappointed. And now for our own Vézelay Magdalen."

Monsignor Poquette-Filposi knelt down in front of a large pink-veined white marble cube on the floor under the shelves of reliquaries. Robert and the twins got the lid off, lifting and sliding carefully–it was about three feet square and heavy. Inside, the box was lined with what seemed to be sheet gold. What looked to be most of a human skeleton was arranged in layers. The skull was on top, though missing the jaw, and it and some of the limbs appeared to have been mummified in some way, dried up with the flesh and skin.

"It smells so strange. Like roses and–chemicals? Ugh! Is it from the marble?" asked Marie.

"No, I think... that is, I'm not sure, actually," said the Monsignor.

"It's some kind of bleach," said Mado.

"To tell the truth, I haven't opened this box for some years. The relic I gave Ser Aspro was from a half-dozen I took at that time...

oh, I think in the early 90s. The odor must have built up since then," said the priest.

Robert looked at all the array of potential DNA sources and, this time, touched the sampler to a part of the skull covered with skin. Sample. Save. View at 20 years old.

"It's the same woman! You made a mistake!" said Mado.

The Monsignor was upset. "You said that they were different... did I somehow confuse the samples? Did they make a mistake and send relics from *this* body to Sens? I don't understand."

Just to be sure, Robert slipped the Personal Sampler down in among the bones and checked another sample. It was the same woman as the other sample from this body.

Marie said, "They're twins, aren't they, Robert?"

Robert nodded. "Like you and Mado, they are identical except for handedness. Saint-Maximin was right-handed, Vézelay was her left-handed twin. I guess that your monk Badillon went down to Saint-Maximin and stole one of a pair of twin saints, and the other is the one that your Count of Provence discovered in the 13th century."

"Then it can't be Mary Magdalen! She wasn't a twin!" said Marie.

"Why not?" asked the Monsignor. We have the Church of the Three Marys. According to that legend, Mary Magdalen arrived in France with her sister Martha. It could be that we have here Martha and Mary."

It was as if he had to speak the idea out loud before it really occurred to him. His jaw suddenly dropped and Robert thought he might faint. The girls took care of him, speaking to him in French and bringing a glass of water from another part of the back-of-the-altar maze.

Robert bent over the marble box again. There was a great deal of hair in the box. Some wisps were still attached to the skull. It was not grey at all, but white, which was what you'd expect from an old woman. Really almost blonde. It must be an illusion, that yellow color you get in an old woman's hair.

He noticed, however, that the wisps attached to the scalp had dark roots.

SEVENTY-TWO

The little Madeleine ... that small bakery seashell, so plump and moist under its piously pleated wimple. These forms had been abolished....

Marcel Proust

Ser Aspro's funeral was as beautiful as the old man could have wished, and as well-attended by friends, culture snobs, and the media.

Robert sat, which mostly meant standing and kneeling, with the family. The twins had insisted he get a new black suit for the occasion (not an easy thing to do in one afternoon). Fortunately, Marie and Madame Rosamonde had lined up some media interviews for him, and it turned out that he could pay not only for the suit but for his prolonged stay in France.

That morning the announcement had been made by some French museum committee that Marie Navet was to be the *Directrice ad interim* of the *Centre Commercial du Louvre*. Robert and Marie seemed to be the only ones who hadn't expected this.

Robert's most spectacular surprise came, however, when Marie and Mado (dressed identically in black dresses and hats with veils) introduced him to their parents, and a grandparent or two from their father's side as well. There seemed to be quite a few Navets, brothers and sisters and aunts and uncles.

After the funeral and a kind of state meal, Marie went flying off to her office. Madame Rosamonde had seen to it that a new office was created in what had been a storage closet. Neither woman wanted to work in the rooms where Aspro had been killed.

Robert was left to walk along the Seine with Mado. He asked about her parents.

"What? Did you think that Marie and me, we sprang grownup from Ser Aspro's head?"

"I guess I thought you were orphans."

"Oh, no. Grandfather just sort of took us under his wing when we were about fourteen. He said he'd educate us and leave us everything. And he did! He had quite a bit put by. I wonder where he got it. Marie can work as hard as she wants to, but she doesn't *have* to, now. If I'm careful, I could get by without having to work any more at all. Except archaeology, but that doesn't pay."

"Congratulations. But I thought Marie wanted to be an art historian or a curator of paintings or something."

"Oh, she loves all that. But she's ambitious, too, and she likes commerce. She likes thinking up things to sell and ways to sell them, and thinking about money. I think she'll be a strong candidate for the post of permanent director. Especially with Madame Rosamonde backing her."

"Hmm. So long as she doesn't stop in the middle of every business conference to slip in a lecture on Retables of the Passion or baroque art."

"Speaking of income, Robert, did you get paid well for that *L'Express* interview?"

"A thousand dollars! It's great."

"Is that all? I think Marie must have given up on you. Or she would have gotten you more. I liked the TV interview, though, what you said."

"Was the translation all right?"

"Yes, it was pretty good. Of course, French law is not what *you* expect. You sounded *so* American! Criminals don't get pardoned here because of insanity or emotions, unless it's maybe after finding their wives committing adultery. I think Fibonacci will get mercy because he informed, and Teabag won't because there was nothing left for him to inform about. He seems to have been a one-man operation, don't you think? The others who helped him didn't understand what he planned to do. They trusted him. But because the scheme regarding museum shops was international, it will have to be tried in a EU court."

"I've also gotten two requests for interviews about the Mary Magdalen relics."

"Of course! Exclusive peek at what Mary Magdalen and her twin sister actually looked like. Next they'll be wanting you to test the ashes of Jeanne d'Arc."

"I'm not sure I *should* do these interviews, money be damned. The people who loaned me the Personal Sampler will not be happy with me, and they certainly aren't going to get involved with–Joan of Arc, is that who you mean? By the way, what does Marie think about the two bodies? Twin Magdalens?"

"No. She agrees with Monsignor Poquette-Filiposi that one body must be Martha and the other Mary of Bethany, the sister of Lazarus. But she does *not* agree that one of them is Mary Magdalen."

"All Pope Gregory's fault for mixing up his Marys?"

"Exactly. She says probably Mary Magdalen is buried somewhere else, in Greece or the Holy Land, or even in the Grotto at Sainte-Baume." Mado paused. "I didn't mention the chemically bleached hair of the Vézelay body to her."

"Just as well. I wonder how a woman would chemically bleach her hair in the first century?"

"Oh, lemon juice and sunshine, probably. Maybe Martha was an amateur chemist."

"You think Martha was the blonde?"

"Sure. She got a little bored with always being Mary's straight man, never getting to sit at Jesus's feet. So she tried that something extra. Why not?"

They walked along together for a while, saying nothing. Finally Mado asked, "So... have you made your reservation for Boston?"

"Not yet, but they tell me I should do it soon, since the planes are heavily booked in the summer. I have two more magazine interviews tomorrow, and then...."

"When do you have to teach again?"

"Late August. But I need to touch base with a couple of graduate students. And I have things to do piling up on my desk there. Manuscripts to read, an article of my own to proofread, a couple of projects I'm already behind on...."

"Yeah. So you're not going back yet, are you?"

"Not if *you* don't want me to."

She stopped and looked up at him. Robert glanced around, a little embarrassed, but then he noticed that there were several couples just standing around talking on the quai. One couple was kissing.

"Robert, don't you think Marie is more your type?"

"What?"

"Business things, computer things, labels. She loves all that stuff, and so do you. And you know she's a virgin? I think you're the virgin type."

"Well, if I did something about it, then she wouldn't be a virgin anymore, would she?"

Mado laughed.

She was perceptive. Some twenty years earlier, Robert had in fact been "the virgin type." He had been secretly engaged for two months to marry Clarrie, and then next year for six weeks to Heather. Both of them were very interested in kissing, and after about a half-hour of heavy tongue-work he could usually get under their blouses. Panties were however unthinkable. Both of them had passed out of his life, but they had left him with a secret weapon. He had discovered that most non-virgin women were suckers for a good kiss, in two different senses of that charming word.

He kissed Mado for about six minutes. When he let go, Mado stared at him for a moment with her glasses askew and about to fall off. She pushed them into place once she had caught her breath, and grabbed his sleeve. She turned and headed wildly into the street, dragging him behind her. She was like a dog that needs to go for a walk

"Taxi this way,"she gasped.

"Finally you get to see my apartment," she said when they were safely inside a taxi. She snuggled up to him and removed her glasses. Robert knew he was about to find out, but he couldn't resist asking anyway.

"Do you really have a barcode tattoo?"

EPILOGUE

For the tenth anniversary of the death of Princess Diana in the Alma Tunnel, the wise rulers of Paris and France had agreed to close the tunnel and the area around it to all traffic. They installed a staircase and also a heavy-duty elevator, allowing even those in wheelchairs to move from the level of the Monument to Diana down below to the site of her death near the thirteenth pillar of the tunnel. Heroic work had been done to find parking for tour buses, some of which had come from England via the Chunnel, others from Germany, Italy, and Spain. Food and water vendors were licensed. Most souvenir vendors were not, but who cared?

For a few days, it was a site of pilgrimage.

Around the monument, a heap of flowers and wreaths covered the entire base of the torch, a replica of that upheld by the American Statue of Liberty. Below, in the tunnel itself, the wise rulers had decided that floral tributes should not be offered, but that notes could be left there, or small objects, which would be collected and sent to her British memorial. Her ex-husband and sons were taking the day to mourn in private at Balmoral along with, presumably, her ex-husband's wife.

A tall, dark woman, neither young nor old, and a less tall, evidently injured man were in the crowd. The woman looked extremely happy and held on to the man's arm as if he might slip away.

The man wore a broad-brimmed hat, and if one peered under it one might have seen that his eyes were brown. When he removed the hat, at the entrance to the tunnel itself, it became evident that his left eye was purple and bruised, as if it had recently undergone an operation. His neck was in a foam collar, and under his shirt a metal brace of some kind made a strict pattern. But he looked as happy to be with the dark woman as she was.

"No claustrophobia?"

"A little. They did a good job removing that particular tumor, I think. And of course once I know it's claustrophobia, and not moral superiority, that makes me hate these underground places, I can actually stand it pretty well."

"Or you wouldn't have survived, dear," said Val Percy.

Fibonacci grunted. *I wouldn't have survived without you, dear Val.*

They walked together toward the thirteenth pillar of the Alma Tunnel.